To my family, who are everything to me

To my parents, who tell me everything is art.

1

The rain lashes down, fierce rods of water that hit the road and bounce back upwards with force. The windscreen wipers whisk manically backwards and forwards across the glass but make little difference to the poor visibility. Slick with rain, the road is awash and the tyres skid and slide across the rivers of water as they stream across the tarmac and pool in the gutters but the drains are already full and can accommodate no more.

There's no moon tonight and even if there were, the cloud cover is so dense that no light would penetrate them. Tall and alien-looking, the streetlights edging the road are so high up as to be useless, and the feeble illumination they throw has all but vanished by the time it reaches the ground.

After a week of unrelenting rain, the river is about to burst its banks and what was once a calm and tranquil body of water is now a furiously flowing torrent. An amber weather alert – which will imminently turn to red – is in operation and no one in their right mind would be driving along the road on a night like this, let alone speeding.

But the people in that car are not in their right minds; or at least one of them isn't.

A desperate struggle between the passenger and the driver for control of the steering wheel is taking place. Wrenched this way and then that, two pairs of hands grapple for control and the car veers wildly from side to side as it races along. One final shuddering lurch and the car plummets nose first into the water where it sits for several seconds, appearing to float, before silently sinking beneath the black waters.

Moments later, a car appears around the bend in the road. The driver of this car is driving well below the speed limit, and the headlights of the first car as it slowly sinks beneath the water glare through the darkness of the night straight into his eyeline. Puzzled, it takes him a moment to realise what he's looking at and when he does, he pulls the car over to the side of the road, turns off the engine and telephones the emergency services.

Once he's finished the call, the driver – a man in his sixties on his way home from visiting his daughter and her new baby – makes no attempt to get out of the car. He knows that there's no chance of him being able to rescue anyone from the water because he's not a strong swimmer and even if he were, on a night such as this, he'd be more likely to drown himself than save anyone's life. Besides, the emergency services made it quite plain that he should make no attempt to go into the water himself, but to leave it to the professionals. He sits and waits patiently, checking the rear-view mirror for the lights of the emergency vehicles, praying that they come soon although he's certain that no one will be getting out of that car alive.

When the blue flashing lights finally come into view, he heaves a sigh of relief. He no longer has to feel responsible. It's in their hands now. Pulling up his hood, he clambers out of the car and jogs through the rain to the team of rescuers climbing out of the vehicle, their torches and lights illuminating the area. By the time he reaches them he's already soaked through and he points, shouting to tell them where he saw the car go into the water. A searchlight mounted on one of the vehicles is swung around and he watches as it pans across the river. Several of the firemen run towards the water, converging on the bank and as he looks in their direction, he sees them pointing to an area of water that appears darker under the glow of the searchlight.

It's a body.

But then the shape moves and what looks like an arm goes up in the air and he realises that the shape is alive.

There's a survivor.

2

MEGAN

Bright light sears itself onto my retinas as I open my eyes and I quickly close them. Steeling myself to open them again, I inhale a deep, shuddering breath, immediately regretting it as the effort sends a piercing pain from the base of my neck to the very top of my head. I lie perfectly still and eventually the pain subsides.

A hangover, that's what this is. A vicious reminder that I can't tolerate alcohol of any sort any more because it leaves me incapacitated for days, the aftermath far outweighing any fleeting pleasure I may possibly have derived from drinking. Something must have happened to make me drink; something very bad indeed to make me break my own self-imposed rule of no alcohol if it can possibly be avoided.

Except it doesn't feel much like a hangover because those headaches used to pound the inside of my skull as if a sledge-hammer were being wielded. A hangover headache is unremit-ting no matter how still I lie. There would be profuse vomiting, too, that would continue long after every morsel of food had been ejected from my stomach.

So. Not a hangover.

I feel hot and my body feels constricted, as if something heavy is weighting me down. Panic suddenly engulfs me, my brain shouting at me that I've been abducted and am tied up somewhere, trapped, unable to escape. I'm now a madman's prisoner and have been taken to the middle of nowhere where I will never be found and will live the remainder of my days as a captive at the mercy of my abductor. Horrors of what will be done to me crowd my mind and I tell myself to calm down, to stop dramatising. I force myself to move my hands and spread my fingers and feel softness beneath them. Slowly opening my eyes just a fraction, I see the outline of a cotton sheet, the pale blue of a blanket on the top of it. It's pulled up to my neck, holding me snugly in place. I press my fingers down and there's the familiar feel of a mattress.

I'm in a bed.

But not my own bed, because as I move my fingers I feel the edges of the mattress on each side. This is a single bed and I have a king-size.

We have a king-size.

Opening my eyes fully, I see that the light that felt as if it was blinding me is a long, narrow, ceiling light. There's a brown patch next to it. I focus on it and decide that it's evidence of a leak at some time. Murmurings of conversation float into my consciousness; the sound of activity, the click of heels on a hard floor, the rhythmic beep of something. A monitor. Or maybe it's a mobile phone. I turn my head, ignoring the pain that screams at me to stop, and try to gauge where I am.

A large room. White walls, beds, some with three-quarter-length curtains pulled around them, showing only the wheeled-legs of the bed.

A hospital ward.

I try to remember how I got here, when I arrived, why I'm here, but there's nothing. A blank. Have I had surgery, some sort of procedure? Possibly, but if I have, I can't remember. Maybe this amnesia is part of the after-effects of the anaesthetic.

'Oh, hello. You're awake. How are you feeling?'

A face appears in front of me, peering down at me. Brown eyes, flushed skin, a tiny hole on her eyebrow where she's had some sort of piercing. Brown hair scraped back from her face. A young, open face, twenty, maybe younger. She's smiling as she waits for an answer, but it's a professional smile that doesn't reach her eyes.

'Where am I?'

'Saturn ward.'

'Why?'

'Don't you remember?' she asks, not answering my question. 'Can you tell me your name?'

'Megan Fordham,' I say, without having to think about it. 'But I don't know why I'm here.'

'You've been involved in an accident. We think you're going to be fine, but we're going to keep you in for a few more days to keep an eye on you.'

I feel cold fingers on my skin as she takes hold of my wrist to take my pulse and although I know she's only doing her job, the touch is comforting. An accident, so not an operation. I close my eyes. Rain beating against a windscreen flows across my closed eyelids, the hypnotic back and forth of wipers attempting to sweep the water away. I was going somewhere, I know that much, so it must have been a car accident, because what other sort is there?

'A car accident?'

She gently places my hand back down on the bed.

'Yes. But you're going to be okay. Bruised but intact.' That professional smile again. She pulls the sheet and blanket tighter, tucks it around me, smooths it down.

'What happened? I can't remember what happened.'

She hesitates, her eyes refusing to meet mine. 'Sister is going to talk to you shortly. She'll explain everything.'

I grab hold of the blanket and push it down and try to pull myself upright, to sit up.

'It's best if you stay laying down.'

I ignore her; ignore the pain driving through my skull with every movement. I feel powerless laying down and I can't stand it.

She sighs and after a moment helps me to sit upright, pushing the pillows behind me to hold me up.

'Better?' she asks.

'Yes.' The rooms spins and I have the urge to vomit but I swallow it down. The pain in my head gradually recedes to a manageable level.

'How did I get here?'

'Sister will explain.' She's backing away, eager to escape my questions.

'Why can't you tell me?'

'Sister will talk to you,' she repeats, turning to leave. But she's not quick enough because I see it; the flicker in her eyes.

I've seen that look before and I know what it means; there's bad news coming and she's not going to be the one to tell me it.

* * *

I awake, my head lying awkwardly to one side, my arm dangling over the side of the bed, wetness on my face where my mouth has been gaping wide. I've been drooling. I remember; Sister was going to tell me why I'm here but, despite being desperate to know, I fell asleep. I wipe my face, haul myself upright and this time, the pain isn't so bad.

It's bearable.

How long have I been asleep? Minutes? Hours?

I have no idea.

A plastic jug and beaker sit atop the square cupboard next to the bed. I twist my body around awkwardly, reach across and drag the jug towards me. I slop water from the jug into the beaker, splashing it onto the top in the process. Picking the beaker up with shaking hands, I gulp down the water, wincing at the pain in my throat as I swallow. The liquid hits my stomach and I have to fight down the urge to expel it; I should have drunk more slowly. Pushing the beaker back onto the top of the cupboard, I flop back onto the pillows and slowly take in my surroundings. There are four beds against the opposite wall, and the curtains on the beds either side of me are drawn, restricting my view to a narrow strip down the middle of the ward. I can just make out what looks like the edge of a door-frame at the end of the ward. I stare at the blue concertina fabric – or is it paper? – and wonder who are occupying the beds next to me. It seems quieter than when I woke the first time and there's a faint smell of food in the air. I have no idea of the time but there's daylight coming in from the windows. Maybe this is the after-lunch lull.

I manage to pull myself upright and lean forward but can't see any nurses or doctors and then remember that there should be a call button somewhere close to hand. Mum always had one nearby in her many stays in hospital. Strangely, the memory pleases me, although Mum is dead, because it means that I haven't completely lost my memory.

I pull back the covers and swing my legs over the side of the bed. The hospital gown I'm wearing has rucked up around my waist and I quickly pull it down to cover my nakedness, although no one is watching. There's a cord draped over the headboard and I grab hold of it and press the red button in the centre. It makes no noise so I press it again, aware that I'm being impatient but not caring, because I've waited long enough.

No one comes so I press it again, keeping my finger on the button this time. Somewhere, it will be buzzing. Two nurses appear at the end of the ward and they stand in the doorway talking to each other. What's taking them so long? I keep my finger on the buzzer and after a moment one of them peels off and heads towards me. She's wearing navy blue. This, I know, means she's a Sister.

'You're awake.' She approaches me, removes the call button from my hand and drapes the cord over the headboard before walking to the end of the bed. She removes the clipboard that's hooked over the end and studies it. 'How are you feeling?'

'Not great.'

'Doctor's prescribed you some painkillers, so they'll help with the aches and pains. You managed to drink something,' she says, spotting the beaker. 'That's good.'

'What happened to me?'

'You were involved in a car accident.'

A memory stirs again; rain, darkness.

'Was I driving? Did I hit someone?'

'Oh, I don't know if you were driving, the police haven't given us that information, but I do know you didn't hit anyone. The car you were in went off the road and into the river during the storm. You were rescued from the water.'

A memory of my hands on the steering wheel fires itself into my brain. I was driving.

Or was I?

Because there are other hands on that wheel, too. Each of us trying to gain control of the car. Fighting for control. I wasn't alone.

'Where's Rick?'

She doesn't answer.

'Where's my husband?' He was with me, I'm sure he was. Or is my memory playing tricks on me?

She hooks the clipboard back onto the end of the bed, and comes round and sits down next to me.

'I'm very sorry,' she says, taking hold of my hand. 'But I have to tell you that your husband never regained consciousness from his injuries.'

Her words don't make sense; can't make sense.

Dead. Rick's dead.

How can he be dead?

'The doctors tried their very best but sadly there was nothing they could do.' She pats my hand, her fingers warm, mine ice-cold. I stare down at them.

'Is there someone I can call for you?' she asks. 'A family member, a friend?'

'No,' I manage to say, after a moment. 'There's no one.'

3

MEGAN

This is only the second funeral I've been to in my entire life.

The first was my mother's; two years ago.

To the day. I knew that, even as the date for Rick's funeral was suggested but I didn't bother to change it, even though Elaine tried to persuade me to because the date was etched in her memory, too. What difference does it make having it on the same day as my mother's?

None.

Besides, although Rick was my husband, I've had nothing to do with any of the arrangements; Keith and Elaine have taken care of all of the organising. Elaine will have done the majority of it, even though Keith will attempt to take the credit. Barely functioning, I've allowed them to take over and deal with it all. The choice of undertaker, flowers, coffin, readings, the newspaper announcement, it's all down to them.

There has been a pretence made that I've been involved; Elaine would thrust a brochure or a picture in front of me and ask if I liked it and I would reply with a yes or a nod, scarcely registering what I was seeing. I don't care about any of it. If it was up to me, I wouldn't bother with a funeral because I don't need the ritual of a crematorium, flowers and a wake to say my goodbyes to Rick. He's gone and is never coming back and all of this is for other people, mostly colleagues and acquaintances of Rick's who I barely know. They weren't a part of our lives together. Today is something that has to be got through because it's what's expected when someone dies; it's the norm, it's required, expected.

What would Rick make of it all? Would he care what sort of funeral he had? What music is played as the coffin is carried into the crematorium? I honestly don't know because it wasn't something we'd ever discussed or even thought about. We'd been married for a year and being young, death and funerals weren't on the radar. Talk about such stuff was for old people who'd fully lived their lives, not us. We had time on our side and decades of life to be lived ahead of us.

Only he didn't.

'All right, lovey?' Elaine pats my hand and peers into my face, a look of concern on her own. She's wearing the same black dress and jacket that she wore to Mum's funeral and I assume it's only the second time she's worn it. She must have put a bit of weight on since Mum died though, because the dress is a bit snug and she keeps tugging it down over her knees every time she moves. She bought it especially for Mum's funeral and I know it was expensive. Not because she told me, but because I'd looked at it for myself and discounted it as a bit too old for someone of my age. It looked good on Elaine two years ago and it still does now, despite her constant tugging of the skirt. It's an elegant style and perfectly suited for a fifty-seven-year-old woman, the age Mum would be too now, were she alive.

When I nod, she pats my hand again and gives it a squeeze. The warmth and feel of her fingers is comforting, reassuring.

Without Elaine to look after me I think I would have curled up into a ball and given up on living. In her loving way, she's practically dragged me out of bed every morning and forced me to continue to function, telling me that the darks days will get better.

I'm not sure if I believe her.

I look down at her hand on mine. My fingers are ice-cold and have been since the accident; I can't seem to get warm, no matter how many layers of clothes I wear or how high the heating thermostat is turned up.

The rattle of a smoker's cough reminds me that Elaine's husband Keith is sitting on the other side of me in the back of the car. He's staring stoically out of the window as we're driven to the crematorium and there's a slight whistle as he breathes in and out through his nose. There's a faint aroma of his citrus aftershave and cigarette smoke and I sense his impatience for it all to be over so we can get to the wake and he can sink his first pint.

Not that I blame him; I want it to be over, too.

Another five minutes and we'll be there. The circus will begin and we'll go through the motions, say the right things and pretend that all this is bringing some sort of comfort and closure. Rick would think the wake a waste of money, as he's not here to enjoy it. I suddenly have the urge to laugh at the thought but stop myself for fear of appearing hysterical.

At least the first part of it is over; the very worst part, which was the hearse leaving our house with Rick's coffin inside, the funeral director in his black suit walking slowly and solemnly in front of the vehicle, his expression fixed. I'd forgotten they do that. They did the same for Mum two years ago and it was a shock then. I'd had no idea they were going to do it because I'd never been to a funeral and had no clue what to expect. There was something unbelievably sad and final about it and I found it worse than the funeral itself. I lost it completely then, as we slowly followed the hearse up the street. I recall screaming and crying that I couldn't bear it, that Mum couldn't be dead, that I couldn't go on. Keith and Elaine couldn't hide their horror at my naked grief and by the time we reached the crematorium, I had to be helped physically from the car and once outside, could barely walk. They held me up, one either side of me, and practically dragged me inside for the service.

I thought I'd never recover from losing Mum; I didn't *want* to recover, I wanted to die, too.

And then Rick, the love of my life, came along and made me want to live again.

And now he's gone, too.

The road noise changes as the driver pulls the car smoothly onto the gravel driveway that leads to the crematorium and I look up to see the squat, square building in the distance growing ever closer. I brace myself for what is to come. It's less than an hour, I remind myself. The service is less than an hour long.

I can get through this.

We come to a halt and I clamber out of the car behind Keith, as Elaine climbs out of the car on the other side. Flakes of snow flutter onto my face, dry and powdery, not like snow at all. The forecasters have predicted a cold snap and weather warnings have been issued, according to Elaine, who watches the weather like a hawk, always fearful of being snowed in despite living in the centre of town. It's bitterly cold and my thin black jacket and dress are no match for the blast of icy wind that whips my hair around my head. I should have worn it in a bun but have left it loose, the way Rick liked it, falling in soft waves to my shoulders and framing my face. He always told me that my naturally blonde hair was one of the first things he noticed about me.

Once out of the car, Elaine takes my hand and grips it tightly and I allow myself to be led like a child. The three of us enter the foyer, Keith leading the way. The celebrant is waiting with several other officials and when she sees us, she breaks away from them and comes over to us. Her mouth is moving rapidly, with so many words, but I can't hear what she's saying; it's as if the sound has been turned off and I'm in a vacuum watching from afar. Am I going to faint? I don't feel light-headed but I do feel strange, as if I'm not really here.

Garrulous and birdlike, the celebrant, Sheila, I think her name is, visited last week to find out everything about Rick's life so she could write the service. When I try to remember what was said, all I can recall is her incessant twittering. Elaine was with me so perhaps she filled in the gaps. I have a copy at home of what she's going to say but haven't bothered to read it.

Rick's life summed up in three pages.

After a few minutes she peels away from us and although I haven't spoken a word, I realise that I don't need to. Nothing is expected of me today, except to be present. This thought gives me comfort. I don't have to do anything. We move now, entering the chapel of rest three abreast, and make our way to the front row, where we settle ourselves in the seats and sit in silence, crow-like in black. I stare up at the lectern and then at the plinth behind it where the coffin will be placed, trying not to dwell on the curtains that will close at the end of the service. Off to the burners; that's what Rick would say, were he here. Once those curtains close, Rick will be gone forever.

The place is filling up now. The sound of footsteps, the murmuring of subdued voices, the rustle as the orders of service are picked up from seats penetrates my brain. I can hear again. Coughing, throat clearing, the creak of seats as people sit down. I make no attempt to turn my head and look at who's here; I'll meet them all as they leave. I remember this much from Mum's funeral.

I hear Elaine mumble something about it being a *good turnout* to Keith. She said this about Mum's funeral, as if how many people turned up was important when the person you loved most in the world was dead. Mum told me that, when my grandparents were old, they made a hobby of going to acquaintances' funerals because they'd reached the age where it became a regular event. It was a bit of a day out; a chance to catch up with old friends with a free lunch and drinks thrown in. That was how they described it. It used to make me laugh, although I have only hazy memories of my grandparents, as I was barely four years old when they died. Now, I can think of nothing worse than a funeral.

Music starts to play and I recognise one of Rick's favourite songs, one of three that I chose. It was my only input to his funeral. There's the sound of doors opening and this time I can't stop from turning my head to look behind me because I know what's happening; they're bringing in the coffin. Four black-suited undertakers are carrying him, their eyes fixed straight ahead as they proceed slowly down the aisle. The coffin looks small between the four men, yet Rick was over six feet tall. Six-foot-two, as he always said, not to forget those two inches. How can someone so full of life be reduced to something inside a wooden box? No longer a person, just a body. He was here one day and gone the next. How can that be?

I turn away so I can't see the progression of the coffin; I can't watch. Instead, I look around to discover that every seat in here is occupied. We have friends, but not this many, but Rick has a lot of work colleagues. I have no family and I assumed that few, if any, of Rick's relatives would bother to attend as he didn't bother keeping in contact with any of them. His parents are long dead and he wasn't close to his only sister and hasn't seen her for years. Despite us being married, I've never even met her. She's younger than Rick and I've never seen so much as a photograph of her. Is she here? Would she bother coming to the funeral of a brother she's had no contact with for years? Would she even know he's dead? Elaine made sure that the undertakers placed the obituary in several newspapers, but not everyone reads the obituaries.

I never do.

Rick was a 'forces brat', as he put it, constantly moving home. He was sent to boarding school at age eleven and then spent holidays with his friends, not his parents, who were posted overseas, hence the lack of a relationship with his sister. She was never a part of his life and when we got married it was in a registry office, just the two of us with two hired witnesses. We told our small circle of friends about it afterwards, pretending it was an impulsive, romantic act, when of course it was no such thing. It isn't possible to get married without giving a month's notice.

Elaine touches my arm, bringing me back to the present and I turn around to face the front. She's speaking; Shirley, the celebrant. I zone out, having no desire to hear her sanitised version of Rick's life. Will anyone here recognise the man they knew?

I stare at the floor and wish for it all to be over.

* * *

We pull into the car park and come to a halt right outside the entrance of the hotel. Too late, I realise that I should have shown more interest in where we were going to have the wake. I vaguely remember Elaine waving a brochure in front of me for a hotel, but it didn't register that it was for the Regency Arms. Not that there's anything wrong with the place, it's just the right side of posh, which means it's not intimidating but they know their stuff. It has a very good restaurant, so although we're not having a full-on meal, the buffet food will be top-notch and the service excellent. No pale sausage rolls with pink meat or curled up sandwiches here, so, in theory, it's the perfect venue. Elaine would have had no clue that it was the very last place on earth I would have chosen to celebrate the life of my lately deceased husband.

It has very bad memories, for both myself and Rick.

I push the thought away; I have enough to cope with as it is. If I allow the memories of that night to invade my brain, I'm done for and won't be able to get through the rest of it.

'Ready?' Elaine grips my hand tightly and although I love her dearly, right now I want to push her away and run for the hills. I think she's worried that I'll *chicken out*, as I overheard Keith saying to her when I fled the crematorium as soon as the doors were opened after the service. Protocol dictated that I should go into the garden of remembrance and greet the other mourners after the service, I should look at the flowers, accept condolences, thank people for coming.

I couldn't bring myself to do any of it.

As the curtains closed on the coffin, it was as much as I could manage to remain in my seat. Had the doors been open then, I would have run full pelt from that place, to put distance between myself and the thought of what was going to happen to Rick's body. When I climbed into the back of the waiting car at the front of the crematorium, the driver looked shocked, although he tried to hide it. I remained there, drawing in juddering breaths, until Elaine came and found me.

So here we are, and yet again, I want to run, escape, pretend this isn't happening. I sense that Keith is itching to get out of the car so he can get to the bar, but Elaine will have warned him that I need to be the first to arrive. Elaine and Mum were best friends since their school days, closer than sisters and always there for each other, but Mum never liked Keith – though she tried her hardest to – and she couldn't understand why Elaine married him. Mum never thought he was good enough for her, although she tried to hide it for Elaine's sake. I think Keith knew how she felt as they were always cool whenever they were in each other's company. Keith and I have little to say to each other, despite Elaine being like a second mother to me, but I always strive to remain polite. Mum often said to me that Keith doesn't like anyone or anything except for his daily pint and cigarette.

'Yes, I'm ready.' I sit up straight, square my shoulders and inhale a deep breath. Time to get on with it; get it over with. After today, I have to move on. No more opting out of life.

'This is the better bit, love,' Elaine says, squeezing my hand. 'Everyone can remember Rick and all the good times. It'll be okay.'

I manage a smile of sorts and she looks reassured although I don't believe her for one minute. It wasn't the best bit of Mum's funeral; there *was* no best bit. I'll try to put a brave front on for Elaine's sake. She treats me like the daughter she never had and always has done, even when Mum was alive because, as she says, 'Keith and I were never blessed'. With another pat and squeeze of my hand she releases her hold on me and gets out of the car, waiting as I clamber out behind her. We stand for a moment and stare up at the imposing façade of the Regency Arms.

Forcing down the horrible memory of *that* night, I walk purposefully towards the hotel entrance.

Let's get it over with.

4

MEGAN

By the time people start to arrive, I'm clutching a large gin and tonic and feeling the better for it. Distinctly unwise, because my tolerance for alcohol is nil, but I don't care because I need it to get through the next few hours. I've already drunk half of it but am making a conscious effort to slow down because I haven't eaten today and it'll go straight to my head. Elaine tried to persuade me to have some toast this morning but I have zero appetite. I'm gearing myself up to visit the buffet to force some food down in an attempt to soak up the gin, because I know I'll be having more than one drink.

Keith is already on his third pint. The first one barely touched the sides and as I watched him drink it, I marvelled at how such a skinny little man could swallow nearly half a pint in one go without any effort. Whose mouth is that big? He put me in mind of a snake swallowing a rodent. He'll be intent on getting his fill of the free bar because the beer is his payment for taking a day off work to be here. He's not completely skinny, a small pouch-like beer gut hangs over the top of his trousers making his arms and legs look even more stick-like.

Elaine, bless her, keeps flicking nervous glances at him but he's ignoring her. It's free and he's taking full advantage of it and if she dares to question him, it'll be *for fuck's sake, leave me alone, woman*. As Mum often said to me, what the hell possessed Elaine to marry him? I've often wondered the same. Despite Keith, Mum remained devoted to Elaine and never allowed him to intrude on their friendship.

Love is truly blind.

Being here isn't as awful as I thought it would be even though I know it's a false feeling and due to the alcohol, I don't care. It's making it more bearable so I'm definitely having more. A thumping hangover will be a small price to pay for getting me through this. It helps that I've never been in this room before, so there are no memories here to ambush me. This is a private function room and not open to the general public. As people have arrived, they've come over to speak to me, given me their condolences, shared a little of their memories of Rick and then faded away with relief as more people have turned up to take their turn. Our little clique of friends have insisted that I sit at their table and I've left my jacket there on a chair reserved especially for me, although I've absolutely no intention of sitting down. When I've finished greeting everyone, I'll wander from table to table, because if I stop, I'll crumble. I have to keep moving. Elaine continues to helicopter around me to make sure that I'm okay and even when she leaves me, I sense her watching me from the sidelines.

'Please make sure to get yourself a drink,' I say to Jake, one of Rick's work colleagues who's the last to arrive. Bespectacled and bearded, his relief at my letting him know that he can go now is almost palpable. He's done his duty and can now reward himself with a much-needed drink. I watch as he trudges to the bar, one of his workmates turning to greet him. Background music is playing, some sort of classical arrangement. Probably the same music the hotel plays for the corporate training courses they host.

I turn to begin my round of the tables when a late arrival comes through the doorway; a girl. Around my age and slightly built, she has shoulder-length white-blonde hair very similar to mine, only hers is an expensive job from a salon. I can always tell. People always assume that my hair isn't naturally blonde because it's so light and no adult could possibly have hair like this.

I do.

The girl's face is pale and devoid of make-up and her huge blue eyes are swimming with tears. She's also very obviously pregnant. Her gaze settles on me and she comes towards me, gives a shaky smile and takes my hand in hers.

'I'm so sorry we have to meet like this.'

I stare at her with a quizzical expression.

'I'm Emily. Ricky's sister.' Her mouth twists downwards when she says his name, and the tears in her eyes look dangerously close to overflowing.

'Oh,' is all I can manage to say.

She steps forward, wraps her arms around me, and pulls me to her. I stand frozen, my arms hanging stiffly by my sides. I don't do hugging, especially not with strangers. She takes a sharp intake of breath and judders and I realise she's crying. We stand awkwardly like this for a while as she sobs until eventually, she pulls away from me.

'God, I'm so sorry.' She stares into my eyes. 'How completely selfish of me. You've lost your husband and I'm making it all about me.'

'He was your brother,' I say stiffly, wishing I could cry like her; what a release that would be. I haven't cried once since the accident.

'Got to let it out, eh?' She gives a shaky smile. 'I'd only just managed to track him down but I'm too late now, aren't I? I thought I had the rest of my life to rebuild my relationship with him, but it turns out I don't.'

I don't answer but take hold of her hand, surprising myself.

'Come on, let's get a drink and find you a seat so we can talk.' I lead her towards the bar and once there, swiftly drink the rest of my gin and tonic and order myself another – unwise, but I find I don't care.

'What would you like?'

'Just a water, please.' She waves a hand at her bump and jealousy engulfs me, shocking me with its intensity. Rick and I will never have a baby now; our future is gone. Dead. I've never wanted a baby but who knows if I would have changed my mind in the future? I no longer have the opportunity to find out.

'So when did you last see Rick?'

'Nine years ago.' She looks down at the floor. 'At our uncle's funeral.'

'Oh.'

'I know. We promised to keep in touch but we weren't close, what with us both sent to different boarding schools at such a young age. I wanted to remedy that though. Finding out I was pregnant made me see how important family is, despite the lack of interest from our parents. I thought this could be a new start.'

Her bottom lip trembles and I hand her the glass of water the barman has just put on the bar. She takes a gulp.

'I never even knew Ricky was married until I saw the obituary. I was surprised when I saw it, because I always assumed he was like me and that our parents had put him off marriage for life.'

I take a sip of my gin and tonic and put it back down on the bar. Truthfully, I could drink the lot down in one go and ask for another, and another and another. Drink myself into oblivion.

'Rick never talked about his family,' I say. 'He said they were ancient history and he wasn't interested.'

'Doesn't surprise me. Stuffed into boarding school at age eleven, we were the kids that our parents couldn't be bothered with. I honestly don't know why they had children because we were treated like nuisances from the get-go. Even before we were sent away to school, we had a nanny or an au pair so our parents could continue with their busy social lives. I wonder what they'd be like if they were still alive now, if age would have made them more interested in us. Probably not. Some people shouldn't have children, should they?' she asks, and then continues without waiting for an answer. 'How long were you and Ricky together?'

'We were only married for a year but met nine months before that. I thought we had years ahead of us.' I bite my lip.

'Married, eh? Still can't get my head around Ricky being married.'

'Shall we go and sit down?' I ask, having no idea how to respond.

'Please. I can feel my ankles exploding as we speak. Who knew pregnancy could affect your whole body?'

'How far on are you?' There it is again, the stab of jealousy as I utter the words. She has a future and I don't; other people will carry on living their lives whilst mine has ended.

'Thirty weeks. Ten more to go.'

I lead her over to an empty table, ignoring Sasha, one of our friends, as she looks over at me as if we're going to join them. I don't have to observe social niceties today; I'm in mourning. I can do whatever I like. I'm not going to introduce Emily to them just so they can have a good gossip about it later. Besides, I have a feeling that our little group of friends will drift away now; they came with Rick and now he's no longer here, I can't see them sticking around. We're a group of couples, and who wants a widow hanging around with them making them feel uncomfortable?

I can't say I'm particularly bothered.

We settle at the table and Emily gives an audible sigh of relief as she eases her feet out of her black court shoes.

'God, that's better. Do you feel like talking?' Her huge eyes search my face.

I've barely spoken these past weeks, since it happened, but I surprise myself with my answer.

'Yes,' I say, quietly, 'I think I do.'

She leans forward and rests her hand on my arm.

'So, tell me what happened to Ricky.'

I study her for a moment, her eagerness to know what happened that night clear to see.

So I tell her.

* * *

'Are you sure you'll be all right?'

'I'm fine, honestly. I'm exhausted and going straight up to bed.'

'It's only eight o'clock, love.'

Elaine's looking at me as if I'm mad. As if going to bed so early must mean I'm definitely *not* all right. Truthfully, all I want to do is collapse into bed, close my eyes, and block it all out. Everything.

Every fucking thing.

The noise of the cab horn tooting carries from outside even though the front door is closed. That'll be Keith nagging at the driver; demanding he sound the horn so Elaine knows it's time to leave; that he's had enough of waiting whilst she *fusses around me*, as he puts it.

Selfish bastard.

'I can stay over. It's not a problem if you don't want to be on your own.' We both know she's lying; Keith will sulk for a week if she doesn't get back in the cab and go home and fry him something in lard that will one day give him a heart attack. Hopefully. An afternoon of drinking requires carb-laden fatty food to soak it all up followed by copious cigarettes afterwards that will stink the whole house out.

How does she tolerate him? She's a kind and lovely person but she cannot see him for what he is; refuses to see him for what he is.

'No, you go.' I usher her towards the hallway. 'You must be tired too because you haven't stopped, what with making all the arrangements. Get yourself home and put your feet up because God knows, you deserve a rest.'

'Well, if you're sure.'

'I am. Absolutely. And I can't ever thank you enough for everything you've done for me.'

She leans in to hug me and turns it into a pat on the arm at the last moment, remembering my aversion to physical affection.

'I'm always going to be here for you, you know that, don't you?'

I smile and resist the urge to open the door and push her outside. I know I'm ungrateful but for the love of God, Elaine, just go.

As I open the front door the car horn toots again. Elaine looks embarrassed and I resist the urge to give Keith the finger.

'I'll see you tomorrow but if you need anything in the meantime, just call me.' She steps outside and hurries down the path towards the cab. I watch her get into the car and then close the door, heaving a sigh of relief that at last I'm alone.

No more talking, no more thinking, just sleep.

I bolt the front door and trudge up the stairs feeling as if I'm ninety years old, not twenty-eight. Once on the landing, I reach the closed door to mine and Rick's bedroom but walk past it, continuing to the front of the house, to what was Mum's bedroom. I haven't slept in our bedroom since Rick died, I can't face lying on my own in that huge super-king bed that he insisted on buying. I don't know if I'll ever be able to sleep in there again.

I haven't changed the room at all since Mum died, everything is exactly as it was; it still has the same wallpaper with tiny pink roses, the same bedding that is a riot of colourful flowers, pinks, purples, violets, and greens. Mum loved bright colours; she hated anything boring or beige and, when she was around, life was fun and never dull.

I crawl underneath the duvet and for a moment I smell Mum's favourite perfume but I know that it's an illusion. This bedding has been washed numerous times since she died, because I change the sheets every week. Maybe she's just here with me, in spirit.

This was Mum's house and then it was mine and Rick's and now it's mine again. Elaine thinks I should move and buy something smaller, more manageable, but I can't see myself ever doing that. It doesn't feel too big for me; yes, it has four bedrooms and two bathrooms and the rooms are huge, but where would I put all of our belongings if I moved? I'd have to get rid of some of them and I couldn't face that, I wouldn't be able to choose what to keep and what to let go.

Rick had wanted to move.

He said that we should sell the house and buy something modern and new and then we'd have plenty of money left over to spoil ourselves. He couldn't understand why I wanted to stay here, said the house was an old-fashioned mausoleum and the garden was far too big to be manageable. I like gardening but Rick hated it, the only time he went outside was when the weather was nice and he could use the barbeque.

I turn over and close my eyes. I need to sleep because tomorrow Elaine is coming round again, and we're going to *sort out the paperwork*, as she puts it. This means we're going to do all of the things that I've been putting off, starting with opening the post that has arrived for Rick that is neatly piled up on the kitchen worktop. We're going to go through everything. She's been nagging me, nicely, about it, and is insistent on helping because she believes I'll just let it all drift on and do nothing about it if she doesn't step in. She still thinks of me as a child even though I'm not and she behaved in exactly the same way when Mum died. There are Rick's clothes to be gone through as well, but I'll do that alone. Some things, I think, are best done on my own and there's no rush for that anyway. Rick would be furious at the thought of Elaine rifling through his belongings. He jokingly called her *the old biddy* behind her back, even though she's not old at all. We'd giggle when he said it, although I'd feel guilty about laughing because Elaine's so sweet.

We used to laugh a lot.

But that's in the past.

I burrow underneath the duvet, making a cocoon for myself, close my eyes and pray for sleep.

Deep, dreamless sleep.

Because tomorrow, I have to start my life over.

Again.

5

MEGAN

'I'm quite sure, I want you to help because it's too much on my own.'

Ironically, despite practically forcing me to sort through everything, Elaine is now playing devil's advocate and making sure that I don't think she's interfering.

'It's just, you know...' She pours boiling water into the mugs of tea that she's insisted on making, stirs the teabag around and adds milk, giving it far more attention than it warrants. Every time she's here she thinks she has to feed and water me. It's kind of her and I shouldn't find it irritating, but I do.

'No, I don't know. Tell me.'

She turns to face me now and leans back against the worktop.

'What if I find something, you know, really private?'

'Private?'

'Yes.'

'Like what?'

She shrugs and pulls an apologetic face but doesn't answer.

'I'm sure whatever's in there will be deadly dull,' I say. 'It's

Rick's office, his workspace. I'm pretty sure I'd be quite safe just dropping the lot of it into boxes and couriering it all to his company for them to sort out, but it somehow feels lazy to do that. The least I can do is check it all before I hand it over to them. Besides, I trust you, Elaine, so if we find out that Rick was a master criminal I know you're not going to blab my private business to the world.'

She laughs but can't quite meet my eyes because she does blab, even if it is only to Keith. She tells him *everything*. I can't be angry with her for doing that, because they are married and there shouldn't be secrets between husband and wife, should there? Unfortunately, Keith has a super big mouth even before he's had a drink and whenever I see him, he invariably slips up by commenting about something I've told Elaine that's supposed to be confidential. He can't help himself. I don't really care, because despite what I've said, I never confide in her about things that I don't want repeated. Whenever Keith slips up and makes it obvious that Elaine's told him something, I make a point of never reacting so he thinks I haven't noticed. In Keith's world, he's as sharp as a knife and I'm dumb and naïve. I let him continue to think that because sometimes it's better to allow people to believe that they're cleverer than you are.

'How about we start with those?' Elaine asks, as she puts the mugs on the table and slides into the chair opposite. I follow her gaze to the small pile of unopened post that's been accumulating since the day Rick died.

'Okay.' I make no move to pick them up.

'Shall I open them?'

'Please.'

She picks up the first one, inserts her finger underneath the flap, rips it open, and pulls out a sheet of paper from inside.

'Credit card statement.' She passes it to me and I glance at it, noting the balance of nearly three thousand pounds before laying it on the table.

She picks up the next envelope and then the next, proceeding through the pile. By the time she's down to the last envelope we've accumulated brochures for two wine clubs, an offer of a new credit card, a charity begging letter and several letters from political parties touting for votes in the next local election. I'm not surprised most of it is junk because we get very little proper mail; even the utility bills are electronic now. This reminds me that Rick has an email account, a mobile phone account, a couple more credit cards, his own bank account, and probably other things that I haven't even considered. They'll all have to be dealt with; more tasks to add to the ever-growing list.

Elaine picks up the last envelope. A4 size and thicker than the others, she holds it up and I see that it's addressed to me. I tell her to carry on and read it for me and she rips it open and pulls out several sheets of paper. I watch her eyes widen at the contents, and she wordlessly hands the papers to me. I take them from her and see they're from Rick's employer. I read it carefully, aware of Elaine's impatience for me to finish.

'Did you know you were going to get that?' she asks, after I've placed the papers down on the table.

'No. Yes. I'd not thought about it but it's a standard sort of thing, so I'm not surprised.'

I pick up the papers and reread them. There are forms for me to fill in and certificates that I need to send. Rick had life insurance as part of his job benefits and I'm to be paid a lump sum of five times his annual salary. It's a lot of money, a hell of a lot; a sad fact that we're worth a lot more dead than we are alive.

'Well, at least you won't need to worry about money.'

I put the letter back down but don't reply. Elaine's face reddens and she looks uncomfortable. Telling someone they'll be okay for money when their husband has just died at the age of thirty-two is crass, and she knows it. I'd expect it from Keith but not from Elaine, but I forgive her because I know she said it without thinking; the knee-jerk reaction to seeing the huge sum in the letter. We sit in silence and drink our tea. The letter from Rick's company reminds me that I have a job, too, and I need to think about what I'm going to do about it. I've been off on bereavement leave for over three weeks but at some point I'm going to have to make a decision about when I'm going back.

If I go back.

'Okay,' I say, swallowing the last of my tea and pushing back my chair. 'Let's make a start in the study.'

I pick up my kitchen chair and wait whilst Elaine gets up. I follow behind her into the hallway, carrying the chair with me. Putting the chair down in front of the door to Rick's study, I take a deep breath and open the door.

'You go first,' I say, staring into a room which looks exactly the same as the last time I saw it. What did I expect to see?

She steps inside and goes over to Rick's desk and, feeling surprisingly okay, I follow, taking the chair with me. I place it next to the enormous black leather swivel chair in front of the grey metal desk that takes up the entire space of the bay window, his chair facing out onto the street. I've always thought the desk looked ridiculous in this room. Too modern, too big and just, well, too much.

'Sit down.' I pull out the swivel chair and motion for Elaine to sit on it. After a moment's hesitation, she lowers herself down, perching on the edge of the seat.

I settle myself on the kitchen chair, my hands clasped on my lap and try to breathe normally. It's colder in here than the rest of the house, probably because the door has been kept closed for so long. Or is the coldness my imagination? The radiator is still working in here, nothing has changed. Rick always kept the door closed and I rarely came in here when he was alive; it was his domain. But it does feel different somehow.

Unlived in. Dead.

This room is what used to be called the front parlour. Most people in the street have knocked them through into the back lounge to make a huge living area but we never did. We used it as a sewing room when Mum was alive because we were both keen on making our own clothes and furnishings. After she died, I had no intention of changing it but Rick was adamant that he needed a study so I gave in and let him have this room. I hadn't done any sewing since Mum died anyway, because it wasn't the same without her here but I still couldn't bear to get rid of anything, so I packed everything into boxes and shoved it all in the garage. Once I'd done that, Rick wasted no time in getting rid of the *old lady vibe*, as he called it, totally redecorating the room. The walls are now painted a bland cream, the rose-patterned vintage carpet that had been in here forever, ripped up and replaced by blond wood flooring. Apart from Rick's huge desk in front of the window, the only other furniture is a grey filing cabinet in the corner and a grey leather recliner on the wall opposite the window where he liked to do his 'thinking' for marketing ideas for work. This room is minimalist, which is how Rick liked it.

'There should be some keys,' I say to Elaine as she looks questioningly at me. 'For the desk and filing cabinet. But if we can't find them, we'll just have to break them open.'

'Oh, I'm sure we'll find them somewhere.' Elaine drags the pen pot and notepad stand towards her, takes the pens out of the pot and thrusts her fingers inside. After a moment, she pulls out a metal key ring with two small keys attached.

She looks at me and I nod. Selecting one of the keys, she

inserts it into the lock above the drawers. It doesn't fit so she tries the other one and *voilà*, it opens.

The top drawer is full of pens, pads of sticky notes, rubber bands, loose envelopes and other detritus. Exactly like my own desk at work; it's office law that the top drawer is always full of crap that seems essential when you throw it in there but is seldom used. The second drawer has a blue coloured file inside and Elaine takes it out and after a brief look inside, we start a pile of work stuff on the floor because I think there's going to be a lot of it. When she pulls open the bottom drawer, Rick's passport comes into view. It's sitting on top of a manilla file. She takes out the passport and file, then looks at me.

'See what it is,' I say, taking the passport from her. 'We have to go through everything. It'll probably be work stuff but we have to check.'

She opens the folder and I see her eyes scanning the thick wodge of papers inside.

'It's some sort of policy, I think.' She frowns.

I lean across to look.

'Yes, it's definitely a policy,' she says, moving the folder onto the desk between us so we can both see it. The header across the top is from a well-known insurance company and Elaine flips through the pages to the back page, where it's signed and dated.

'It's life insurance,' Elaine says. 'It says here that in the event of either of you dying, the other is to receive five hundred thousand pounds.'

'Oh my God.' I stare at her in shock.

She turns to me, her eyes searching my face.

'See. There.' She points to my signature. 'Don't you remember signing it, it's only dated four months ago?'

I look at the signatures and then at her, my eyes wide.

'You do remember, don't you?' she asks.

'Of course,' I stammer, as the silence becomes uncomfortable. 'I'd forgotten about it.' She stares back at me, her feelings written all over her face.

She doesn't believe me.

* * *

I splash water onto my face and run a brush through my hair then peer at my reflection in the bathroom mirror. A bit of make-up wouldn't go amiss; my skin is so pale as to be almost translucent apart from the dark, panda-like circles underneath my eyes.

But I can't be bothered.

The murmur of Elaine and Keith's voices drift up through the ceiling from the kitchen below but I can't make out what they're saying. I came up here two hours ago, citing a headache. As soon as we'd finished in Rick's office – the filing cabinet was dispensed with quickly, as most of the drawers contained very little – I made my excuses and escaped. I'll tell Elaine that I've been asleep although I haven't; I've been wide-awake and mulling things over in my head. I'll have to go downstairs and speak to her because she won't leave until she's satisfied that I'm okay, despite my telling her that I'd be fine. I said that she must have lots of things of her own to do but she wouldn't listen; she said she was 'going to run the hoover round the study for me'. I didn't have the energy to argue with her even though the study is fine and doesn't need vacuuming at all. She likes to keep busy and it's her way of coping. I'm annoyed that Keith is here, though. He seems to think he can turn up here and make himself at home whenever he chooses. He never dared do that when Rick was alive, or Mum for that matter, but once Mum had died, he took to pitching up whenever he fancied, as if he lived here. He obviously thinks he can start doing that again now Rick is gone.

A glance at my watch confirms that it's three thirty-five. How long has he been here? He has a job of sorts, something to do with house clearances, but appears to work whatever hours he chooses. Or not work, more often. Elaine is the grafter of the two of them and I feel bad that she's taken so much time off work to look after me. I'm going to insist that she let me pay her for the time she's been off as I know her employer won't. She works as a doctor's receptionist and the pay is low and benefits zero so I've never understood why she's so loyal to them. She's worked there forever but they have no loyalty to her, so I know she'll be out of pocket. She won't take money from me so I'll just send it straight to her bank account.

I scoop my hair up into a ponytail and then tuck it into a bun, leave the bathroom and head downstairs.

'Feeling better, lovey?' Elaine asks as I walk into the kitchen. 'Cup of tea, something to eat? I can make you a sandwich. There's a nice bit of chicken in the fridge.'

'I feel loads better, thank you, and I can make myself something to eat, you don't need to wait on me.' The words came out more sharply than I'd intended but the sight of Keith seated at the kitchen table, his feet propped up on the chair next to him as if he owns the place, puts me in an immediate bad mood. I pick up the kettle, take it to the sink and fill it up.

'Would you like one?' I ask with a smile, as I flick the kettle on, in an attempt to make amends for my curtness.

'A tea for me. What about you?' She looks over at Keith.

'I'll have a tea if you're making one, Meg.' He looks up from the newspaper he's reading and grins at me. I turn my back on him to take the mugs out of the cupboard so I don't have to look at him or return his smile. She's already told him about the life insurance money and the payout from Rick's company; the sickly grin and the way he's called me 'Meg' as if we're the best of friends has just confirmed it.

I stare at the kettle as I wait for it to boil and wonder if it would look really rude if I took my tea into the lounge to drink it. I already know that it would and that I'm not going to do it because it's not fair to Elaine. I throw teabags into the mugs and when the kettle boils I pour on boiling water and add the milk. Forcing a pleasant expression onto my face, I turn around and carry the mugs over to the kitchen table before returning for my own.

'Have you decided what you're going to do?' Keith asks, folding up the newspaper and looking up at me as I slide into the seat next to Elaine. I sense, rather than see, the warning look that Elaine flashes him.

'Do?' I fix a bewildered expression on my face although I know exactly what he's getting at.

'About the house? I don't suppose you'll want to stay in this big place all on your own.'

I take a sip of tea, nearly scalding my lips in the process. I had all this from him when Mum died. He suggested then that I sell up and move in with him and Elaine so they could 'look after me'. As if I were five years old and needed taking care of. He has the same greedy look in his eyes now that he had then; there's a lot of money to be made in selling this house and, for some bizarre reason, he seems to think he's entitled to some of it.

'I don't know what I'm going to do.' I look him straight in the eye. 'It's too early to even think about it.'

'Well, you know, if you want to come and live with us, the offer's there. We've plenty of room and we promised your mum we'd always look out for you.' He smiles and I want to punch the barely concealed greed off his face. It's a blatant lie too, because they live in a very small three-bedroom semi that is barely big enough for the two of them, so I'd be expected to pay for an extension to make it bigger. I know this because he suggested it in the weeks after Mum died when I was barely functioning. He was round here all of the time and the expectation that I go and live with them was constantly dripped into my ear, the inference being that I wouldn't be able to cope alone. Thank God I met Rick and didn't give in.

'Thank you, That's very kind of you but I'm twenty-eight, not a child. I don't need looking after.'

His face flushes slightly and he's unable to conceal the dislike in his eyes. I stare back at him and he eventually looks down, unfolds the newspaper and pretends to read it.

'Well, the offer's there,' he mutters. 'If you find it a bit much being on your own.'

We sit and drink our tea and after a while, Elaine begins to gossip about someone in their street, nervous twittering about someone else's family which is an attempt to cover the silence. When I've finished my tea, I stand up, pick up the mugs and take them over to the dishwasher and put them inside.

'Thank you so much for everything you've done for me,' I say, turning to face Elaine. 'I couldn't have got through these last three weeks without you.'

'I'm glad we could help.' Elaine smiles. 'You know if there's anything you need you've only to ask.'

'I know, and I do appreciate it, honestly I do, but now I need to get on with things, try and get back to some sort of normality and you do, too. And I know you've taken a lot of time off work to be with me and that's really good of you but I also know you must be out of pocket, so I'm going to send you some money to make up for it.'

'Oh, you don't need to do that...' At the mention of money, Keith looks up from the newspaper he's pretending to read.

'I'm not arguing about it because it's only fair and the money is nothing compared with what you've done for me.'

'Listen to what the girl says, Elaine.' Keith glares at her, afraid she's going to talk me out of it.

'Anyway, I must get on now,' I say, mustering up a smile. 'This morning has really helped and I feel ready to tackle some of the other stuff that needs sorting.'

'I can stay and help, if you like?' Elaine offers.

'No, honestly, I'll be fine, I've taken up enough of your time, you must have things of your own to do.'

I've barely finished speaking before Keith is up out of the chair, newspaper tucked underneath his arm, heading for the door, hustling Elaine out of her seat. He pushes her out into the hallway, telling her that 'they need to get on' and several minutes later, I close and lock the front door behind them with a sigh of relief.

At last, peace.

The shrill of my mobile ringtone shatters the silence, making me jump. I pull it out of my sweatpants pocket, certain that it's a spam call. Calls have been few and far between these last weeks, most people preferring to send a card to express their condolences. I don't blame them, because what can you say? I stare at the screen for a moment in bafflement before realising who it is.

Emily.

6

MEGAN

I let the phone ring and eventually it stops. I slip it back into my pocket but seconds later, it rings again.

I ignore it.

I don't have the headspace to talk to her right now and – despite what I said to Elaine – it's not because I have any intention of sorting stuff out. I just want to be on my own. I'm hoping that Elaine will take the hint and go back to work now because although she's only trying to help, treating me like a child is doing me no good. I'm extremely grateful for her help, but it's time for me to man up and start dealing with things, because if I don't, it's a slippery slope to misery.

I've no intention of becoming the person I was after Mum died.

I so very nearly gave in and moved in with Elaine then because it would have been the easy option. She would have taken over and made decisions for me and I could have drifted along without having to make any effort to take control of my life. It was only meeting Rick that stopped it from happening then. But now, I'm a very different person.

After Mum died, meeting a man was the furthest thing from my mind. Rick came into my life and despite being gorgeous and everything that I would normally have looked for, I wasn't in the least bit interested. At first. Because Rick was persistent; he wouldn't take no for an answer.

When Mum was alive, of course I had boyfriends but they were casual; nothing lasted longer than a few months because I wasn't intending on settling down. I was young, I wanted to travel and after that, find a good job that would make use of my degree in textiles and design. Mum becoming so ill wasn't on the horizon; she was young and vibrant and had everything to look forward to.

Only she didn't.

The cancer diagnosis, when it came, was a horrific shock; she'd visited the GP because of indigestion and instead of coming away with a prescription for antacids as she'd expected, she was given an emergency appointment for the hospital. That appointment was the catalyst to a decline as rapid as it was devastating. The speed with which she became seriously ill was overwhelming and we were both still coming to terms with her illness when she died. The shock was mind-numbing and I couldn't cope; I didn't want to cope.

I wanted to die, too.

Elaine, despite her own grief at losing her best friend, did her best to help me after Mum's death but in all honesty, I didn't care about living because I could see no future.

Mum was everything to me and me to her, because it had only ever been the two of us. My father has never been in my life and the little I knew about him wasn't appealing; a handsome charmer who'd skipped town the very minute Mum found out she was pregnant. A father like that I can do without. I've made no attempt to find him and never will. I know his name and a little about him but quite honestly have no interest in finding him.

Even now, I can't help smiling when I remember how Rick and I met. He always insisted that it was fate. We crashed into each other in the town centre, literally, crashed into each other. He was on his way back from a meeting with an important client and I was going to the cemetery with flowers to put on Mum's grave. It was three months after she'd died and I was going through the motions of going to work and behaving in a near normal way but inside, I felt dead too. I'd called into the florists after work and was hurrying along the high street to the car park, head down against the sleet that had started to fall, trying to protect the flowers from the wind, when I'd barged into Rick. I wasn't looking where I was going and the flowers went flying up into the air and I nearly fell over, only saved by Rick catching me. He gently set me on my feet, grinned at me and made an inane joke about 'women falling at his feet'.

I promptly burst into tears.

Somehow, we ended up in a nearby pub, the battered flowers drying out underneath the table, whilst Rick listened as I talked about losing Mum. Not a great start to a romance, but somehow, it worked for us and I found a reason to live again.

I push the memories away.

I can't think about it all now; it's in the past and I have to look to the future.

The first thing I need to do is go back to work.

I don't love my job as it's not a career and it was only ever supposed to be temporary but for now, it'll force me back to some sort of normality. Fielding calls for small businesses and arranging appointments and chasing their invoices isn't a long-term career choice but for now, it's all I can cope with. It's familiar and doesn't require too much brain power. It'll get me up in the morning and out of the house and into a routine. I could easily work from home instead of going into the office but I won't do that because I'll achieve nothing if I don't get out into the world. Yes, I have things to sort out but none of it is urgent; it'll all get done in time. I could easily not bother working at all because the life insurance money and Rick's payout from his company are more than enough to keep me in comfort, but I need something to occupy me. If I go back to work and get back into a routine, then I can decide what I'm going to do. Decision made, I pull out my phone and type a message to Jeremy, my boss, to tell him that I'll be back into the office next week. I press the send button before I can change my mind, feeling ridiculously pleased that I've actually made a decision.

I go into the lounge and stand looking out of the front window. The street is quiet, which isn't surprising for a late afternoon in February. Most people will be at work and it's not as if I see many of my neighbours anyway. Although I've lived here nearly all of my life, the houses in this street have changed hands many times. I can count on one hand the number of neighbours who came to Rick's funeral. It was nice of them to bother but truthfully, I struggle to remember their names although we always say 'hello' if we happen to pass one another in the street. The irony is that Rick never spoke to any of the neighbours and only acknowledged them if he was forced to. He wasn't deliberately rude; they just weren't on his radar.

I pull the curtains closed to shut out the gloom; it'll be dark in less than an hour. Turning on the lamps gives the room a warm glow and I pick up the remote control to turn on the TV to put a stop to the silence in the room and the noises in my head. My phone rings again and I pull it out of my pocket to see 'Emily' on the screen. She's not going to give up. Pressing the answer button, I take a deep breath.

'Hello, Emily,' I say. 'How are you?'

'Hi, Megan. I'm fine,' she replies. 'But more importantly, how are you?'

'Um. Okay.'

'I keep thinking about you, and Ricky, and how things could have been different if I'd just found him sooner.'

I don't answer because what do I say to that?

'I'd like to see you,' she says. 'Before I go home.'

'Home? Where's home?'

'Up north. Newcastle.'

'Oh.'

'So can I come and see you?'

'Yes, of course.'

'Great. Is seven o'clock tonight all right?'

'Tonight? Um, okay.'

'Great, I'll see you then.'

Before I can respond she ends the call and I stare uselessly at the phone. I should ring her back; tell her it's not convenient, make an excuse, put her off.

Or maybe I should just get on with it.

* * *

At exactly seven o'clock, the doorbell rings.

The TV is on a quiet murmur in the background so the silence isn't too loud and I've turned on the electric fire flames to make the room feel cosier. After I spoke to Emily, I made myself a sandwich and a cup of tea and forced myself to eat it in the spirit of *getting on with things*. I then went upstairs and put on some make-up. Not much; a little tinted moisturiser and a slick of lip tint, I've also let my hair loose and brushed it around my face.

I'm tired of looking and behaving like a victim.

I go out to the hallway and open the front door. Emily is standing outside looking pale and cold.

'Hi. Come in.' I pull the door open wide and she steps into the hallway, bringing the cold air in with her. I close the front door and usher her into the lounge.

'Let me take your coat,' I say, as she stands hesitantly, looking around. 'And I'll hang it up for you.'

She unbuttons it, shrugs it off and gives it to me before lowering herself down onto the sofa. Her bump looks huge, the rest of her body tiny. Her bump seems much bigger than when she was at the funeral but maybe it's her clothes; she's wearing leggings and a tight-fitting jumper today, making her arms and legs appear stick-thin. I remember her saying she has ten more weeks to go but it doesn't look possible for her to get any bigger but then, what do I know? I quickly turn and take her coat out into the hallway and hang it on the peg next to Rick's jacket. It's still hanging there as if he's going to walk through the door at any moment.

'This sofa is lush,' she says, as I go back into the lounge. 'I could easily fall asleep on it.' She leans her head back and closes her eyes.

'Are you feeling okay?'

'Oh, yes.' She opens her eyes and smiles. 'Just tired. I don't think my body was made for carrying a baby elephant around.'

She's a similar build to me except for the bump; slender and not very tall. I'm five-feet-four in my stockinged feet. Rick used to say I looked as if a gust of wind would blow me over but I'm much stronger than I look. I settle into the armchair opposite her.

'You don't have a Geordie accent,' I say, remembering that her home is Newcastle. She looks surprised and then laughs.

'Ha'way man, what d'you mean? Listen to me; I live there and I can't even do the accent. I don't have any sort of accent. One of the benefits of a private school education.'

'Rick was the same. He used to call me the country bumpkin or the Swindoo.'

'Sounds like Ricky, although your accent's so slight it's barely noticeable. The Swindon accent is nothing like the Bristol one.' Emily laughs. 'I changed trains there and I could barely understand them. Even stronger accent than the Newcastle one.'

She leans forward, her eyes searching my face.

'But anyway, how have you been, really? Have you got someone staying with you?'

'No.' I shake my head. 'Elaine, my late mum's best friend, has been round every day but she's not been staying here. I'm fine on my own.'

'Really?'

'Well, no, not really but I just have to get on with it, don't I? I can't ask Elaine to come and stay here, she has her own life and she's done more than enough for me already.'

'You're very brave.'

No, I'm not.

'I still can't believe it,' she goes on. 'All these years of looking for Ricky and I get here too late.'

'I'm sorry.'

'Oh, God, how selfish of me, there I go again, thinking of myself. You've just lost your husband and I'm making this all about me. I'm so sorry. Is there anything I can do?'

'Thank you, but there isn't.' I shake my head. 'So, when do you go home?'

'The day after tomorrow. I'm not looking forward to the journey, hours and hours on a train.' She pulls a face.

'It's a long way in your condition, although you must be

excited.' I nod towards her bump. 'About the baby. You and your partner.'

'*I'm* excited. The father? Well, let's just say he's not in the picture.'

'I'm sorry to hear that. Although my own father was never in the picture and I never felt as if I was missing out. My mother was all I needed.'

'I don't want him around.' She shrugs. 'I'll be okay. He'll get the message eventually.'

'What message?'

'That we're over.' She frowns, bites her bottom lip. 'I'd rather not talk about him. So, you're coping?'

'Not really.'

'Oh, God, poor you.' She gets up from the sofa, comes and sits next to me and takes my hand, holding it in her small, cold fingers. 'I'm probably the only person in the world who has any idea how you feel, because I've lost him too.'

I turn my head to see her huge eyes searching my face, tears welling in the corners of them. We sit in silence for a moment and then I slide my hand from hers and stand up. 'I'll go and put the kettle on. Tea or coffee?'

'Just a glass of water for me, please.' She pulls a face. 'I've had my quota of caffeine for the day.'

'I have milk, or fruit juice, if you prefer?'

'No, honestly, water's fine.'

I go out into the hallway and through into the kitchen. I'm standing at the sink filling the kettle when her voice calls from the hallway.

'Is it okay to use your loo?'

'Of course,' I call.

I put the kettle on the stand, flick it on and go into the hallway to tell her where the toilet is, looking up just in time to see the back of her as she disappears up the stairs. The door is open to the bathroom so she'll have no trouble finding it.

'Just here would be great.'

I slow the car, pull over to the side of the road and stop. It's past ten o'clock so the roads are quiet with little traffic about. I wouldn't dare pull over on this busy main road if it were daytime.

'I'll wait here whilst you walk to the hotel entrance,' I say as she opens the car door.

'Honestly, there's no need, it's only a couple of minutes away.'

'Humour me,' I say. 'It's dark, you're a woman on your own. I won't be able to sleep if I don't see you safely through the door.'

She smiles but I sense a hint of annoyance from her. I've only just met Emily but already I've discovered that she's not the best at hiding her feelings.

Unlike me.

'So I'll see you tomorrow?' She gets out and then leans into the car, ready to close the door.

'Yes, I'll pick you up at the car park at the back of the hotel at one o'clock?'

'Perfect. You're sure you don't mind me coming?'

'Of course not.'

'I'll say goodnight then.'

She closes the door and I watch her hurry along the street, wrapping her thin coat around her as she goes. She must be freezing. When she reaches the hotel, she turns, gives a little wave and disappears through the doorway.

That hotel again; the Regency Arms; that bloody place. The

memory of that night will never go away but I can cope with it now, because if I can have my husband's wake there, how can a memory possibly hurt me?

It can't.

I push the gearstick into first and head home, pushing the memory of Rick's anger out of my head. Concentrate on the here and now, that's what I have to do. This evening didn't morph into the stilted misery-fest that I expected; Emily talked about Rick when they were very young but, as he was older than her and went off to boarding school when she was five, her memories were limited. She saw him in the school holidays sometimes, but due to the age difference, they weren't close. When he went to university, he mostly stayed away in the holidays and didn't bother coming home. She cried then, for what she'd missed. She barely mentioned their parents who died in a car crash when Rick was only twenty-three. She talked a lot about her feelings and I let her because I'm not a talker, I never have been. I'm a good listener.

I told her how I was going back to work next week and she said she wished she had a job. She clammed up then and said she should be going and I was shocked to see how late it was. She took out her mobile phone to call a cab, because that's how she'd arrived, and without thinking, I offered her a lift.

Tonight is the first time I've driven since *that* night.

Rick's car was a write-off obviously, but I still have mine, safely parked in the garage where it's been for the last three and a half weeks. It felt strange holding the car keys in my hand again. Strange but also good.

It means I'm getting back to normal; doing normal things.

I concentrate on the road. It's not far to get home; less than a fifteen-minute drive, perhaps even less as there's no traffic. I drive past the river and it's calm, benign, unrecognisable from that night. In no time I've arrived and I pull up onto the driveway and turn off the engine.

That's one ghost laid.

Tomorrow, I'm going to the funeral directors to collect Rick's ashes. Elaine said that she would go and get them but I refused her offer. Rick was my husband, not hers, so it's for me to do. I can't let someone else do it. I haven't decided where I'm going to scatter them or if I even will; maybe I'll just keep them. People do that, don't they? Isn't there a joke about having them on the mantelpiece?

Somehow, I found myself telling Emily about it on the way to the hotel and she asked if I minded if she came with me. How could I refuse her?

So she's going with me.

7

EMILY

I never intended going to the funeral.

I knew when it was, of course I did, because it was announced in the local newspaper which I'd been scouring for news since the day I found out Ricky was dead.

That's how I found out he was dead; from the newspaper.

I'll never get over that, never. My lover dies in a tragic accident and I learn of it from reading the headline in the local paper. There I was, queuing at the newsagent waiting to pay for a magazine and it was there, staring at me from the rack, *Local Man Dies in Tragic River Accident* with a picture of Ricky beneath the headline.

I stared at it in disbelief and then my legs crumpled and I couldn't breathe; it felt as if all of the oxygen had been sucked out of the shop and I was trapped in a vacuum. In the split second of seeing that headline, my future was gone.

Someone must have called an ambulance but I have no recollection of it. When the paramedics arrived, they insisted on taking me to hospital because even though I'd come round by then, I was in such a state of shock that I couldn't speak.

Once we arrived in A & E, I didn't have to wait around too long before a doctor came to examine me. Or at least, I don't think it was very long but I can't be completely sure because time had ceased to mean anything. I'd found my voice by then and I lied and told him I'd come over a bit faint with the standing still and waiting to be served. He looked a straight up sort of guy, short back and sides, sensible shoes, and I had a feeling that the truth – that my secret lover and the father of my child had drowned in a tragic accident – would be unpalatable to him.

Because I'm the other woman, you see, so undeserving of any sympathy. Although Ricky was planning to leave her and move in with me, in the eyes of Joe Public, *I'm* the bad person, not the cold bitch he was married to.

Even now, I try not to think about how Ricky died because he hated the water and going into the river would have been his very worst nightmare. He couldn't swim, not properly anyway, he used to laugh and say he'd perfected the doggy paddle but he wasn't the least bit interested in swimming. I never said it to him but I think he was afraid of water and didn't like to admit it. 'Who wants to swim in perpetually cold and wet England?', that's what he used to say. Squash and cycling were much more his thing. Knowing the panic he must have felt, trapped in that car, makes me shudder. Why did he have to be driving along that road, in that awful weather?

Just my luck.

I was still in shock when they let me out of hospital although I was just about managing to function by then. I got home to my flat, locked the front door, crawled into bed and stayed there for the next three days. Now and then I'd haul myself out of my pit to go to the toilet and make myself tea and toast and then crawl right back in. I lay underneath that duvet and wallowed and cried, and on the fourth day, when I was done, I dragged myself out of bed and into the shower where I stayed until the water ran cold. Although I wanted to give up and lie there, I couldn't wallow forever, because I needed to figure out what the fuck I was going to do.

Because Ricky dying was definitely *not* in my plans.

I loved Ricky.

Well, I say loved, maybe that's stretching it a bit, but I was definitely fond of him. He definitely loved me though, and he was going to give me a future, despite me getting accidentally pregnant – or maybe even because of it. We hadn't been together for long when I found out and quite honestly, I was sure he'd run for the hills if I told him. It was strange because actually, I wasn't even going to tell him; I was going to take care of it and there would be no need for him to ever know and we'd continue as we were. My intentions were blown out of the water because one night he told me he loved me and wanted to be with me and I came over all emotional – not like me at all – and I just blurted it out without thinking. No one had ever chosen me over their wife, you see, I'd always been the bit on the side, and I got carried away in the moment.

He froze after I'd uttered the immortal words, 'I'm pregnant' and I could have bitten my tongue off because as I stared at his shocked face, I knew I'd ruined everything.

Only I hadn't.

A big, slow, cheesy grin spread across his face and he pulled me into his arms and said I'd made him the happiest man alive. What could be better, he asked, than having a baby to complete our lives? Well, I could think of a million things that would be better, but I didn't tell him that. I pretended to be as delighted as he was. And there are nurseries and stuff for after it's born, so it wasn't as if I'd have to be looking after it all of the time. And we'd be well off and well able to afford it once he was divorced, because Ricky kept assuring me of that.

He'd get half the house, which was worth an absolute bomb because it was in an upmarket and much sought-after area. He also had a well-paid career so I'd be able to stay at home and not have to go back to work after I'd had the baby. For the first time in my life, things were going my way. I knew we could have a good life together and although I didn't actually love him, that wouldn't be a problem because I liked him enough and we had fun together. I always make the effort when I'm with a man; I'm good company and attractive and I made Ricky feel good. If it all went pear-shaped, well, with a baby, he'd have to look after me, wouldn't he?

But not now.

Why couldn't she have died and he survived? He'd have got all the house then and it would have saved the hassle of getting a divorce.

Just my luck.

So why did I go to the funeral?

Well, as I say, I wasn't going to but the more I thought about it, the more I thought, why shouldn't I? I'm mourning too, even if it is mostly for myself. Why should she get to keep everything? I'm having Ricky's baby so that should entitle me to something. If he was alive and he'd changed his mind and stayed with her, he'd have to provide for his child so why should death make a difference? The more I stewed about it, the more determined I became to get what I'm due.

Because I've got nothing.

I live in a rented flat that without Ricky here to subsidise will be nigh on impossible to keep. My wages as a mobile hairdresser used to be good but since I met Ricky, they've become sporadic. With Ricky funding my lifestyle, I haven't bothered working much of late because I used to do a lot of evenings and that didn't fit in with seeing him. A lot of my clients have drifted away to other hairdressers now I've not been so reliable, so I'd have to look for new clients. Also, now I'm quite heavily pregnant, it's not good to be on my feet all day.

But I need money.

The statutory maternity pay I'll receive is frankly laughable and I have no one else to look after me. And once the baby is born, do I really want to be dragging it around with me whilst I cut hair? No, I don't. Since Ricky's death, the germ of an idea of how to get what I'm owed has begun to grow and I've come up with a plan. If it doesn't work, what have I lost?

Nothing, that's what, because I *have* nothing to lose. Nothing ventured, nothing gained.

And the first step in that plan was the funeral. I visualised my entrance before I even got there. Ricky had told me about his family and his sister, how he doesn't ever see her and hasn't done for years. We were the same like that; I never see any of my family either. I have a brother somewhere but I've no intention of looking for him, I never knew my father, and my mother? Well, who knows if she's even still alive. Who cares? I left home at sixteen and I've never been back, never wanted to go back.

Although Ricky did know where his sister was, despite what he told Megan. He never bothered to contact her, though, because he gave it a lot of thought and decided that they'd managed this long without seeing each other, what was the point? Also, I think the thought of what Megan would say about it stopped him because he said he couldn't talk to her about any of it – she used to come over all funny whenever he spoke about family. Stiff and even colder than normal, Ricky said. Frozen. I think it was because she was jealous and didn't want to share Ricky with anyone. Anyway, the upshot is that I know his sister is safely out of the way and there's little chance she's going to pitch up and scupper my plan – she got married and moved to Australia a few years ago and is settled in Adelaide. I don't think, realistically, that she'd even have any idea that Ricky is dead. I googled her name and none of the ones that came up lived in Australia and also, she's married now, so her name will be different. I looked on Facebook too and there's tons of women called Emily Fordham so I think I'm pretty safe.

So I'm not stupid; I've thought this through.

But my plan means that I need to get into Ricky's house, and the easiest way to do that is by getting close to his snotty wife. Pretending to be Emily, Ricky's sister, seemed the obvious way. I even had ready what to say to her if she guessed I was lying. I was going to tell her the whole truth about me and Ricky and spare none of the details, but she fell for it so, so easily. It was funny really, because the way Ricky talked about her, I had this image of a cold, calculating, cool-headed smart arse but she didn't come across like that. She seemed a bit vague. And gullible, luckily for me. Maybe she really is missing him.

The biggest shock, though, was seeing how much she looked like me. When I walked in to the wake and saw her standing there greeting people, I did a double take. I could be *her* sister. I knew we looked alike because Ricky made no secret of that fact and as he used to say, everyone has a type they're attracted to. Ricky was my type; tall, dark and good-looking with velvet brown eyes that a person could drown in. Although equally, he could have been short, blond and ugly – as long as he could give me a future and wasn't a nasty piece of work. But no matter, he was gorgeous and there was no need for me to fake anything with him. Except the love bit.

It's so bloody unfair.

Anyway, on the day of the funeral I didn't put any make-up

on because I had to look as if I was grieving and also, it was a bit of method acting. I read that somewhere, the need to live the part. I had to make myself feel like a different person, and I did; I felt bare and exposed because I'd never normally leave the flat without a face full, even at six months pregnant I always make an effort because you never know who you're going to meet. Ricky loved a bit of glamour, that's what he called it; glamour. He loved all of it; the make-up, perfume, nice clothes, sexy underwear; the fact that I bothered because he never got it at home. He said I was the technicolour version of *her*. According to Ricky, she's strictly black and white, both in and outside of the bedroom and as dull-arsed as they come. She likes crocheting, for fuck's sake.

My hair is dyed, yes, I'll admit that, but nature needs a little help sometimes and I like to make the most of what I've got and it's done well, because I am a hairdresser, after all. *Hers* is natural, I can always tell because well, being a hairdresser, I can spot these things a mile off. I was shocked when I saw her in person even though I'd seen her photograph in the newspaper, I mean, I hate to admit it and it sticks in my throat, but she's seriously beautiful.

Absolutely stunning.

And it's all wasted on her.

As I said, her hair is a natural pale blonde that most women would die for and her skin is flawless, even without make-up. Not a blemish on it. She didn't have a scrap of it on, not even tinted moisturiser. Not a thing, no lippy or mascara, nothing. She's beautiful in that ghostly, ethereal sort of way but with a bit of slap and a bit of effort, well, she'd be breathtaking. Film star beautiful. I can see why Ricky fell for her and he did tell me that he was bowled over by her looks and couldn't believe she wanted to be with him.

Until he found out how seriously weird she is.

He said the house is like a museum; he had to sulk for weeks for her to let him have the front parlour as his office. Front parlour? What the fuck's that? He said it was like something out of the nineteen-fifties and she nearly had a nervous breakdown when he cleared out all the old crappy furniture and ripped up the flowery carpet. He said his office was the only room in the house where he felt comfortable and not as if he was trapped in a time warp. That's why he spent so much time here, because he couldn't stand living there, it gave him the creeps. Just a few more weeks and we'd have been together.

Why is life so cruel?

When I introduced myself and spun her a load of rubbish about being Ricky's sister, she fell for it *so* easily. She seemed genuinely interested in me and we sat down together and I reminisced about Ricky. It was very weird, because all the time we were talking, I wanted to punch her in the face and then climb on top of her and beat her to a pulp. Not that she knew what I was thinking because I'm a very good actress. I sometimes think that if I'd had a different upbringing, I could have been an actress, had a proper career. Been something. Made something of my life.

Anyway, by the time everyone started drifting away, I made sure that we exchanged phone numbers. She never talked to anyone else whilst I was there so I was feeling quite pleased with how it went. Although there were a lot of people at the funeral and they were obviously there for Ricky, they didn't seem like they were her friends as well as his. Ricky used to say she was a bit of a loner apart from her dead mum's creepy old best friend who was always hanging around like a bad smell. She drove him mad, always popping in and poking her nose in. Helicoptering around Megan as if she was a little kid. Ricky called her the *old biddy* and did his best to put her off coming round but he said she wouldn't take the hint, even when he was quite brutal about it. Quite often he'd come home from work and he knew she'd been there because there'd be a disgusting casserole or something in the fridge, as if they couldn't manage to cook a meal on their own.

He was so excited about divorcing her. 'Not normal', that's what he called Megan. He'd been blinded by her looks and she thought she had him trapped into marriage but he was leaving her to live with me, and the really gutting thing is that he if was still alive, he'd have told her by now. He'd be with me. He was going to wait until the second anniversary of her mother's death had gone by because he knew what a state she'd get in about it and he didn't want to get the blame for her doing something stupid. He was thoughtful like that. On the first anniversary she'd gone into mourning all over again; barely speaking to Ricky for weeks on end and moping around the house with a long face, as if her mother had just died. I mean, I'm not unsympathetic, but get a grip, for God's sake.

I know there's no point in dwelling on it because my situation is what it is, but sometimes it's really hard when I realise how close I came to having it all.

But I have to move on.

After the funeral I made myself wait until the Tuesday before ringing her. When she didn't answer, I did wonder if I'd imagined her liking me. But then I reminded myself that she's the old-fashioned sort who'd think it was her duty to speak to her late husband's sister so it was just a matter of time; all I had to do was keep ringing her and wait for her to give in. I rang again later on and when she answered, I made my face look all sad because although she couldn't see me, how you look affects your voice. Method acting again. I was pretty pushy and pretended I was leaving town and wanted to see her before I went. I invited myself around because she clearly wasn't going to ask me. She seemed a bit hesitant but agreed that I could visit, because she could hardly say no to Ricky's sister, could she? I silently punched the air when I'd hung up.

Step one of the plan completed.

Which was to get inside the house. When I arrived, I told her I'd got a cab but I hadn't; I walked from my flat, which takes a good half an hour. I just don't have the money to waste on cabs but she never batted an eyelid, falling easily for my lie. A lie of no consequence but it reassures me that she's gullible and that I'm fooling her.

She had a bit more colour when she answered the door because she'd put a bit of make-up on, just a touch, and it looked good on her. I immediately felt like a tramp because I'm still sporting the grieving sister persona but I reminded myself that it's all in a good cause. I gave her my lie about living in Newcastle – far enough away for there to be no possibility of her knowing anyone there – and she surprised me by commenting about my having no accent. Not as dim as I thought. Luckily, I'm quick-thinking and told her I didn't have any accent at all due to my private school education. I don't normally have much of an accent although occasionally it slips out so I'll have to be careful. When I made the comment about the Bristol accent it made me realise that I need to flesh out my back story a bit more; I have no idea if the train from Newcastle changes at Bristol and she obviously didn't either but I need to be careful. The devil is in the details. We seemed to get along well again, although she's such a cold fish that it was hard work keeping the conversation going at times.

After we'd chatted about how sad we both are, she got up to

make a drink and I used that opportunity to go upstairs on the pretext of using the toilet.

Step two of the plan completed.

I do feel better for having a plan; it's making the loss of my life with Ricky more bearable.

When she offered me a lift back to the hotel at the end of the night, I definitely had to be quick-thinking then because obviously, I'm not staying at a hotel. I told her I was staying at the Regency Hotel because I knew she wouldn't be able to stop right outside the place because it's pedestrianised. When her eyes widened slightly, I realised it was where she'd had the wake. I had an anxious moment then, trying to remember if I'd mentioned where I was staying when I spoke to her at the funeral. I'm pretty sure I didn't and she never mentioned it so I think I'm safe. We passed the spot where the accident happened on the way and she never batted an eyelid; nothing, never even flinched. I felt sick as we drove down that road because that was the last journey Ricky made and she carried on as if everything was normal, never even mentioned him or the accident.

Cold-hearted, that's what she is. Not normal.

When we got to the hotel, she insisted on waiting at the end of the street to watch me go safely inside the hotel. I could have done without that. The receptionist looked up at me, giving a quizzical look as I strolled in. I had to think on my feet because I couldn't just turn around and go back out in case she was still there. I clutched my bump and with a pained expression, asked if I could use the loo as it was an emergency. Her expression softened a little and she directed me to the toilets, although I knew where they were because I'd been in the hotel bar many a time.

I went into the toilets and I did use them, because it's a bit of a walk home from Old Town to my flat, and when I came out, instead of going past reception, I slipped out through the back entrance into the car park. It rained on the way home, of course, and I got soaked but despite that, I felt positive about things.

Very positive.

Because tomorrow, she's picking me up to go with her to the funeral directors.

We're going to collect Ricky's ashes.

Together.

8

MEGAN

Awake, I lie still, the nightmare of last night gradually receding. Soon I'll feel calm enough to get out of bed and begin the day. Every night since the night of the accident the dream has been the same; the storm, the torrential rain beating against the windscreen, the headlights illuminating the black waters of the river, the darkness swirling as they swallowed the car, the stifling panic and terror at being trapped.

Both of our hands on the steering wheel, fighting one another for control.

I never told the police that bit; how the wheel was wrenched this way and that in an attempt to stop the plummet into the river. I told them the car skidded on the wet road and we veered into the water because it was perfectly possible that it was the way it happened.

Some truths never need to be shared with anyone.

What would be the point in the truth about that night coming out? It's done. Over. Cannot be changed.

Strangely, I never dream of the hours before the drive home; our last supper at the Regency Arms.

I throw back the duvet, clamber out of bed and head for the bathroom, pushing it all from my mind as I do every time I wake up. Will there ever come a day when I don't wake like this? I hope so; I remind myself that it's not even a month since it happened. Time heals. I turn on the shower and brush my teeth, then strip off my nightdress and step underneath the running water. Ice-cold at first, I force myself to stay underneath the water as I turn the dial to 'hot' and the ancient boiler does its work, and as the water eventually runs warm and then hot, it washes away the final vestiges of last night's dream. When I get out ten minutes later and towel myself dry, I feel awake and alert, the nightmare banished.

For now.

I go downstairs and force myself to eat some cereal, each spoonful a trial. After breakfast I look at the kitchen clock and try to imagine how I'm going to fill the hours until I pick up Emily from the hotel. The morning stretches ahead of me interminably, seeming like days, not hours. I could sort Rick's things out as I told Elaine I was going to do, make a start, at the very least.

Stop putting things off.

Rick's study is done and that wasn't so bad, was it? And if I find it too much, I can stop. Maybe if I do it little by little, I'll be able to get through it.

I load the breakfast dishes into the dishwasher, take a roll of dustbin liners from underneath the sink and go out into the hallway. I stop and stare at Rick's jacket hanging on the peg and after a moment, reach up and take it down. I check the pockets but there's nothing inside any of them. As I move the material the familiar smell of the aftershave that he always wore brings him to life for a fleeting second and I can almost believe that if I turn around, he'll be behind me.

It's my overwrought imagination.

I press my nose to the inside of the coat and breathe in deeply. Nothing. It smells of nothing.

I open up the dustbin bag, roll up the jacket, shove it inside and drop the bag to the floor. I'll take all of his clothes to one of the charity shops in town so that someone in need can have the benefit of them. This jacket, in particular, was a very expensive brand and has hardly been worn.

I head up the stairs and when I get to the top, I shake out another bin bag, go into the bathroom and open the wall cabinet; bottles of aftershave, razors, shaving foam and assorted bits and pieces fill the shelf. I pick each item up and drop it into the bag, doing it quickly before I can change my mind. Rick's half-used charcoal toothpaste that tasted disgusting goes in, too, followed by his bottle of mouthwash. I repeat the process from the ledge in the shower and the cupboard beneath the sink. I scan the bathroom to see if I've missed anything and try to remember if I threw his toothbrush into the bag. I must have done because as far as I can see, all trace of Rick has gone. But I can't remember putting his toothbrush in there. I'm about to check if it's in the bag when I remind myself that it doesn't matter.

The bathroom looks strange when I've finished, and I spread my own things out to fill the gaps. It still doesn't look right, but I don't suppose it ever will. Maybe I'll move into Mum's bedroom permanently, make the en suite in there my own and leave this for guests.

Not that I ever have any.

Pulling the top of the bag together, I tie it in a knot and take it onto the landing and put it at the top of the stairs. Taking a deep breath and readying myself, I walk across to our bedroom and open the door.

The room looks dusty, neglected. Sad.

As if all life has been sucked out of it.

Elaine wanted to dust and hoover in here but I stopped her; I told her not to come in here and to leave the door shut. I stand for a moment and close my eyes to see if I can sense Rick's presence, is his spirit still here?

No, there's nothing, or if there is, I can't feel it. I don't believe in any of that anyway; it was the same when Mum went. I desperately waited for a sign from her but there was nothing.

I open my eyes and stare at the bed; the bedding is black with swirls of muted reds, as are the curtains. Very masculine, very Rick, not my choice at all. The sheets haven't been changed since before he died. Before Rick, when this was just my bedroom, my bedding was pale blue and white, the curtains a shade darker. Rick said we needed warmth in a bedroom, that blue made him shiver and made everything feel cold. Cold to the touch.

Like me.

I push his words away. No dwelling, remember? On impulse, I cross to the bed, pull the cover off the duvet, throw it on the floor and then grab hold of the bottom sheet and wrench it from the bed. I have to pull it hard to get it to release from the corners of the mattress and I think how satisfying it would be if it ripped. It doesn't, of course, and I pull off the pillowcases and then hurl the pillows at the wall. They hit the ancient anaglypta paper that Rick hated so much and flop to the floor with an unsatisfying flump and I wonder where this sudden anger has come from. I open another bin bag and roll all of the bedding into a ball, pushing it inside the bag and tying the top in a knot when I'm done. I go out to the landing and drop it next to the bathroom bag and look at my watch, convinced I've been doing this for hours but I'm mistaken; only half an hour has passed. I go back into the bedroom and open the wardrobe doors, to be confronted by Rick's shirts. Each one is perfectly arranged on a hanger, the top button done up. I did that; I took a peculiar pride in ironing his shirts, despite detesting ironing. The shirts are expensive because Rick was very particular about his shirts and he never bought cheap. I take the first hanger out and am about to unbutton the shirt when I change my mind. I grab a handful of hangers from the wardrobe, take them out and throw them onto the bed, repeating the process until all of Rick's clothes cover the mattress. There are too many clothes and they're too heavy to put into bin bags but it doesn't matter because I have a much better idea. When Rick moved in, he brought his own suitcases with him. I don't need them because I have my own in the cupboard underneath the stairs. I'll get his cases, fill them up and the charity shop can have the cases, too. I head downstairs, taking the bags of rubbish with me, renewed with a new sense of purpose.

I can do this.

I drive into the car park at the back of the Regency Hotel and pull into the nearest empty space. It's only quarter to one because I left home extra early so I could drop off all of Rick's stuff at the charity shop. Once I'd pulled his clothes out of the wardrobe and packed them into cases, I wanted all of it gone. I didn't want to be seeing those cases all of the time. That would be worse than Rick's stuff still being in the wardrobes because at least I didn't have to see it all, even though I knew it was there.

So it's done.

Not that the woman in the charity shop was the slightest bit pleased with my donations; far from it. She had a look of distaste on her face when I manhandled both of the bulging cases into the shop, despite them being high-end, barely used and worth a small fortune. Did I expect her to be grateful? Yes, I think I did, at least a bit. But she wasn't, so I left the cases in front of her desk and walked out, ignoring her loud voice telling me that they would only take three carrier bags of donations at a time. No way was I taking any notice of her and dragging that lot home again.

I lean my head back on the headrest, turn the radio up louder and prepare to wait. I feel surprisingly good now I'm driving again; it's a bit like getting on a bicycle once you've had a fall. A flicker in the mirror catches my attention and I see Emily coming through the entrance of the car park and walking up to the back entrance to the hotel. She hasn't seen me and I watch as she picks her way across the pothole-strewn tarmac. Once at the door she steps underneath the porch and waits. I open the car door, climb out and wave to her. After a moment she waves back and walks towards me.

'Sorry, didn't see you there.' She smiles, hitching a large handbag onto her shoulder. 'Just went out for a bit of fresh air. Blow the cobwebs away.'

'Rather you than me.' I climb into the car and push the passenger door open. 'It's not exactly pleasant.'

'Oh, I don't feel the cold.' She clambers into the car, pulling the door shut with a thump and reaching for the seat belt. 'I've got my baby to keep me warm.'

I put the car in reverse and zoom backwards, swing around and out through the entrance I came in.

'You okay?' I detect concern in her voice.

'Fine.' I keep my eyes on the road and stretch my lips slightly upwards in an attempt at a smile. 'It's been a bit of a morning.'

'Oh, why?'

'I took all Rick's clothes to the charity shop.'

'Oh,' she says, after a pause. 'That must have been a hard thing to do.'

'It was.' I slow to a stop at the traffic lights. 'Not helped by the woman in the shop behaving as if I'd taken in two suitcases of cow manure rather than a shed load of designer clothes. Talk about ungrateful.'

'You'd think they'd be glad of anything they can get.'

'You would. I'm afraid I was a bit off with her and just left them there. No way was I taking them away again.'

'It must have taken a lot to do that, sort all his clothes out.'

'It did.' I pull away. 'But it's done now. Next step, the ashes.'

'Are you sure you don't mind me coming with you?'

'Of course not,' I reply. Why do people do this? Ask if you're sure about something when you're practically doing it? Elaine constantly does it and I don't get it. Why do people need constant reassurance? Or maybe it's me; maybe I'm the odd one.

'We're here.' I pull in to the car park and manoeuvre into one of the three empty spaces. There are only six spaces in all but I don't suppose these places get super-busy. I turn off the engine and turn to Emily.

'Okay?'

She nods, her face pale, her eyes huge.

I climb out of the car and wait whilst Emily heaves herself out. I lock the car and head towards the entrance, Emily beside me. The door opens magically as we arrive and I guess that we're on camera.

'Mrs Fordham?' A black-suited man of about fifty steps outside and ushers us through the door. He looks familiar, and I wonder if he was at the funeral. Maybe he was, but I can't really remember.

'Yes. And Mr Fordham's sister.' I nod towards Emily.

'Mr Weaver.' He does a head incline that's almost a bow and leads the way, showing us into a stiflingly hot room decorated in green flock wallpaper and floral carpet. A huge flower arrangement in an elaborate gold vase sits on a gilt table at one end of the room, a long velvet-covered sofa at the other.

'I'll be back in just one moment.' He disappears through a different door and I wonder how long we're going to be here. I don't want to be here; aside from the stifling heat, there's no need to hang around. Everything has been paid for and completed, and all I want is Rick's ashes.

'If you'd like to come through.' It's seconds later and he's back, beckoning us to go with him. We follow him through the doorway into a larger room with a hotel-like reception desk. Like the previous room, the heat is stifling. A large, cardboard box is sitting on the desk and I presume the urn is inside. My first thought is that it's much bigger than I expected. I can't get my head around the fact that all that's left of Rick is inside.

'There's just a form for you to sign and then we won't keep you any longer.' Mr Weaver stands by the box and I almost expect him to thrust his arm out, game show-style. It's hysteria, I know. I just want to get out of here.

'Where's the form?'

'Jacqueline's just bringing it.'

A fifty-something brunette with an over-made-up face appears from a doorway behind the desk, approaches the counter and slides a printed form towards me.

'If you could just sign there.' She taps the paper with her index finger and gives me a sad, closed-lip smile.

Feeing more claustrophobic by the minute, I take the proffered fountain pen from her and scribble a signature. No biros here. I give the pen back to her and as she takes it from me, she turns to Emily and gives her the same practised smile and opens her mouth to speak but Emily suddenly makes a strange squeaking sound. I turn to her in alarm.

'Got to get some air,' she gasps, clutching her throat. She runs from the room, and I quickly pull the cardboard box from the desk and hold it in my arms. It's heavy and the woman is saying something about carrying it to the car for me but I shake my head, telling her it's fine, wishing that she'd stop talking and just leave me alone. I turn and head to the door and Mr Weaver holds it open for me and I march through it, just managing to mutter 'thank you' and then somehow, he's ahead of me in the waiting room, opening the door to the car park. I step outside into the fresh air with relief. I'm behaving badly but I just want to get out of this place. I'm sure I can't be the only grieving relative who's behaved this way and the place is obviously affecting Emily, too. Although maybe it was the stifling heat. It might help if they turned the thermostat down in there. Does it really need to be a heated to a tropical temperature?

The door quietly closes behind me and I look around the car park but I can't see Emily. I'm momentarily confused; where is she, where did she go? This building is at the side of a busy dual carriageway into town, there are few buildings around so there's nowhere for her to go. And then I spot her, slumped on the low wall that runs around the perimeter of the car park. She's partly hidden by my car and is holding her head in her hands. I walk over to her and put the box down on the floor with relief.

'What's wrong, Emily, do you feel okay? Do you want me to go and get you a glass of water? Call a doctor?'

'No, I'm okay. I'm sorry.' She's crying, tears streaming down her face. 'It just got too much. The thought of Ricky being in that box. I couldn't stand it.'

'Why don't we get in the car? We can sit in there. It'll be more comfortable than the wall.'

She nods. I pull out my car keys, press the button to open the doors. I pick up the box and put it in the boot and then go round the other side and open the passenger door. She gets up from the wall and walks to the car on legs that look shaky and scrambles into the passenger seat. I close the door and go around to the driver's side and get in.

'Are you sure you don't want anything?' I ask as I strap myself in. 'I'm sure they'd be happy to provide a glass of water or something if I go back in and ask.'

'No.' Her voice is loud, almost a shout.

We sit in silence and I turn on the engine to warm the interior of the car. Despite being inside the funeral directors for such a short time, the car feels cold, especially so after the heat of the waiting room.

'I'm sorry,' she mumbles.

'It's okay.'

'No, it's not.' She turns and looks at me. 'I've made it all about me again and I'm so sorry about that.'

I shrug.

'And it's not just, you know, about the urn.'

'No?' I ask.

She takes a deep, shuddering breath.

'No, it's not. You're Ricky's wife, so I feel I have to be honest with you.'

'Okay.'

'There are things you don't know,' she says, quietly, 'about me.'

9

EMILY

She arrived early to pick me up – of course she did, because she's the sort who's early for everything. She probably always has a clean hankie, too, because she behaves as if she's fifty years old. I told her I'd been out for a walk and she lapped up my lie, just as I knew she would. It did throw me a bit, though, her sitting in the car waiting for me, because I walked straight past her and didn't even notice she was there. I need to be careful because it would be very easy to slip up if I get over confident, even though she is a bit dim.

The whole journey to the undertakers she was blathering on about going to the charity shop with all of Ricky's clothes. That's why she was a bit early. I hid my surprise when she told me; I didn't think she had it in her, to be honest, I thought she'd get the old biddy round to sort everything out for her. She started whining about the woman in the charity shop not being grateful so she just left the two suitcases full of his clothes in the middle of the shop and walked away. I wanted to hit her but I bit my tongue and made myself agree how ungrateful she was but inside, I was fuming.

What a stupid bitch.

Those clothes would have been worth a lot of money because Ricky didn't buy cheap. He liked to look good and made a lot of effort with his appearance. He spent a lot of time and money sourcing his clothes for the right look and *she* took them to the charity shop. What a waste. I could have sold them online and made myself a small fortune. Unlike her, I need the money. She *gave them away*, that's how well off she is. I know for a fact that those clothes won't even get as far as hanging on a rail in that bloody shop because all the volunteers will pick the best stuff out and keep it for themselves. I know they will, because it's exactly what I would do and I can't be the only person who thinks that way, can I? I mean, they work there for nothing selling people's old crap so they have to have some perks, don't they?

After she told me what she'd done, it put me in a really spiteful mood and so I wanted to hurt her, make her feel a tiny little bit of how I feel. I could have told her about Ricky and the baby, because it would devastate her and I could have sat and watched that devastation. I would have enjoyed it. I was so tempted to let her know what he thought about her, tell her some of the names he called her behind her back but I stopped myself because that would blow my plan out of the water, satisfying though it would have been to vent. So I kept my mouth shut. But it's definitely in the plan to tell her in the future so at least I have that to look forward to.

So here we are, on our way to collect the ashes of my lover and her husband. How bizarre is that? I take a sly look at her as she drives and I feel such hatred for her. I have to stop looking at her and turn and look out of my window because everything is just so unfair.

I so want to punch her.

As I watch the cars go by, I start to think about money a bit more. There'd be insurance, wouldn't there, now that Ricky's dead? I know there's no mortgage on that house because Ricky told me; he said he didn't feel bad about leaving her because if she was so desperate to stay in that museum of a place, there was no reason she couldn't get a mortgage herself and buy him out. He didn't understand why she'd want to stay there but if she insisted on it, she could. Although if they sold up and she took her share of the proceeds there'd be more than enough to buy a really nice house of her own, but Ricky said he couldn't see her doing that, because she was tied to that house. The only way he could see her leaving it would be feet first.

She loved that house.

'More than she loved me', that's what Ricky used to say. I didn't like it when he said that because it made me think that he wanted her to love him; that if she showed him some affection then he'd love her right back. I always changed the subject when he said it, and mentioned the old biddy or the front parlour because it always made him laugh. I didn't mind talking about the house or her weird old friend, but I didn't like talking about *her*, because it made me feel jealous, so maybe I did love Ricky a bit and wasn't just fond of him.

'We're here.' We pull into the car park of the undertakers and I set my face in an expression that is absolutely not a reflection of how I'm feeling, because right now I hate her guts, and it's not just because she gave Ricky's clothes away.

We pull into a space and she turns off the engine and looks at me.

'Okay?' I do the big eyes and the sad smile and nod, and we clamber out of the car and walk across to the entrance. Megan doesn't really wait for me and I have to do a quick walk to catch up with her. I look at her perfect hair as I reach her and resist the urge to pull it so tightly that I wrench a handful out by the roots.

The door opens as we get closer and a creepy little man dressed in black does a peculiar curtsey thing and waves us through. The heat hits me as we walk into the room and my armpits are already sprouting water as the creepy bloke disappears through another door. That's the thing with being pregnant, my thermometer has broken and I veer between boiling hot and ice-cold; there is no in between. Megan waves her hand in front of her face so she must be feeling the heat too, although she still looks immaculate. God knows what their heating bill must be and aren't bodies supposed to be kept cold? I mean, I know they keep them in big fridges but what about when they get them out for viewings? It wouldn't take long for them to go off in this heat. Although I never did understand why you'd want to go and see one of your relatives once they're dead. What does that achieve?

He's back, the creep.

'If you'd like to come through?'

I gulp in some air in an attempt to cool down. I feel all flustered; I think it's the thought of seeing Ricky's ashes in a box, or whatever it is they put them in. And the heat, too, that's not helping. I follow behind Megan and tell myself to concentrate.

Ten minutes and it'll all be over.

* * *

Bloody, bloody, bloody Jackie Saunders.

Why did there have to be someone I know working there? Just my luck that she happens to work in *that* undertakers. I used to do her hair for her – a colour far too dark for a woman of her age in my opinion – but I hadn't seen her for a while because since I met Ricky I haven't been working much. Obviously, I knew she worked in an undertakers because she was always banging on about it as if it was something to brag about, but I didn't know it was that one. She used to talk as if she was an actual undertaker when all she did was answer the phone and make cups of tea and stuff. If I'd realised it was *that* place, I'd never have set foot in there. My own fault, I suppose, because I tend to turn off from listening when I'm doing someone's hair and go off into a world of my own. Next time you're at the hairdressers, you may think your stylist is having a conversation with you but trust me, they're not. They're just very good at saying 'yes' and 'no' in the right places, whilst not listening at all. It's a skill we all learn, like putting perm rollers in or trimming men's eyebrows.

The minute I saw her behind that desk, my heart sank and I just knew she was going to drop me right in it because Jackie has a big mouth and a foghorn voice that could wake the dead. I knew there was always the possibility of someone 'outing me' in front of Megan but the chances of it happening were, I thought, slim, because this is a big town.

I never even thought about it happening today.

Whilst Megan was signing the form, Jackie turned to look at me and smiled and I knew that at any second she was going to open her trap and call me 'Shelley'. And that would be it, game over, because how could I explain being called by a different name in a town I'm supposed to have never been to before? I couldn't. And that would be without Jackie saying anything else – and she would carry on talking, because she can talk for England and never takes the hint to shut up. I could see it all coming out: how I lived here and not Newcastle; how my name is Shelley Beech and not Emily Fordham.

Absolute nightmare.

Ultimately it wouldn't matter because I'd still be able to get what I wanted even if I was outed but it would be better the way I've planned, more enjoyable. So I did the only thing possible.

I pretended to be ill.

I deserve an Oscar, honestly, I do. Although, truthfully, my face probably was as white as a sheet and I did feel pretty sick, what with the boiling heat and the fear of getting caught. I muttered something about needing air and ran out of there as fast as I could. I knew that Megan would follow me, because she's the polite sort who does the right thing and I'm gone six months pregnant, which always puts people in a flap. Handy actually, because her following me minimised the risk of big gob Jackie dropping me in it. I just prayed that Jackie didn't take it into her head to follow, too. I came outside and headed straight towards the low wall running around the outside of the car park and sat on it; mostly because it was out of sight. If Jackie decided to come out and poke her nose in, hopefully she wouldn't be able to see me. Although my legs do feel a bit wobbly so it is a relief to sit down. I have my head in my hands but I can see through my fingers and Megan has just come out of the door and thank God, Jackie isn't following her. She stops for a minute and looks around the car park with a puzzled expression on her face, as if I've vanished into thin air. Then she spots me and walks towards me. I keep my head down with my hands over my face and wait for her to get to me.

'What's wrong, do you feel okay? Do you want me to go and get you a glass of water? Call a doctor?' She's looking down at me and I lower my hands.

'No, I'm okay. I'm sorry.' Somehow I'm crying and tears are streaming down my face. Wow, that's a whole other level of method acting because I didn't even realise I was doing it. 'It just got too much. The thought of Ricky being in that box. I couldn't stand it.'

'Why don't we get in the car?' she asks. 'We can sit inside. It'll be more comfortable than the wall.'

I nod and she unlocks the car, chucks the box in the boot and I pull myself up and clamber into the car whilst she holds the door open.

'Are you sure you don't want anything? I'm sure they'd be happy to provide a drink or something if I go back in and ask.'

'No.' My voice comes out much louder than I intended.

We sit in silence and she starts the car and the heating blasts through the vents.

The silence is getting a bit uncomfortable so I apologise for making it about me again and she's so cold and unfeeling and just sort of shrugs. No wonder Ricky preferred me; living with her must have been like living with the ice queen. I need to move to the next stage of my plan and I can't waste time waiting around until the right moment, so it has to be now.

'And it's not just about the urn,' I say.

'No?' She looks at me and I feel pity for Ricky, that he had to live with that cold bitch. So I take the plunge and say it; the thing that I've been rehearsing in my head.

'There are things you don't know,' I say, quietly, 'about me.'

She looks at me, her eyes wide and I think I might have over-egged it a bit because it did sound a bit dramatic. I'm playing for time because I'm trying to get it all straight in my head so I don't say the wrong thing and muck it all up. My original plan was to tell her I was staying in town for a bit longer; that way I'd have had the chance to make her my friend, push the sister-in-law thing a bit more, but I can see that it won't work that way because she's not the friendly type; she's the dutiful type. I'll have to jump straight to step three of my plan and cross my fingers that it works out. It's risky, but she's a do-the-right-thing kind of person, and I'm counting on that.

'What sort of things?' she asks.

'Well, I lied about going home tomorrow.'

She doesn't move, not an inch, and I try not to flinch under the gaze of her cold blue eyes.

'Lied?'

'Yes.' I force out more tears, helped by the thought of being penniless. 'When I said the father of my baby wasn't in the picture, that wasn't the truth. Coming here to find Ricky wasn't the only reason I left Newcastle. I also came here to hide from my ex.'

'Okay.' She says the word slowly and I stay silent for a beat before speaking to raise the drama.

'I can't go home tomorrow, or ever, because if I do, he's going to kill me.'

'Kill you?' she repeats.

I nod, biting my bottom lip.

'I've got a restraining order on him but that won't stop him. He will kill me, I know that. He says that he'll never let me go and if he can't have me, no one else can. He says he'll wait until after the baby's born, but after that, I'm dead.'

'But surely there's something the police can do? He must know he'll get caught.'

'He's clever. There are never witnesses around when he threatens me, but I believe him. I lived with him, I know what he's capable of. And he knows that he'll probably only do ten years, even if they can pin it to him, because no one gets life these days. He says it'll be worth it.'

'Is that why you split up, because he was violent to you?'

I turn my head away. 'I'd rather not talk about it.'

We sit in silence, the only noise, the blast of the heater vents.

'So what are you going to do?' she asks.

'I don't know.' I sigh. 'I don't have a lot of money so I'll have to try social services, see if they can help. I could get a job but I don't think anyone's going to take me on at the moment.' I look down at my bump so she gets the drift. 'I'll stay a couple more nights at the hotel as there's a reduced-price offer on as I'm already staying there but I'll have to look for something cheaper. A guesthouse or maybe an Airbnb until I can find a place of my own, although I'll likely have to settle for a room in a shared house.'

'With a baby?'

I shrug. 'Wes cleaned me out. I had savings when I met him but they're all gone now.' I don't know where the name Wes came from, it just popped into my head, as if he was real. I should probably write all of this down because my back story is getting bigger and more complicated by the minute. Lying is exhausting because you have to remember what you've said. It'll be much easier once I can tell her the truth. But for now, I have to lie.

'You look worn out.' She puts the car into gear and reverses out of the space. 'I think we should get you home.'

I put my head back and close my eyes.

Done; step three of my plan completed.

Now it's up to her.

10

MEGAN

In order to move on, you have to face the past.

I read that somewhere, I don't remember where. Is it true, though? Isn't it easier to bury the past and not think about it? I think it is, as long as it wants to stay buried and doesn't keep rearing its ugly head. What's the point in dragging everything up and going over it all again and again when you can't change it? Especially when one of you is dead.

No, there's absolutely no point.

I stare at the urn containing Rick's ashes. I took it out of the box last night and put it on the coffee table because I couldn't think of anywhere else to put it. It wouldn't fit on the mantel-piece because it's way too big but I didn't want it in my bedroom. It doesn't feel right putting it in one of the spare rooms, or the garage with all the unwanted clutter, as if it were a piece of old junk, so what am I going to do with it?

Maybe I should scatter the ashes and throw away the urn.

Where would I scatter them, though? The Regency Arms, a voice in my head shouts, the last place you went to. It would have to be in the car park because I can't see them allowing me to cover their restaurant with my deceased husband's ashes.

But I'm having a sick joke with myself, because the Regency Arms has no good memories for me at all.

The Regency Arms was the last place we went to as a couple and then the venue for Rick's wake. Wake? Why do they even call it a wake? I've never understood that because it's not as if anyone is ever going to wake up at their own funeral. That last night we went there, Rick was nice to me. At first. He complimented me on how I looked, was the charming man I'd fallen head over heels in love with.

He told me I looked beautiful.

He often told me that but somehow, after a while, it began to feel like an insult, as if I'd used my beauty to lure him into marriage under false pretences. But I never pretended to be anything other than what I am and if I didn't match up to his idea of what I should be, is that my fault? I never lied to him, made him think I was something I wasn't. I never expected him to be anything other than he was, I didn't marry him to mould him into a different person; all I wanted was for him to love me as much as I loved him. And I still loved him, despite what he said to me that night, despite everything he's done, despite his rage at me.

And now he's gone; replaced by a plastic container that's trying, and failing, to look as if it's made of bronze.

'What should I do, Rick?' I ask it. 'Do you want to be scattered somewhere or should I put you in a dark cupboard and leave you there forever?'

Predictably, the urn doesn't reply.

Maybe I should give it to Emily.

The sound of a key being inserted into the front door lock drifts in from the hallway. I sigh. It'll be Elaine, who clearly never took the hint about going back to work and not coming round here all of the time. The door opens and she steps into the hallway, pushing the door closed against the wind and rain.

'It's vile out there.' She smiles at me. 'And how are you today?'

'I'm okay. I didn't think you were coming today?' The words come out more sharply than I intended and she looks hurt. I feel disgusted with myself; talk about ungrateful. 'I mean,' I get up from the sofa, 'I thought you'd be going back to work today.'

'No, no work today.' She smiles again, puts her bag on the floor and slips her coat off, hanging it on the peg where Rick's used to be. 'I've still got a couple of days until I have to go in so I thought I'd come and give you a hand.'

'That's so kind of you,' I lie. 'Come and sit down. I'll make us some tea in a minute.'

'I came to say thank you, as well, for the money you sent to my account. There was no need to send me so much.'

'It's only what you've lost from not going to work. I also wanted you to know how grateful I am for everything you've done but I couldn't think of a nice present to buy you. I just don't seem to have the headspace for it at the moment.'

'Oh, it's nothing, you know I'm always here for you. We're family, always have been, haven't we, even if not by blood?' She comes into the lounge, stopping in her tracks when she catches sight of the urn.

'Oh, you've collected it.' She looks crestfallen and I realise that I never even mentioned it to her.

'Yes, I went yesterday. I took Rick's sister with me. She asked if she could come and I couldn't really say no, could I?'

She sits down in the armchair facing me and although she tries, she can't hide her distaste at what I've just said.

'Seems odd she wanted to go seeing as they haven't been in contact for years and years.' She purses her lips.

'Well, like I say, she asked and I didn't feel I could refuse,' I say.

'I would have thought she'd have gone home by now.'

'She was supposed to be going home today.'

'Supposed?'

'Yes. Well, the thing is, she's in a bit of a bind. Her ex, the father of her baby, is a nasty piece of work and she says she can't go back to Newcastle because she's scared he'll kill her.'

'What?'

'I know, awful, isn't it? He's told her that if he can't have her, then nobody else can either. I do wonder if that's why she was trying to get in contact with Rick again after all those years. Maybe she was hoping he could help her to escape from him, you know?'

'Oh, I see.' She thinks about it for a moment. 'Yes, I suppose that would make sense. She should go to the police and report him.'

'She's already done that and, from what she's said, he's been warned off but as he's been careful never to threaten her in front of witnesses, there's not a lot they can do. She says he's even told her that he doesn't care if he goes to prison for killing her, because it would be worth it.'

'My God. What's she going to do?'

'Find a room to rent or something.'

'What, you mean here?'

'Yes. She seems to think that it's far enough away from Newcastle that he won't find her.'

'Rent a room, with a baby?'

'That's what I thought. It's not really practical, is it, sharing a house with strangers with a new baby?'

'Not really, but no doubt the council will find her something.' She gets up from the sofa. 'I've brought cake. Lemon drizzle. I did a bit of baking this morning.'

'Sounds lovely.' I get up. 'I'll make us some tea to go with it.'

'You seem a bit brighter.' She puts her head on one side and stands and studies me. 'A bit more like your old self.'

'Well, I'm trying. I have to get on with it, don't I? Try and get back to normal, whatever that is.'

'Sadly, you do.'

I go out into the kitchen and Elaine gets her bag from the hall and follows me.

'I've been thinking,' I say, flicking the kettle to boil. 'About Emily.'

'Oh yes?'

'She doesn't have a lot of money and I feel sort of responsible for her because she's Rick's sister. I feel like I should ask her to stay here whilst she sorts herself out. It must be costing her a fortune at the hotel and it can't be much fun living out of a hotel room.'

Elaine busies herself getting the cake out of the tin and putting it onto a plate but she doesn't say anything.

'You don't think I should?' I ask.

She slowly puts the lid back on and returns the tin to her bag before replying. 'I just think,' she says quietly, 'that you should be careful.'

'Careful? In what way?'

She sits down at the table. 'You don't know her. She's a stranger to you.'

'I know but she's Rick's sister, the only family he had left in the world. I can't just ignore her, especially as she's pregnant. I probably wouldn't feel so responsible for her if she wasn't.'

'I know, but she's still a stranger. You don't know anything at all about her and you're very vulnerable at the moment.'

I make the tea, take the mugs over to the table and sit down on the chair opposite Elaine.

'Why do I get the feeling that you don't like her?'

'I never said I didn't like her; I don't know her. I only met her briefly at the funeral.'

It hits me then; she's jealous. The expression on her face when I told her I'd taken Emily with me to collect the ashes, she didn't like it one little bit. Perhaps she thought I should have asked her instead. Maybe I should have. Yes, I definitely should have. I'm an idiot.

'I hear what you're saying, Elaine, but I still think it's the right thing to do. It's only fair that I offer her a place to stay whilst she sorts herself out. Just for a couple of weeks until she finds herself somewhere permanent. I mean, aside from anything else, that baby is going to be my niece or nephew and it's not as if I don't have plenty of room.'

'Well, it's your house.' Said in a way that very much tells me she disapproves, Elaine picks up the plate of cake and offers it to me.

I pick up a slice and take a bite.

'I know it's my house, but I do value your opinion and you know how much you mean to me and how much I rely on you. Like you say, we're family, and if you genuinely think it's a bad idea, I won't do it.'

She's pleased by my words; I can tell by the hint of colour that appears on her cheeks. She finishes her mouthful of cake before replying.

'I'm not saying it's a bad idea, it's a very kind offer and I understand why you want to do it but I don't want to see you taken advantage of, that's all I'm saying. She's a stranger and you know nothing about her other than what she's told you.'

'I know, but she's pregnant and I can't stand by and see her homeless or living in one rented room, can I? If she has a bit more time, maybe the council will come up with something. Surely they have to help in cases like this.'

'I don't know about the council; I don't think just because you're pregnant that you jump the list any more. That's a thing of the past and something she'll find out for herself. All I'm saying is, be careful. I probably shouldn't say this, with her being Rick's sister, but I'm just going to put it out there...' She pauses, as if having second thoughts about what she's going to say.

'You can say it, Elaine, I won't be offended. I'd appreciate your honesty.'

'Okay. Well. I know I only talked to her for a short while at the funeral but there's something about her that doesn't gel. I can't put my finger on it, but what I do know is that you shouldn't put your trust in someone just because they want you to.'

* * *

We're upstairs, Elaine and I, staring at the unmade bed in mine and Rick's old bedroom.

'Are you sure about this?'

'Yes. I'm going to sleep in Mum's bedroom in the future, make that my bedroom. I can't face sleeping in here on my own without Rick. I'm going to make the en suite my bathroom and Emily can have use of the main one.'

'We'll need to empty out all of your wardrobes then.' She looks at the triple built-in wardrobes along the back wall.

'Only of my stuff. Rick's is all gone. I took it to the charity shop yesterday.'

'What? All of it?' She looks shocked.

'Yes. I packed it into his suitcases and dropped it off at the shop before I went to collect the ashes.'

'You should have said, I would have helped.'

'I know you would but I felt it was something I needed to do on my own and it wasn't as bad as I thought it would be. They're just clothes, aren't they, at the end of the day? Just inanimate *things*. They don't mean anything. Someone else will have the benefit of them and that makes me feel better because they're not being wasted.'

I fling open two of the wardrobe doors and show Elaine the empty rail.

'See? Plenty of room.' I open the doors to mine. 'And these will be lost in Mum's massive built-in wardrobe.' I grab a handful of hangers, take them off the rail and go out onto the landing and into Mum's room.

My room.

I arrange them on the rails and head back for more. In no time at all, all of my clothes are in their new home and I repeat the process with the chest of drawers whilst Elaine vacuums and dusts the wardrobe. We make the bed up with the old blue set that I used to have on there before Rick moved in, but I don't bother to change the curtains.

Elaine insists on cleaning the bathroom – although it hardly needs it – after I've transferred all of my bits and pieces to the en suite and several hours later we go downstairs feeling that we've achieved something. We go into the kitchen and I'm filling the kettle with water when I notice Elaine sweeping crumbs from the table. There's also a mug on the table that wasn't there when we went upstairs.

Keith's been in here.

I bite down my annoyance. Whilst we were upstairs sorting the rooms out, he sneaked in here and made himself a drink and helped himself to a slice of cake.

As if he lives here.

Elaine has a key, she's always had one, but clearly now Keith has one, too, and I don't like that. I never gave it to him so Elaine must have got him a copy made. No doubt he nagged her relentlessly until she gave in. I don't like that he can swan in here any time he likes and treat the place like his own but I don't want to upset her by demanding that he relinquish his key. It's only the fact that Elaine is a dear friend who's done so much for me that I'm not banning Keith from the house.

'Tea?' I ask.

'Please.'

'Thanks for helping today, I really appreciate it. Shall we go out for something to eat after we've had this? My treat? There's that new Italian place on Farringdon Road, we could go there?'

Elaine hesitates for just a fraction too long and I know what she's thinking.

Keith. How can she go out for dinner when he's sitting at home waiting for her to get back and cook his tea?

'Only if you want,' I say. 'No worries if not.'

'No, no, that would be lovely.'

'Great.' I slide the mugs onto the table. 'I'll be back to work next week so it's nice to have the house straight before then. I won't feel like sorting stuff out when I'm back in the daily grind.'

'You're going back to work?' She looks surprised.

'Yes. I need to get back to normal. Once I've got back into the routine, I'll reassess my options, think more of a career rather than just a job. It was only ever a stopgap and I don't know why I've stayed there so long.'

'That's very brave of you.'

'Not really.' I take a shuddering breath. 'But if I concentrate on doing something and keeping myself busy it takes my mind off losing Rick.'

'But what about Emily?'

'What about her?'

'If you're at work, she'll be on her own here all day.'

'She'll be fine, I'm sure she'll be able to amuse herself.'

Elaine purses her lips and takes a sip of tea. I know that's not what she meant but it's a bit rich saying that, when she knows damn well that her husband comes in here whenever he feels like it without asking.

'Although I may be jumping the gun,' I say, 'because I haven't even asked her yet. She might not want to stay here.'

'Oh, I'm sure she won't refuse,' Elaine says.

No, I don't think she will.

'We need dinner. Let's go out, my treat, and then I'll ring Emily, see what she thinks of the idea.'

11

EMILY

What a cow.

When she said, 'let's get you home', I thought she meant her home, not the hotel. I laid my head back on the headrest and closed my eyes because I was exhausted with all that method acting. I drifted off to sleep, what with the warmth of the heater and the movement of the car. Plus it was relief, too, at getting away with it after the near miss with Jackie. When I woke up from my lovely sleep I couldn't believe my eyes; we were in the car park at the back of the hotel and Megan was staring at me, with her reptile gaze, clearly waiting for me to get out of the car. I'd just offloaded and told her how I could never go back to my home because my ex was going to murder me and that I was now homeless, and she was abandoning me; a six-months-pregnant woman in one hell of a state.

Okay, I wasn't actually in a state and it was all lies, but that's not the point is it, because she didn't know that, did she? I'd been so certain she'd invite me to stay at hers because it's not as if she hasn't got the room and I am Ricky's sister. Well, obviously I'm not, but she thinks I am.

Ricky was so right about her and now I'm seeing it for myself I can see that he wasn't exaggerating.

She's a cold, weird, unfeeling cow.

And just to rub it in even more, when she'd driven out of the car park, I had to walk all the way home to my flat. And she never even mentioned meeting up again either; nothing, nada, not a bloody thing. That bothers me because I need to keep in contact with her and keep this *we're family* thing going but I knew I'd have to leave it for a day or two and wait for her to contact me because I don't want to look desperate.

Even though I am.

But I've heard nothing from her and now it's nearly seven o'clock and more than twenty-four hours since I last saw her. Not so much as a text message to ask how I am. Her lack of contact has started me wondering if she fell for the abusive ex story after all. She appeared to believe what I was saying but how can I know for sure – am I kidding myself about my acting abilities? She can hardly come right out and call me a liar, can she? She's odd and a bit dim and naïve but what if she's not as easily fooled as I think? Or on the other hand, maybe she totally believes that I'm Ricky's sister but doesn't feel any responsibility for me? What if she doesn't care one bit about Ricky's family? I keep going back over the events of yesterday and trying to remember if she seemed suspicious, if maybe I missed the signs. But no, she wasn't any different, she was the same cold fish that she's been since the first time I met her at the funeral.

It's a worry, I won't lie. My plan is to tell her the truth after the baby is born when I can prove that Ricky is the father. If I tell her the truth now, I face three more months of scraping by and I definitely will end up in a rented room somewhere because I've run out of money. Social services aren't suddenly going to furnish me with a nice new home; I'll join a very long list and be pretty much at the bottom of it. I feel so angry when I think about Ricky dying because I have nothing; this baby has nothing. Not a cot, a pram, absolutely sod all. We were going to buy it all together, go baby shopping, as Ricky called it. We'd even booked a 3D scan for a week's time to find out if we're having a boy or a girl. I could have found out from my NHS check-up at twenty-eight weeks but I told them I didn't want to know because we wanted to be together when we found out. I would have had the scan sooner but Ricky wasn't comfortable doing it until he'd dumped her. I'll have to ring them and cancel it now because there's no way I can afford to pay for it.

My baby is entitled to something from Ricky's estate, a very *big* something, because it's his child and he should provide for it for the rest of its life. Why should she get everything? I'm hoping she's not going to contest my claim because that would make things much more difficult for me. I'd need to get myself a solicitor and they don't come cheap, and even if they did I still couldn't afford it. I'm relying on her not contesting it because I'm guessing she won't want her late husband's private life gossiped about. I'll tell her I'll go public if she doesn't cough up. Straight to our local newspaper for a start. She won't want it splashed all over the front page, will she? They're always scratching around for stories so I think they'd definitely publish it. And if they're not interested, there's always social media or one of the downmarket magazines who peddle low-life true stories.

I'll give it until tomorrow and if I don't hear from her, I'll have to bite the bullet and ring her. I'll have to keep to the story that I've told her – that I have to move out of the hotel in a couple of days – and if there's no offer of a bed at her house, *Ricky's* house, I've come up with a plan B: I'll tell her I've found a room in a shared flat to move into.

My flat.

I'll pretend I'm renting a room in my own flat, genius, eh? She won't know any different and if nothing else, if she gives me a lift in the future at least I won't have to tramp home miles from that sodding hotel.

My fingers twitch towards my mobile phone lying on the sofa next to me. The temptation to message her is strong but I resist. I'll wait just a little longer. I need her to come to me.

I sit back and flick through the TV channels but I can't concentrate on anything. After ten minutes of staring at a depressing soap, I heave myself off the sofa, go out into the kitchen and pull open the top drawer next to the sink. It's the one full of assorted bric-a-brac and useless crap that every kitchen seems to have. I rummage through the debris until I find what I'm looking for.

A pen and a notepad.

The notepad is new and unused and I can't recall buying it. I take them with me back into the lounge and settle down on the sofa, wrapping the throw around myself because it's cold in here. The heating is turned off, as it is most of the time now because I can't afford to have it on. When Ricky was alive the flat was always toasty warm and I never needed to worry about the bills. Perhaps I should have saved some of the cash he gave me instead of spending most of it on expensive food and luxuries. That life feels like a lifetime ago, not mere weeks. With a sigh, I open the notebook and stare at the blank page and try to think. After a few moments I begin to write and I make it as neat as I can, because I'll be reading this again.

It's my back story.

The first page is Emily's facts; her age, her education, some of it is true and some things I made up because I didn't actually know and Megan won't either, because Ricky barely told the cold bitch anything. Next, I write down the fictional growing-up memories of Ricky. There aren't many of them because I told her he went away to boarding school when I was five so I couldn't remember a lot. The lies about Newcastle and Wes, the abusive ex, come next. I write down the history of our relationship that I haven't actually told her yet; where we met, how long we'd been together and the shock I felt the first time he was violent. After a while, I begin to enjoy myself and the words flow and it's so easy making it all up. It almost feels like the truth and I think that I might have a talent for this. When my mobile phone shrills from beside me, I'm so engrossed in my story that I jump and the pen skids across the paper. I stare at the blue streak across the page, annoyed. I'll have to rip that page out and rewrite it now because it's spoilt the neatness. I put the pen down, pick up my phone and when I see who's calling, I smile. I answer the call, turning the corners of my mouth downward. You can tell when someone is smiling at the other end of the phone.

'Hello?' I make my voice flat, dull and depressed-sounding.

'Emily? How are you?'

'Okay,' I reply, in a *not okay* voice.

'I'm so sorry I haven't rung before,' she says, 'but things have been a bit hectic.'

What's so hectic that she couldn't pick up the phone or message me? She's not even at work, what does she do all fucking day? Selfish, that's what she is. Okay, she's lost her husband but I've lost my brother, I have a violent ex who wants to kill me *and* I'm six months pregnant.

'Oh, that's okay,' I eventually reply when the silence has stretched to embarrassment point. 'What's happened to me is nothing compared to what you're going through.'

'Are you still at the hotel?' I'm disappointed by her lack of interest. I expected a bit of grovelling, a show of concern.

'Yes,' I lie, 'although I'll be checking out tomorrow. It's just too expensive to stay any longer.'

'So...' She pauses. 'I've had an idea and please tell me if you don't want to take it up, I won't be offended. But would you like to come and stay with me whilst you get yourself sorted with somewhere proper to live? I have plenty of room.'

'Oh my God,' I gabble. 'Thank you so, so much, you're an absolute lifesaver. That's so kind of you, but really, are you sure?'

'I'm sure; it'll give us a chance to get to know each other properly. I can pick you up from the hotel tomorrow. What time are you checking out?'

'I have to be out by ten thirty.'

'Perfect. I'll wait in the car park at the back.'

'Thank you so much.'

'No problem, see you in the morning.'

I start to say goodbye when I realise she's already ended the call. Weird. I'm elated though and she might think I'm only staying for a week or two but once I'm in that house, I don't intend leaving until I've got what I want.

Possession is nine-tenths of the law, right?

Whatever that means. I abandon my notebook and head to the bedroom to pack a case to take with me. I can't take too much as I'm supposed to be staying at the hotel and had only planned on staying for a few days. I can pop back here when she's not around and get some more stuff. I drag my suitcase from underneath the bed, wipe the dust bunnies off it and begin to pack. By the time I've finished the case is so full I can barely close it. I drag it off the bed and onto the floor. I don't fancy humping this all the way to the hotel in the morning. I'll have to get a taxi.

I'll treat myself, because things are looking up.

* * *

'I've put towels in the bathroom but there are plenty more in the cupboard on the landing, just help yourself. I've got my own en suite so you'll have this all to yourself.'

'Thank you, it's so kind of you.'

'I'll go downstairs and put the kettle on but if you need anything, just let me know. Come down when you're ready.' Megan backs out of the bedroom, seaside landlady-style and when she's gone, I study my surroundings.

Beige, non-descript, bumpy old wallpaper, blue stripy bedding and horrific black and red curtains. Huge, chunky dark wood doors cover one wall opposite a giant, dark wood dressing table with an old-fashioned stool upholstered in red velvet. Matching bedside tables with revolting beige lamps. Faded blue carpet with beige swirls that make me feel seasick.

Absolutely hideous.

No taste, obviously.

It's much warmer than my flat though, and it's cosy, despite the horrendous decor. I sit down on the massive bed and bounce up and down. Soft but firm, just how I like it. I can be comfortable here until *my* inheritance comes through.

I drag my case closer to the wardrobe and open it, not bothering to heave it onto the bed. It weighs a ton. Thankfully, Megan carried it upstairs for me; she never commented on the weight of it and carried it as if it weighed nothing. I'll admit I was impressed, she's much stronger than she looks. Maybe she's a gym bunny and pumps iron.

I open two of the wardrobe doors and marvel at the size of the interior. If I brought every single item of clothing here that I own, it would still be lost in that amount of space. They certainly built these old houses big. I hang up my clothes and then cross the room to the dressing table. It has two huge drawers and I pull open the top one and shove my underwear in. It looks lost in there. I didn't bring any toiletries with me because they would have taken up too much space. Hopefully there's some in the bathroom.

The only thing left in my case is the notebook. I stare at it, trying to decide where to put it. Not in the drawer, because there's not enough stuff to hide it. The wardrobe? I pick it up and stare at my clothes hanging on the rail. Is Megan the sort to snoop? Maybe not, but I'm taking no chances. I push the notebook into the pocket of a pair of dungarees and stand back to make sure it's not visible. It's not. I close the suitcase, put it on the floor of the wardrobe and shut the doors.

I look around at my new home. I was hoping there might be a television in here. I wouldn't have to spend so much time with her then. I can use my pregnancy as an excuse, pretend I'm tired and stuff, but it's going to be pretty boring up here on my own. I have my phone and I can watch stuff on there but it's small, not a patch on the forty-inch screen in my flat. I wander over to the window and stare out over the back garden. It's long and mostly laid to lawn aside from a patio formed from large grey slabs.

Plain and dull, like her.

I don't get any sense of Ricky being here, his spirit or whatever. Not that I believe in any of that but I did wonder if there might be a bit of him lingering, but there's nothing.

She said she was putting the kettle on so I suppose I'd better go downstairs and start acting. I can't be bothered but I can't hide away up here forever. I have to play the part. I'm hoping that she'll be going back to work soon and then I can have the place to myself in the daytime. I can watch TV and do what I like but more than that, I can have a good snoop around; find out the lay of the land regarding finances and stuff because I need to know how much to aim for. I don't want to ask for too little if she's got shitloads of money. I remember Ricky saying something about her having a job because she was out of the house all day. Yes, definitely, she does work, in an office or something, although she has a degree of some sort but doesn't use it. Ricky said it was a waste and she should get herself a proper career. I didn't like hearing that about her because I don't have a degree and it made me feel a bit lacking. Although I am a properly qualified hairdresser, even if I did skive off a lot of the course and barely scraped through.

I check my appearance in the age-spotted mirror on the dressing table; hair tied back in a ponytail, no make-up, black leggings with loose fitting T-shirt and humungous jumper. I look tired, my face puffy and pale. My ankles are a bit swollen, too. Nine more weeks and it'll all be sorted.

I open the bedroom door and listen.

Silence.

God, I hope she's not one of those people who likes peace and quiet.

I take a deep breath in and slowly blow it out.

Okay, here goes, step four of the plan.

I'm in.

12

MEGAN

I put the phone receiver down and quickly type a message to the client before taking my mug out of my drawer and heading off to the kitchen. I like my day to have a routine; start work at eight thirty, coffee at ten thirty, lunch at twelve, break at three, home at four thirty.

I fill the kettle, set it to boil and throw a spoonful of instant into my mug from the huge tin next to the sink. It's a cheap supermarket brand but it's not so bad with a good splash of milk.

'How's it going?'

Sam, one of my fellow coworkers, appears. He goes straight to the wall cupboard and takes out a mug.

'Not bad,' I say. 'Getting back into the swing of it.'

'Jesus, look at that.' He thrusts the mug towards me. 'There are some right filthy pigs working here.'

'I know.' A brown, dried-on, scummy ring circles the mug, a tinge of pink lipstick visible on the rim. He turns on the tap and pushes the mug underneath it, picks up a disgusting-looking sponge and proceeds to scrub it.

There's a reason I keep my mug in my drawer.

He dries it with a grubby-looking tea towel, sets it on the countertop next to mine and tosses a teabag in.

'Seriously, though, I mean, how are you really?'

'Getting there. I think. It's definitely helped coming back to work. Takes my mind off things.' It's the truth; I thought I'd find it hard but after a week back here, I can actually not think about Rick for minutes at a time.

'Well, you know, if you're up for it, there's the regular Friday night meet-up at the pub tonight after work. If nothing else, it's a good chance to rip Jeremy to shreds without being overheard.' He grins, looking over his shoulder to make sure Jeremy, our boss, hasn't silently materialised behind us. He hasn't, nor will he, because if he wants a coffee, one of us minions is summoned to make him one. Whoever is summoned for the job always uses the filthiest mug possible and makes it with lukewarm water to ensure the cheap coffee tastes even more disgusting.

'Thanks. Maybe I will.' I definitely won't. Rick's been dead barely six weeks, I'm not ready for pub nights just yet and especially not with Sam.

The kettle boils and Sam turns around, picks it up and immediately pours water into both of our mugs. I'll have to wait until he's gone and tip mine away; the coffee will be tainted now with the boiling water. I like my coffee made with water that hasn't been boiled to death. Maybe I'll empty the kettle and start again.

'I hear you have a lodger now.' He throws the remark out in a casual way but his behaviour makes sense now; he followed me into the kitchen so he could find out what's going on in my life. Tell one person anything in this office, tell the entire twenty-five people. Because I certainly never told him about Emily. I told Rosie; only because she asked if I was okay living on my own. She's obviously already broadcast it to everyone else. Not that it's a secret; if it was a secret I wouldn't have told her.

'Not a lodger. She's Rick's sister and she's just staying whilst she sorts out somewhere permanent to live. She's moved from out of town and is looking for a home here.'

'Oh. Right, I see. Well, when she's gone, if you want another lodger, I'm your man. I'm fully house-trained.'

He grins, leans back and folds his arms, showcasing his gym-honed muscles. Sam's been through most of the women in this office and somehow still managed to stay working here, despite a nasty break-up with one of them.

'I'll bear that in mind,' I say, knowing that I definitely won't. I go to the fridge, get the milk out and slop some into my disgusting coffee. I hold the bottle towards Sam but he waves it away.

'No fats for me. Or carbs. It's protein all the way.' He pats his washboard stomach, his eyes lingering on mine for a moment.

I abruptly turn away and put the milk in the fridge, pick up my coffee and head back to my desk despite knowing that I won't drink it. Does he really think I'm in the mood for flirting? Because that's definitely what was going on there – he's so obvious. I've worked here long enough to know Sam's modus operandi for lining up the next woman in his life, and what just happened was a prime example of it.

I put my coffee on my desk, knowing that I'll return to the kitchen to throw it down the sink once the coast is clear. I sit down, open up my emails and try not to feel angry about what just happened. It was disrespectful and inappropriate to behave that way, but I have to remember that Sam is thoughtless and thick-skinned; he didn't do it to upset me. His relationships with women are usually brief and not necessarily exclusive so he'll have no conception what it's like to be widowed or to lose one's partner.

I glance up to see Sam weaving his way back to his desk. Our desks are too far apart for us to be able to chat and I'm thankful for that. As I turn back to my screen I see Rhona, who sits at the desk opposite, staring at me. She smiles and I smile back and then resume staring at my screen. She saw me looking at Sam and, as she's one of the worst gossip hounds in here and will be going to the pub after work, by the end of tonight the rumour mills will be spinning. Not that I care or am interested in what other people think of me. No doubt it would be the same no matter where I worked, and aside from the incessant gossiping and intrigue – surely a by-product of the job being so deadly dull – this job is okay. I don't have to use my brain very much because it isn't exactly taxing. It gets me up in the morning and out of the house and I have the company of other people, but that's about it. I can work from home if I choose and I might do so after I've been back for a while but for now, I need to be here. With people. I pick up my coffee and then put it back down again, unable to bring myself to drink it.

A lodger.

That's what Sam called Emily. I definitely didn't call her a lodger when I told Rosie, so clearly, it's been lost in the Chinese whispers that circulate this office. It felt strange at first, when Emily moved in, especially as she's in mine and Rick's room. I didn't tell her we used to sleep in there but I wonder if she's guessed. For the first few days, before I came back to work, she stayed in her room a lot, said she was tired and that she liked to have a nap in the afternoons.

Elaine popped round the first afternoon she moved in. She wanted to make sure I was okay, she said, but I knew her real motive was to meet Emily properly.

To the casual observer, Elaine was very nice to Emily when she introduced herself to her in the kitchen. She'd brought home-made cake with her, again, and she insisted that Emily sit down and have a slice whilst she made some tea. But I'm not a casual observer and I've known Elaine for all of my life and when she's not keen on someone, to me it stands out a mile. She asked Emily a lot of questions, about where she was brought up, which part of Newcastle she lived in, that sort of thing. All done in a very nice, chatty way but she was questioning her, there was no doubt about that. Emily answered her questions and appeared not to be bothered by them but when Keith turned up and introduced himself, it wasn't long before she made her excuses and went upstairs for a lie-down. Probably because he was his usual crass self and seemed to think it was okay to make a lame joke to her, saying 'maybe you should stop eating enough for two otherwise you won't be able to fit through the door much longer' as she was eating a slice of Elaine's cake. I told him not to be so rude and he sniggered and said he was only joking. Elaine smirked too until I flashed her a warning look. He only came round so he could get a look at Emily too, because Elaine will have told him she was moving in and from his rudeness to her, Elaine must also have told him she wasn't keen on Emily staying. When Emily had gone, Keith wolfed down half the cake, spitting crumbs everywhere and then sloped off, too. Elaine asked me when I was going back to work, even though I'd already told her. She raised her eyebrows as if she was surprised at my answer and asked if I was sure Emily would be okay at home all day on her own. I told her that of course she would, that Emily wasn't a child, deliberately misunderstanding her. Then I made my excuses and said that I had to go out and I know Elaine was annoyed with me but that's too bad; I'm also not a child.

The phone on my desk rings, the name of a local builder flashing onto the screen. I take a deep breath, putting all thoughts of Emily and Elaine aside, and pick up the receiver.

* * *

The smell of bacon hits me as I open the front door. After hanging up my coat and slipping off my shoes I go through to the lounge to find Emily lying sprawled across the sofa, her mouth gaping open, her arms flung wide. She's snoring like a train. My furry throw is stretched over her bump, her bare feet poking out of the end. A plate with bread crusts lies on the floor next to the sofa and a game show is blasting from the TV. How she can sleep through the noise is beyond me. I go back out into the hallway and through to the kitchen to find the source of the bacon smell. My large frying pan is sitting on top of the fat-spattered hob, a perfect ring of congealed fat around the inside of it. The butter dish lies next to it with a knife stuck in the butter, the dish cover abandoned on the countertop. An open loaf of bread with slices spilling out of the bag completes the tableau.

I pick up the pan, wipe the fat out with kitchen paper, put it into the sink and turn on the hot tap. Whilst the sink fills with hot soapy water, I tidy the bread away and wipe the tops over. By the time I've dried the frying pan and have put it away in the cabinet, it's taken me exactly ten minutes.

'Oh, God, I'm so sorry. I intended doing that but I must have dozed off. You should have left it; you've been at work all day.' Emily is standing in the doorway rubbing her eyes, her hair fuzzy and sticking up in spikes.

'No worries, it only took a minute, besides, you need your rest.'

She yawns loudly, making no attempt to disguise it. 'I swear

I could sleep for twenty hours a day; it was only his kicking that woke me.' She rubs her bump. 'Seven and a bit more weeks of this and then I'll have no choice but to stay awake, will I?'

His. She said his.

'You're having a boy?' I ask in surprise. She's always referred to her bump as 'the baby'.

'Yes.' She grins. 'I just found out today. What with me being a new patient and everything, the midwife insisted on scanning me to make sure my dates were right and well, I couldn't resist finding out whether it was a boy or a girl. I was going to wait and find out when it was born but when they asked me if I wanted to know, I said yes.'

'Well, that's lovely that you're having a boy. I take it you didn't mind what you were having?'

'No, I don't mind at all but I'm glad, now, with losing Ricky, that it's a boy. It's a sign, isn't it?'

'A sign?'

'Yeah. That it's meant to be. Because of losing Ricky. And he's going to be your nephew. It'll give you something to look forward to. I'm going to call him Ricky. You don't mind, do you?'

'No, I don't mind.' Do I mind? I'm not sure. It's Rick, anyway, not Ricky. Ricky. Makes me think of Mickey Mouse.

'Great.' She yawns again.

'So,' I say. 'I was going to order a takeaway for dinner, seeing as it's Friday. We always used to do that, me and Rick. Our Friday night end-the-week treat, we called it. Flop in front of the TV and put a movie on. What do you fancy? Chinese? Indian? Or something with no spice like pizza?'

She looks uncertain.

'Sorry. Silly me, I forgot you've already eaten.'

'No, it's not that. I can eat for England as well as sleep. I can't *stop* eating, actually. God knows how I'm ever going to get back to a normal size afterwards.'

'Oh. So what is it then? Don't you fancy takeaway?'

She sighs. 'I don't have any money.'

'Oh, that's okay. I'll get it. I wasn't suggesting you had to pay for it.'

She comes into the kitchen and sits down at the table.

'But you've paid for everything. I haven't contributed a thing towards food or anything since I've been here.'

'That's okay. You've just moved from the other end of the country, it'll take time to settle in, find a job. What is it you do?'

'Mobile hairdressing. I had a busy round when I was in Newcastle but I'll have to start from scratch here. I've thought about starting up a round now but it hardly seems worth the expense of advertising as I'll barely get going and then I'll have to stop again after the birth. I think maybe it'll be best to try to get into a salon after Baby Ricky's born. Rent a chair. I'm trying to claim some benefits for now, but you know how slow it is to get things set up.'

I don't know actually, because I've never claimed. I sit down opposite her.

'You've put your claim in motion, though?'

'Oh yes, I've filled all the forms in and everything. Once it's sorted, it'll be fine. The thing that really bothers me is that I haven't got any baby things for him, not even a cot or anything. Well, I have, but it's not here, it's back in Newcastle and I can't go back and get it, can I, not with Wes after me. When I told the social about my situation they didn't seem forthcoming with any solution. I guess I'll just have to find a way of funding it on my own.'

'So what are you going to do about your flat and your job? You can't just leave and never return, can you?'

'The flat's not a problem. I share with another girl and she'll just get someone else in to rent my room and pay the rent with her. And as for my job, like I said, once Baby Ricky is born and I'm settled, I'll go back to work and get a job in a salon or rent a chair. The only reason I'm not looking for work right now is because my blood pressure is a bit high and the midwife advised me to rest. Too much standing up, she said, would not be good for us.'

'So you're never going back to Newcastle?'

'No. I can't risk it, especially once Baby Ricky's born. I can't put him in danger. If I show my face up there, Wes will carry through on his threat and that will be the end of me.'

'What if he comes here looking to try and find you?'

'He won't. He'd never even think to look in Swindon because he doesn't know about Ricky and no one else knows where I am. I never even told my housemate where I was going. I lost touch with all my friends once I met Wes. He said he didn't like sharing me. Anyway, he thinks Sunderland is another country and that's only seven miles away from Newcastle so there'd be no way he'd come this far south. I'll find somewhere around here to live and everything will be fine.'

'I see.'

'Is there something wrong?' She looks worried.

'No,' I say. 'Not as such, Emily, but there is something I need to talk to you about.'

13

EMILY

The water's gone cold and as I've drained the tank of every last drop of hot water, I'll have to get out of the bath. Which isn't easy seeing as it's so full that any movement will send the water lapping over the sides. Erring on the side of caution, I wiggle my foot around until I manage to hook the chain of the plug with my toes and pull it out. As the water swirls around and glugs down the plughole, I haul myself upright and heave myself over the side of the bath. I grab the towel from the rail and wrap it around me. It's soft and thick, large too, plenty big enough to go around my bump. This house may be furnished with ancient furniture but I'll give Megan her due, she doesn't stint on quality when she does buy new stuff.

Since she went back to work at the beginning of the week and I have the place to myself all day, I've got into a nice routine. I stay in bed until around twelve, get up, have a leisurely soak in the bath and then get dressed. I need my sleep and I have to make the most of the opportunity to lie in bed because once the baby is here, it'll be very different. Am I going to stay in bed tomorrow? I'm not sure; it's the weekend, so she'll be around, but does that matter? I can always use the excuse of being pregnant for sleeping a lot, although truth be told, even before I was pregnant I always stayed in bed until lunchtime if I didn't have anything planned.

Some people might call it laziness; I call it self-care.

I comb my wet hair and study myself in the mirror. The pregnancy is showing in my face now; my cheeks look even puffier than a couple of days ago and despite all the sleep, I have dark circles underneath my eyes. Is it possible to have too much sleep? Maybe it is.

I open the bathroom door and pad across the landing to my bedroom. A noise from behind me startles me and I spin around in alarm, clutching the towel tightly. I knew things were going too well; someone has broken in whilst I've been wallowing in the bath and now they're going to attack me, rape me, kill me.

'For fuck's sake!' I shout, when I see who it is. 'You scared the life out of me.'

Keith grins as his eyes travel up and down my body.

'And stop looking at me, you fucking perv. What are you even doing here again?'

'Mind your own,' he says. 'I can come in whenever I like.'

'Why though?' I demand, hugging the towel even tighter. 'Why do you want to come in? It's not as if you live here, yet you can't seem to stay away from the place.'

'Jobs to do.'

'Bullshit. You're just a sleazy creep.' I turn and go into my bedroom and as I grab hold of the door to close it, he's still watching me. 'I'm going to tell Megan you're round here all the time. I bet she doesn't know, because you don't do it when she's here.'

His eyes flicker and his grin slips slightly.

'But if you stay away,' I add, 'and stop creeping around, I might not tell.' This time it's my turn to grin.

'Is that right?' He puffs his skinny chest out. 'I'd keep my mouth shut if I was you, *Emily*, because I might decide to tell Meg a few things about you.'

What does he mean? Does he know something about me or is it just hot air?

'Well, then maybe I'll tell your wife how you keep coming round here to ogle me when I'm coming out of the bathroom,' I spit at him, to show him that what he's just said hasn't hit a nerve.

He makes a snorting noise and I slam the door shut and lean back against it so he can't get it. I don't think he'd try, but you never know. He's a weedy weasel of a man, but when's that ever stopped a bloke from throwing his weight around and thinking he's something? Never, that's when. The sound of his footsteps going down the stairs reassures me that he's leaving. Sure enough, the slam of the front door echoing up the stairs confirms he's left. He's always coming round here when I'm here on my own and although he has a key and Megan must have given it to him, I'm pretty sure she doesn't know how often he's here. The first time I met him was when he came round with his creepy wife. I didn't like him on sight, even before he made a nasty comment about the size of me. And it bothers me that he's been so openly hostile straight off the bat because I did try, even after his rubbish joke, to be civil to him but he didn't want to know. Whenever I see him he makes a comment about me being lazy or fat or a freeloader. I mean, who the hell does he think he is? And I didn't like her, either – Elaine. Bringing her shitty dry cakes round, sucking up to Megan the whole time, it's sickening. Dead nosey, too, questioning me as if she has a right to know everything about me. Keeps asking me if I'm applying for jobs and what I'm planning on doing. I wonder if she sends him round to check on me and find out what I'm doing? Although what she thinks I'll get up to in my condition, God knows.

That said, I haven't exactly been idle; Keith did nearly catch me out on Monday afternoon when Megan was at work. I thought it was a good opportunity to have a snoop around with her safely out of the house so I could find out how the land lies. I don't want to aim too low and find out later that she's got way more money than I thought. I want my fair share to bring up Ricky's baby and to get that, I need to know how much money she actually has. I know she's got this house but Ricky must have had life insurance, mustn't he? And maybe savings, too. Everyone does, especially if they're married. I thought I'd start my search in Ricky's office, because that would be the obvious place to keep documents and stuff. And it was a good job I did start there, because it's at the front of the house and has a big bay window so I saw creepy Keith before he saw me. He was walking up the path, cool as you like, and I'd just that minute found a file that looked promising when I happened to look up and see him. For a woman with a due date of just over seven weeks away, I moved like lightning getting out of that room. By the time his key was opening the door, I was sitting on the sofa in the lounge with a throw over me to hide the folder. Too late, I realised that I'd left the study door open which is always kept closed, but I'm hoping Keith wouldn't know that, because he doesn't live here.

I never even thought about him turning up because when Megan was here, he only came round with his snotty wife.

When he came into the house, I stayed quiet and when he walked into the lounge he jumped out of his skin when he saw me. I didn't have the TV on and it was deathly quiet so he probably thought I was upstairs. It was hilarious but I kept a straight face and looked all shocked and pretended that he'd frightened me. I might as well have not bothered with the act because he didn't give a shit; he never apologised for startling me, just gave a sort of sneer and when I asked what he wanted, said 'Mind your own'. He says that a lot. I was surprised at his rudeness because I thought he'd be like his wife, all smiles and creeping, but secretly hating me, but him, no – like I said, he's openly hostile and that makes me nervous.

Because, you know what they say, it takes one to know one.

* * *

I wake with a start and for a moment, I wonder where I am before realising I'm in Megan's lounge.

I move and a piercing pain shoots through my neck and I wince, slowly pulling myself up onto my elbow and wiping drool from my mouth. I think I was about to fall off the sofa because my head was hanging off the pillow and my arm was trailing on the floor. The TV is blaring and I rummage around underneath me for the remote control. I can't find it and then spot it on the floor next to the plate.

I lean down, pick it up and turn down the volume. There's a faint clatter coming from the kitchen and I sit bolt upright; I bet creepy Keith is in there snooping around or helping himself to food. Has he been in here watching me whilst I've been sleeping? I shudder at the thought. Heaving myself off the sofa, I silently pad down the hallway to the kitchen so he doesn't hear me coming. When I get to the doorway, I'm surprised to see Megan at the sink washing up.

'Oh, God,' I blurt from the kitchen doorway, sounding as if I actually care. 'I'm so sorry. I intended doing that but I must have dozed off. You should have left it, you've been at work all day.'

She turns and tells me not to worry but I can tell by her face that she doesn't mean it, of course. Not that I give a shit. She thinks I'm a slob but I'm pregnant, you know, and anyway, now I've found out how much money she has, I don't know why she doesn't get a cleaner in a couple of times a week to do the dross. Why do it yourself when you have the money to pay someone?

A yawn hits me and I basically suck the room in; I can't help it and I just give in to it. Baby yawns, I call them. She stares at me and can't hide her horror. Jesus, has no one ever yawned in front of her before? I give her the spiel about pregnancy making me tired and then drop the fact that I'm having a boy into the conversation. She looks surprised and I tell her all about my midwife appointment today.

All absolute bullshit, but she laps it up. The midwife sent me for an extra scan because she thought I was a bit big for my dates. After they'd done all the measuring and stuff, they decided I wasn't big for my dates after all. The bonus was that I found out I'm having a boy and I didn't have to pay for a 3D scan to find that out. So then she says how lovely it is, blah, blah, blah, all the usual rubbish that people spout and when she's finished, I tell her that I'm calling him Ricky.

I study her face as I say it. She looks a bit shocked but she can't really object because he was my brother and I'm doing a really nice thing, aren't I? I think maybe I'm just telling her I'm calling him Ricky to be spiteful because I'm not sure if I will give him his father's name; I'll see what he looks like when he gets here. I quite fancy Brad, after my all-time favourite man, Brad Pitt. I could give him Ricky as his middle name. Maybe. Or maybe not.

'No, I don't mind,' she says.

'Great.' Another baby yawn escapes me and there's a definite hint of disgust on her face now and I have to swallow down a laugh. Then she starts prattling on about ordering a takeaway, how her and Ricky used to do it every Friday, or something, as if it's important. Why do I even need to know that? And then she asks me what I'd like; Chinese, Indian, blah, blah, blah.

So I keep quiet and don't say anything but fix this worried look onto my face, bite my bottom lip and tell her that I don't have any money. Because I decided earlier, before I fell asleep, that I should probably address the money issue with her soon, and now seems like a good opportunity to get it over with.

I studied her as I said it and I thought, you have loads and loads of money so why should I pay for anything at all? Even though actually, I do have some money, because the social have been remarkably amenable and whilst it's not a lot, a payment went into my account today. The certificate I got from the doctors saying I need to rest, helped. But I need that to pay my rent to keep my flat so I definitely won't be contributing anything here, ever.

After a minute she tells me, 'it's okay' and that she wasn't suggesting I had to pay for it, which makes me feel that she's thinking the exact opposite.

To give myself time to think what to say next, I waddle into the kitchen and sit down at the table, walking as if I'm about to give birth at any moment just to emphasise that I'm pregnant and need looking after. She has no idea how agile I really am and probably thinks that I can barely heave myself around. I sit back in the ancient chair and pretend to be thinking. This room is probably the most hideous room in the house; ancient wooden cabinets and shelves full of faded photographs of people who are probably dead, in horrible old-fashion wooden frames. If that's not bad enough there are dust-gathering pots and creepy ornaments that look as if they were bought on a day-trip to Weston in 1975.

It's like a museum.

Does she dust them all? What a waste of time; they all want sweeping into the bin. After a suitable pause, I say, 'But you've paid for everything. I haven't contributed a thing towards food or anything since I've been here. I'm really grateful but I feel bad for not paying. I'm trying to claim some benefits but you know how slow it is to get anything.' This is her cue to tell me that it's not a problem and that I'm not to worry, but does she?

No, she does not.

She asks me if I've started the claim, what job I used to do, what I'm going to do about my flat in Newcastle. Question after question. Nosey bitch. Luckily, I'm quick-thinking and give her chapter and verse of why I can't work now and what I'll be doing once the baby's born. All lies, obviously, because why should I get a job when she's rich and half of it is rightfully mine? I throw in about having nothing for the baby, because I'm on a roll now and she's pissed me off, to be honest. Let her see how shit someone else's life is. And all the time she's chipping in, interfering, asking questions, interrogating me. And when I've finished telling her, she just says, 'I see.'

I see? What does that mean? She's got a strange look on her face that I can't quite fathom and I wonder if I've over-egged it a bit so I ask her if something is wrong and then she says that there's something she needs to talk to me about.

I'm not going to lie, I'm seriously worried now, because what she's said sounds ominous. Like she's going to tell me to leave, or something. I brace myself; is this where I have to tell her who I really am? Just when things were going so well, too. I can't be arsed, if I'm honest; I'd be quite happy to lie through my teeth and stay here until the baby's born. I can put up with her and it's comfortable here. And warm. And free.

'It's about money.' She pulls a face. 'And I don't want you to be offended by what I'm going to say.'

I stare at her. Just spit it out, you weirdo. Get it over with.

'The thing is, you're going to need things for the baby: a cot, a pram, everything really, so I'd like to help, if you'll let me.'

14

MEGAN

Putting the last piece of toast into my mouth, I pick up my phone, type a quick message and then toss it back onto the table. I'm on my own, as usual. Emily won't surface until at least twelve o'clock and even then, she doesn't spend much time downstairs. She prefers to stay in her bedroom. At least, she does when I'm here. I'll be gone by the time she gets up, anyway, as I have a couple of classes to go to at the gym and I'll stay on for a late lunch afterwards.

I never bothered with the gym in the weeks after Rick died; it was the furthest thing from my mind but once I went back to work I thought it would be a good idea to try to get back into fitness. I always used to go to straight to the gym every morning before work, getting up an hour earlier to fit in a session. At weekends, mornings were always a longer session because I had the time. Now that I've got back into the routine, I realise how much I've missed it. How much good it does me. It gives me something to focus on because whilst I'm working out, I can clear my mind of everything.

The sound of the front door opening and closing tells me

that Elaine has arrived. I haven't seen her all week because now she's back at work, too, she only has time to visit at weekends. I was expecting her to turn up today, but maybe not this early. It's barely nine o'clock.

She comes into the kitchen, leans down and kisses me on the cheek.

'How are you?' she asks.

'Good,' I say. 'And you?'

'All good.' She slides a tin onto the table and settles herself in the seat opposite. 'Coffee and Walnut.'

'My favourite.' I don't have the heart to tell her that most of the cakes she brings go into the bin after a few days. I only eat cake to be polite when she's here and the one she brought last weekend, Emily turned her nose up at. She made a comment that it was 'too dry and not sweet enough'. She says she prefers proper cake from Mr Kipling. Emily eats a huge amount of food but not Elaine's cakes and I wonder if she's trying to make some sort of point, because she's not fussy about anything else she puts into her mouth.

'I'll look forward to a slice when I get back from the gym.' I'm hoping she'll take the hint that I'm going out and am not going to sit here, drinking tea, eating cake and gossiping.

Her smile slips slightly, but she doesn't stand up again, so clearly she hasn't taken the hint. I feel slightly mean and then remind myself that I'm not obliged to do what Elaine wants all of the time. I care about her but I'm an adult, I don't need mothering any more and maybe she needs to check I'm not doing anything before she comes round. Maybe the time for gentle hints has passed, maybe I'm just going to have to be blunt.

'How are you finding being back at work?' she asks.

'Much better than I expected. Everyone was very kind,

which helped, but then after a few hours it was just how it used to be and I think I needed that. How was it for you?'

'Manic.' She rolls her eyes. 'Hardly any of my work had been done whilst I was off so I've been playing catch-up all week and the reception area was a tip, paper and dirty coffee cups everywhere. I wonder what some of them do all day.'

'You're wasted there and they don't deserve you because you always go above and beyond. You're under appreciated and underpaid.'

'I know, but I couldn't leave my patients.'

Elaine works as an administrator in a doctor's surgery and has done for the last twenty years. She's overly loyal for a place that pays her the minimum wage and has absolutely zero perks.

'So where is she?' Elaine enquires.

'Emily?' I ask, as if I have someone else living here. 'Upstairs in bed.' I look up at the ceiling. 'She's not up yet.'

She purses her lips and gives a disapproving look. She doesn't bother to hide her dislike any more; if Emily's around when she turns up, she questions her relentlessly on how the hunt is going for accommodation and a job. The atmosphere is awful and I cringe at each question asked. Elaine thinks she's looking out for me, protecting me from being taken advantage of. Emily disappears to her room with an excuse as soon as she possibly can and once she's gone upstairs, Elaine then accuses her of being antisocial.

'Has she found anywhere to live yet?'

'No. She's looked at a few places but so far hasn't found anything suitable. They've offered her a couple of flats but they had too many stairs to get a buggy up and down and neither of them had lifts. You'd think they'd only offer suitable accommodation, but apparently it doesn't work like that.'

'Well, she'd better get a move on, hadn't she? She'll be giving birth here at this rate. How many weeks is she now?'

'Another six weeks to go, I think.'

'The social will have to help her, surely?' Elaine persists. 'They're obliged to find her somewhere. I mean, don't pregnant women jump the queue? It's the guaranteed way to get a council house. Are you sure she's really trying her best to find somewhere to live?'

I shrug, not reminding Elaine that this is the exact opposite of what she originally said about council houses. 'I don't think being pregnant guarantees anything now. I'm sure they'll find her something eventually but it's not a problem her staying here. I don't mind. The baby is going to be my nephew, after all. My only nephew.'

'You're too nice.' She leans closer and lowers her voice. 'I don't like to say it but I think she's taking advantage of you, Meg, and so does Keith.'

Do I care what Keith thinks? I absolutely do not. I don't believe he cares one bit if I'm being taken advantage of, other than he'd like to be the one taking the advantage and no one else.

'What makes you say that?' I ask.

'It's obvious. She's here sponging off you and you only have her word for it that she hasn't got anywhere else to go. It's all very convenient for her, isn't it? Does she even contribute anything, pay her way at all? Does she do anything apart from eat all of your food and laze around all day?'

'What makes you think she lazes around all day?'

'Well, what else does she do? Does she do anything to help at all? Because I've been round and seen you doing the cleaning at the weekend although you're at work all week. I've never seen her lift a finger. I bet you don't come home to a cooked meal after a day's work.'

I get up, pick up my plate and carry it over to the dishwasher. 'I don't think you should talk about her like that, Elaine. Emily is Rick's sister. My sister-in-law. She's family. I'm finding it a little disrespectful, if I'm honest. I know you mean well but it just makes me feel awkward, you slagging her off and grilling her with questions whenever she makes an appearance. And you have no idea what she does all day because you're not here, you're at work. Rick's gone and I can't do anything about that but the very least I can do is help his sister. I know he'd want me to and if he were here, he'd be helping her himself.'

Her face reddens and she realises she's overstepped the mark.

'Anyway,' I say, after a moment, breaking the uncomfortable silence and letting her off the hook, 'seeing as you're here, would you mind giving me a hand to move a couple of boxes into the garage out of the way?'

'Of course I don't mind.' She looks relieved to be off the subject of Emily. 'What boxes?'

'Some deliveries. I've shoved them in the study for now, but they'll be in the way if I decide I want to work from home, so they need moving. I could probably manage them on my own but it'll be much easier getting them into the garage between the two of us.'

My phone bleeps from where it's lying on the table and a message flashes onto the screen. It's from Sam. I lean over, pick it up and slip it into my pocket. I can tell Elaine's seen his name flash up because she can't hide the interest on her face.

'Shall we, then?' I stride out into the hallway and she follows behind. I wonder if she'll leave after we've done this because I've already told her I'm going to the gym. If she doesn't, I'll just have to come right out and tell her that I have a class starting in twenty minutes.

I open the study door, go in and grab hold of the nearest box. It's not particularly heavy, just large and awkward to get hold of.

'If we get them both outside and lean them up against the wall, I'll open up the garage. I'll lead, you follow.'

She grabs hold of the other end and we slide it into the hallway.

'What's inside?'

'This one's a pram and that's a cot,' I say, nodding at the other box in the study as I open the front door.

'Oh.' Her face is a picture of disapproval but after her telling off for slagging off Emily, she daren't comment. We drag the box over the front door threshold and then lean it up against the wall and go back inside for the other one.

'This one's a bit heavier, so mind your back. If we can get it over the step, we can just push it into the garage.'

We manhandle the box outside and lean it up against the other one whilst I unlock the garage and pull open the doors. The sight of Rick's state-of-the-art barbeque as I go inside hits me in the chest like a physical force. I have to stop to catch my breath. He loved that stupid barbeque. My reaction is irrational because it's not as if I haven't been in this garage countless times lately but each time it hits me anew.

'You all right, lovey?' Elaine's looking at me with concern.

'Yes.' I blink rapidly and pushing all thoughts of Rick away, I stride past her and grab the box. We push and pull the box inside the garage, neither of us speaking and I'm grateful for that because right now, I don't have any words. We repeat the process with the second box and by the time we're done, I feel almost normal again.

'Thank you for that,' I say, once they're inside and in place and I've got my voice back. 'Emily doesn't want them in the house just yet. She says it's tempting fate to have everything where she can see it.'

Elaine frowns, looking around at the other boxes of baby equipment scattered around the garage.

'How does she afford all this then? She can't be hard up if she can splash out on a new pram and a cot and all this other stuff. I've never seen so many boxes. It's like a warehouse in here. None of this comes cheap.'

I don't reply but walk out of the garage and wait for her to follow me. She stands silently beside me whilst I close and lock the doors.

'Honestly, Meg, that's a small fortune's worth of stuff in there. Where does she get that sort of money from, when she says she has to claim benefits and go on the council waiting list for a place to live?'

I go back inside the house without answering her and pick up my gym bag from the floor underneath the coat pegs. If she doesn't take the hint that I'm going out now, she never will.

'How does she afford it all, you tell me how, because I must be missing something?' she persists, refusing to let it drop.

'I don't know, Elaine,' I say with a sigh, not meeting her eyes. 'It's none of my business where Emily gets her money from and nor is it any of yours.'

* * *

'How do you feel?'

'Hot,' I reply, taking a slurp of my smoothie.

Sam sits back on the sofa, slipping his arm along it. His fingers would touch my arm, if he moved them just a fraction.

'Yep. That was some session.' He stretches his arms above his head, showing off his muscles. He's doing it for my benefit, he can't help himself. I can't help noticing that he has no hair underneath his arms, none at all. I wonder if he shaves his armpits but decide not; no stubble. Maybe he has them waxed. They're also the exact same smooth honey tan as his arms. A definite sunbed tan. Maybe I should get myself one to dispel the winter pallor.

'Chilli chicken and salsa salad?' A waitress is standing in front of us, a plate in each hand. One is my panini and the other Sam's salad. She's asking us both the question but her attention is firmly fixed on Sam.

'Yep. That's me.' He lowers his arms and gives her a smile, holding her gaze for just a fraction too long and she blushes from her neck to the roots of her hair. She slowly lowers the plate onto the table in front of him, making the normal action a seductive performance. In comparison, my panini is almost thrown in my direction.

'If you need anything else, just let me know,' she breathes at Sam.

He treats her to another smile and she pivots on her heel, sauntering off with an exaggerated swaying of her hips.

'You can't stop yourself, can you?'

'What?' He turns to me with a mock offended look and then grins.

'I'm just being friendly, that's all! I'm a friendly kind of guy. Can I help it if I'm irresistible?' He puts his hands out and laughs. I laugh too. He's making out he's joking but I know he's not. He is hot, there's no denying it; handsome and toned to perfection, he merits a second look from most women he comes into contact with.

'Do you know,' he picks his plate up and forks a huge piece

of chicken into his mouth, 'I think cardio pump has to be my all-time favourite class.'

'Second favourite for me. Boxing is the best.'

'That's because you like hitting me.'

'Rubbish.' I laugh. 'And we never actually make contact, do we?'

'No, more's the pity.'

I throw him a warning look and he grins.

'So, how's it going with the lodger?'

'Will you stop calling her the lodger? You know very well that she's my sister-in-law.'

'Okay, how's the sister-in-law?'

'I don't see a lot of her because I'm at work and when I'm there she spends most of her time in her bedroom. I mean, she does make a token effort to stay downstairs after dinner in the evenings for an hour or two, but we don't really spend any time together as such. She's okay, though. Seems nice enough, although she does have a way of making me feel like I owe her something, as if it's my duty to look after her now that Rick's not here, even though he hadn't seen her for years before he died.'

'What does she do to make you feel like that?'

I shrug. 'It's hard to explain, I can't really put it into words but I feel like I have so much and she has nothing and that somehow, it's my fault her life is a bit of a mess. She doesn't come right out and say it but the odd remark here and there makes me think that she's definitely thinking it. Or maybe I've got it all wrong and I'm reading her all wrong. It doesn't help that she's absolutely nothing like Rick, in looks or personality. No resemblance at all. Chalk and cheese.' I sigh. 'It's not her fault but I can't see any family similarities at all and I've looked, believe me. I thought there'd be something about her of Rick, you know? I thought having her stay might be a comfort, sort of a reminder of Rick but it hasn't turned out that way and you're right in a way – she is like a lodger, except that she doesn't pay. It's just so sad that Rick's never even going to meet his nephew and although I keep telling myself I should do it for his sake, part of me wonders why I'm bothering. Is that a really awful thing to say?'

Sam puts his plate on the table and moves closer.

'No, it's not. You don't owe her anything. You said yourself that Rick hadn't seen her for years and they never bothered with each other. Who's to say he would have wanted to get close to her again? Tell her to move out. You don't have to look after her, she's not your responsibility.'

'No.' I shake my head. 'I couldn't do that. She's due in a matter of weeks and I couldn't be that nasty. No, I have to let her stay until she finds her own place.'

'You're too nice.'

'No, I'm not. Stop saying that.'

'You are, though.' He gazes at me and I look away.

'So,' he says. 'Changing the subject, are you still coming out tonight? That little Italian in Old Town? I've booked a table for eight o'clock, if you're still up for it.'

He looks uncertain; not his usual cocky self. I like him more when he's like this; for me, over-confidence is a definite turn-off.

'Yes, I'm still coming.'

'Great.' The grin is back. 'I'll pick you up at half-seven?'

'No, it's okay, I'll drive myself.'

'Oh.' He looks disappointed. 'You sure? It's no bother for me to come and get you.'

I put my head one side.

'What?'

'You know I'm not staying over at yours after, don't you? It's just a meal, that's all. We're just friends. I'm not ready for anything else.'

'Of course I know you're not staying over at mine, I'm not a complete bastard, you know.'

'That's okay, then, because if that's what you're expecting, we might as well cancel the meal now.'

'I'm not, I promise.' He takes my hand in his huge fingers and holds it. 'I've told you, I'm not the guy you think I am. I'm here for you. I know what you've been through and I'm not about to force myself on you or take advantage. If anything develops, that would be my dream come true, but first and foremost, we're friends.'

'Okay.' I pull my hand away and pick up my panini. It looks distinctly dry and unappetising but I'll force it down because I need the calories after all that exercise.

'You haven't mentioned to anyone at work that we've been meeting up, have you?' I ask.

'Not a word.' He laughs. 'I can keep my mouth shut sometimes, you know.'

15

EMILY

Bloody hell.

She's only gone and given me her credit card.

And the pin number.

I honestly thought she was going to ask me to leave, but no, I got that completely wrong, which just shows that I can't read her as well as I thought I could. Slightly worrying, but there it is.

Then when she said she'd like to help with buying baby things, I thought, here goes, she's going to want to go shopping with me, and how excruciating is that going to be? I had a vision of the two of us trundling around the baby shops together and the thought wasn't in the slightest bit appealing. The widow and the pregnant lover, not that she knows that but still, a bit cringing. And there would also be the distinct possibility of bumping into someone I know when I was with her, which would have been an added stress. But I could force myself to do it and even pretend to be grateful to her, as long as she was paying for everything. Pretty big of me, I think, because she is still alive and Ricky is dead. But I would have done it, because I wasn't lying when I said I had nothing for the baby. The lack of baby stuff has been playing on my mind a bit, what with prams and whatnot costing a small fortune. Me and Ricky had looked online and picked out a few things to go and look at before he died and I couldn't believe the price of it all. It's not something that can be scrimped on, either, because I don't want second-hand crappy stuff for my baby, thanks very much. Why should I?

But no, she didn't want to come with me, thank God, she just wants to pay for it all.

Absolutely fine by me.

I said no at first, of course, because I had to make it look as if she was being too generous and I have my pride and couldn't possibly take it. I then let myself be persuaded very easily because I couldn't risk her believing what I was saying and withdrawing the offer. Once that was settled, she didn't hang around, either; she got straight up out of her chair, went and got the card and gave it to me, right there and then. I eventually managed to mumble 'thank you' and for once, I was nearly lost for words.

I was itching to start spending but I waited until the Monday when she'd gone back to work. As soon as I got up in the afternoon and was washed and dressed, I was straight down the town to order a pram and a cot. I couldn't resist buying some nice clothes for him too, because he'll need something to wear, won't he? He has to wear something and it's not as if I can knit. I didn't skimp, either, because if Ricky was here, he'd have bought the best, so why should I go cheap? I had a lovely time, I'll admit, and I'd have carried on and bought more but I was getting tired so I came back here and thought, I'll go another day, I've got plenty of time.

And I did. I went the next afternoon and because I bought so much, I couldn't carry it all so I got a cab home. I paid for that with the credit card because that's legitimate, isn't it? I can't lug huge bags and boxes of stuff on the bus.

When I got back, I packed it all away in the wardrobe in my bedroom which is so big that it's lost in there, so there's plenty of room for more. I didn't want boxes cluttering up the bedroom and also, it's out of sight in there so she won't know exactly how much I've bought. Not that she comes in my room, except when she cleans it and changes the bed on a Sunday afternoon, and she always asks me first if I mind. I think it's weird how she's too tight to employ a cleaner but has handed a credit card over to me. Anyway, there's no need for her to know about every single thing I've bought. She knows about the cot and the pram and other big stuff because that's being delivered, so I had to tell her because she'll see it. But she doesn't have a right to know every single thing that I buy because he's my baby and not hers. She'll find out how much I've spent when she gets her statement although maybe she won't bother checking it because she has so much money. It was a nice feeling, though, knowing that Brad is going to have everything he needs when he arrives.

I've decided on Brad for his first name; Brad Ricky. Yeah, maybe not Ricky for definite, but maybe Ryan, after Ryan Reynolds, my second-most favourite man. Ricky doesn't really sound right, does it? Although I'll wait and see because I don't have to make a decision just yet.

I didn't plan on going shopping again for a while but when I got up the next day, I thought of a few more things that I'll need so I went into town again. I got a cab there this time because my due date isn't far away so I shouldn't be on my feet for too long waiting at bus stops and the like. And it's just sort of carried on like that ever since; when she gave me that card two weeks ago, I never intended buying so much, but it's sort of snowballed. She's not commented on it at all, even when the deliveries started. She's well aware of how much stuff she's lugging into the garage, because obviously I can't do it, and she hasn't mentioned it so she must be happy about it otherwise she'd have taken the card off me, wouldn't she?

Besides, I know how much money she's got because I've been through that study with a fine toothcomb. She's got a lot more than just the insurance money, I can tell you. There's a massive payout from where Ricky used to work and he had some sort of pension thing that she's getting all the contributions he made refunded to her.

She's actually a millionairess.

By rights, half of that money should be mine but for now, she's got it all, every last penny, so why shouldn't I buy what I want? Because I've moved on from just buying baby stuff now; I've bought myself a fancy new hairdryer and straighteners, because I had to leave all mine behind at the flat. Quality equipment, because if you buy cheap, you buy twice. It'll come in handy when I start hairdressing again. That's if I do, because I might not do once I get my share of the money. New clothes were also a necessity because I came here with just one suitcase and I'm sick of wearing the same crap all the time. None of my bras fit me now, either, and it's uncomfortable spilling out of the top of them. So I had a bit of a splurge and got myself some nice clothes, and I got a few bits and pieces to wear after the birth, too, because obviously, nothing that I've brought with me is going to fit me once he's born.

Because I've made a decision: I'm not going anywhere until I've had this baby.

She must want me to stay, too, because she never asks any more how the house search is going, or when I'm moving out, and if she wanted rid of me, she'd be nagging at me. Her only questions now are to ask how I'm feeling and if I'm managing okay, whatever that means.

Unlike that nosey cow Elaine.

Now when I hear her come into the house, I stay in my room because I've had enough of the Spanish Inquisition every time I see her. If I have the misfortune to be downstairs when she pitches up, I make an excuse as soon as I can and escape to my room to get away from her. She constantly questions me about finding a place to live, asks what the social are doing for me, that sort of thing. Who does she think she is? Bloody cheek. It's none of her business. At first, I used to give vague answers, you know, remain polite but distant, gabble on whilst never actually telling her anything. Now I don't bother because what, exactly, is she? A nosey old bag who's got nothing better to do than come around here and poke her nose in, that's what she is. Why has she got a key to come and go as she pleases? She doesn't live here, she's got her own house. She's just a friend. Although why a twenty-eight-year-old woman would want a friend as ancient as her, God knows. She might be her dead mother's best friend but why is she still hanging around like a bad smell? It's just peculiar. She needs to go and get a life.

So apart from her, and her creepy vile husband – don't get me started on him – things are pretty good at the moment.

I miss Ricky, of course I do, but my life could be a whole lot worse.

* * *

'Thanks.' I close the front door and push the boxes up against the wall, sort of out of the way. A high chair, a baby bouncer, a baby milk maker and a steriliser. I researched everything online before I bought it all and the milk maker in particular looks amazing. It's sort of a coffee maker for babies so there's no messing about with cooling the milk down once you've made it. This baby will definitely be bottle-fed. No way will I be breast-feeding; I value my perky boobs and have no intention of having them wrecked by a baby hanging off them all hours of the day and night. That's if they're still perky once I've pushed the baby out, because at the moment they're like two huge, bouncy balloons. Only much heavier. My midwife told me that a lot of new mums start to express the milk right away; says there's even a machine you tuck into your bra that works off an app so you can carry on doing other things. I smiled and told her I'd think about it, but I had a job to hide my disgust. It sounded like milking a cow. No, Brad will be having good old, powdered milk. It was good enough for me and it'll be good enough for him.

I stare at the boxes lined up against the wall and ponder whether to take the smaller things up to my room. The wardrobe is full up now but I could shove it underneath the bed, I'm sure there's a little bit of space left. I no longer bother lugging stuff home from the shops with me, it's so much easier to pay for next-day delivery. No, I'll leave it for her; she can put it all in the garage when she gets home from work because she just sits at a desk all day pushing a pen around. It'll give her something to do.

The delivery man got me out of bed this time, his incessant ringing of the doorbell waking me from a lovely sleep. It's over the top, if you ask me, wanting me to sign for it. He could have just left it outside like they usually do but maybe he was new to the job. A bit keen. I told him when I took it in that the next time, he could leave it outside and not to worry about getting a signature. This is a good neighbourhood and no one is going to steal anything. I smile to myself at the thought of it; it wouldn't be a problem if any delivery were to go missing because I'd just order it again. I glance at my watch, it's only eleven o'clock, far too early to get up yet.

I waddle back up the stairs, wrapping my lovely new dressing gown around me. Thick and luxurious, I'm pleased I bought it because otherwise I'd have had to come down in my nightie, which is a bit tight and short now. I should treat myself to some new ones. Baby brain, that's what it is, because I could have bought them when I got the dressing gown, but I just didn't think of it. I'll have to go back into town to get them but I don't know if I can be bothered this afternoon. Maybe tomorrow. I'm a regular in Next now and the last time I was in there the assistant gave me a leaflet about opening an account; said I should order online because there's more choice that way and it saves a visit to the shop. I was tempted, although I'd have to do it in her name because of the credit card and I don't know how that would go. She probably wouldn't even notice, she has so much money. Maybe I will. I'll think about it.

I take off my dressing gown, crawl back underneath the duvet, wrap it around me and snuggle down. I close my eyes and am drifting off into a blissful sleep when a noise jars its way into my brain. I open my eyes and slowly haul myself upright. I stay motionless and listen.

The front door. It was definitely the sound of the front door.

Which means he's here again, for fuck's sake.

I get out of bed and wrap my dressing gown around me for the second time today. I'm getting royally pissed off with creepy Keith turning up whenever he feels like it. I caught him in the kitchen yesterday, sitting at the table tucking into a pile of toast, treating the place as if he lives here. And that's only the times I know about. What about when I'm asleep or out shopping and he comes in here? Who knows what he's doing then. He could be poking around my bedroom for all I know.

I drag myself out onto the landing and lumber down the stairs into the hallway but there's no sign of him and the study door is still closed. I go into the lounge but he's not in there either so I head to the kitchen.

'Oh, it's up then,' he says with a sneer as I walk in. He's sitting at the table eating a slice of the horrible cake that nose-bag, Elaine, brings around every weekend.

'Make yourself at home, why don't you?' I say.

He laughs, crumbs dropping from his mouth.

'Haven't you got a job to go to?' I demand.

'Yeah, course I have. Unlike you.'

'I'm pregnant,' I sniff. 'In case you hadn't noticed.'

'Oh, I've noticed all right, lumbering around like a big, fat, pig. You just need trotters to complete the look.'

I boil just looking at him; what a disgusting, skinny excuse for a man he is. I can smell the cigarette smoke from two feet away and God knows if he ever washes. He always looks distinctly grubby.

'You shouldn't be here and you know it,' I say, determined to keep my temper in check. 'I notice you never come around when Megan's here, so she clearly has no idea you come and go as you please.' He rams a piece of cake into his mouth and chews washing machine-style, mouth open. 'You're disgusting.'

He swallows and burps loudly, all for my benefit. 'Be a good girl and put the kettle on, fatso.'

'You must be joking,' I snort. 'I'm not your servant. I've got every right to be here but you haven't. You need to leave, now, or else I'm telling Megan how you're here all the time and I don't think she'll be pleased about it. She'll soon have that key off you when she finds out how you treat this place.'

'Is that right?'

'Yeah, it is right. I hope you enjoyed today's visit because it's your last one.'

He jumps up from the table and in seconds is leaning over me, his hand gripping my arm.

'Don't you threaten me, you slag.' He spits the words into my face.

I recoil and try to twist out of his grip but he squeezes tighter and then suddenly releases me. I stagger backwards and grip the door frame to stop myself from falling.

'You've done it now.' I rub my arm. 'Attacking a defenceless, pregnant woman. You wait until I tell her what you've done.' Hopefully there'll be a bruise there later.

Evidence.

He turns and goes back to his seat and sits down. 'Put the kettle on, then.' He grins.

I turn away. I'm not speaking to him any more. I'm going upstairs and I'm messaging Megan, right this minute. I'm not putting up with this creep for a minute longer.

'You and me need to have a talk, fatso,' he says, loudly.

'No, we don't,' I shout over my shoulder.

'You sure about that?'

I turn around. 'Quite sure. Why the hell would I want to talk to you? You're a disgusting creep.'

I want to go upstairs but something about his grin is worrying me. He's too cocksure. He should be fretting that I'm going to drop him in it with Megan but for some reason, he doesn't seem bothered at all.

'Like I said, put the kettle on because me and you need to have a little chat.'

I open my mouth to speak but he talks over me.

'About your notebook.' He winks.

Ah, that's it, he's been snooping. But it's okay, because even if he's read every single page of that notebook, it proves nothing. It's simply the story of my life, that's all. There's nothing incriminating in there because I'm not *that* stupid. If push comes to shove I can say it's a diary. That's all it is, a diary in notebook form that I've been writing down because the pregnancy is getting to me. It's cathartic, that's what I'll say. It's helping me feel better about my situation.

'I don't know what you're talking about,' I say.

'Yeah, you do.' He sneers. '*Shelley.*'

16

MEGAN

I tap on Emily's door and wait.

Is she asleep? There's no noise from inside so she could be because she sleeps an awful lot. I told her the other day that I was going out tonight but she may have forgotten. I could just go but somehow it feels rude to disappear for the evening without reminding her. I feel slightly bad that I was out last night, too. I joined the rest of the office for drinks at the pub after work and although I only intended staying for an hour or so, the time just flew by. When I arrived home the house was in darkness and Emily was in her room so of course I didn't disturb her but I haven't seen her at all today, either. When I left for the gym this morning she was still in bed and when I came back this afternoon she was in her room although I knew she'd been up. She'd been downstairs and cooked herself some lunch because the frying pan was wedged into the bottom of the dishwasher and the kitchen stank of sausages. I tap on the door again, telling myself that if she doesn't answer this time, I'll just leave without letting her know. At least I'll have tried. There's no answer. I turn to head back downstairs when the door is pulled open just enough for her to poke her head through the gap.

'Yeah?'

She looks rough. Incredibly, for someone who sleeps so much, she looks tired, with big dark circles underneath her eyes. Her skin is flushed and spotty so I guess that's the pregnancy taking its toll on her body.

'Hi.' I smile. 'I just thought I'd let you know I'm eating out tonight so I won't be here to cook dinner, but there's plenty of food in the fridge, so just help yourself.'

'Okay.' She moves to shut the door.

'Are you feeling all right?' I ask, quickly, before she closes the door. 'With the baby and everything?'

'Yes, fine, apart from this stinking cold.' She stares at me, barely concealing the fact that she's looking me up and down.

'So you're okay apart from the cold?'

'Yeah. Why wouldn't I be?'

'It's just that I've hardly seen you over the last couple of days. Have I done something to upset you, Emily?'

'No.' She looks surprised. 'No, of course not.' She gives me a strained smile. 'Sorry. It's not you; it's nothing to do with you. Aside from this rotten cold, I'm not sleeping well and Wes keeps pestering me, wanting to know where I am. It's really getting me down.'

'Oh, I'm sorry, I didn't realise he was still in contact with you.'

She pulls a face. 'I keep blocking his number but then he uses a different phone to message or call me the next time. I could do without it because he gets proper nasty and vicious. I know it's only words but it's not nice reading what he says he's going to do with me when he finds me.'

'Do you think you should contact the police, make a complaint about him? Get them to warn him off or something?'

She looks alarmed and shakes her head.

'God, no. What if by doing that he found out where I was and came after me? I can't take that risk. No, it's best I just keep blocking him, he'll get bored of trying in the end. He doesn't really want me, he just doesn't like it, because I've left him instead of him leaving me. He'll hook up with someone else eventually and then he'll leave me alone.'

'Okay, well, you know, if there's anything I can do to help, you only have to ask.'

'Thanks.' She looks me up and down, again. 'You're done up. Going somewhere nice?'

'Just out for a meal with a friend.'

'Have fun,' she says with a straight face, and with that she closes the door. I stand for a moment and stare at the wood panelling on the door before heading down the stairs.

* * *

'So this boyfriend of hers, he was abusive, was he?'

'Yes. I'm not sure if he actually hit her, because she was a bit vague on details and I didn't like to ask but he was definitely verbally abusive and very controlling. He sounds like a complete thug. He lives in Newcastle and never leaves the place, so Emily says she's safe down here, but he still keeps ringing and messaging her. She blocks his number but then he uses a different phone to contact her again.'

'Why doesn't she change her number if she's that bothered?'

'I don't know. I hadn't thought of that. I'll suggest it to her.'

'I'm surprised she hasn't already done it.'

I think about it.

'You don't think,' Sam says, 'that she actually wants to keep in contact with him? That she's going to get back with him and is just using you?'

'Using me? For what?'

'Yeah, for a free place to stay.'

'No.' I shake my head. 'Why would she want to stay here if she's going to get back with him?'

'I don't know. But you say she hardly spends any time with you and you're not getting any benefit from her living there, are you? You've said yourself that she's no comfort. I mean, it's not as if you're talking about Rick's childhood or anything.'

I shrug.

'Look, just because she's Rick's sister doesn't mean that she's not a grifter, does it?'

'Sam!'

'I'm just putting it out there, that's all. You know nothing about her, other than what she's told you.'

'Isn't that all we know about most people?' I ask.

'Maybe. Although in my case, you misjudged me anyway.' He raises an eyebrow.

'How so?'

'You had me down for some sort of gigolo, when clearly I'm a thoroughly decent, stand-up kind of guy.'

'I never said you were a gigolo.' I laugh. 'I just said you'd been through most of the women in our office.'

'Which I haven't.'

'Well, you have been out with a few of them.'

'Two, to be exact, but I'm single and so were they, so where's the harm?'

'Okay. You've lost me now, because I don't know what point you're trying to make.'

He throws his head back and laughs. 'No, nor me. I've talked myself into a corner that I can't get out of, trying to warn you not to let your sister-in-law take advantage of you.'

'She's not.' I pick up the water bottle and pour some into my glass. 'You want some?'

'Yeah, seeing as we're both driving.' He grins.

'Another bottle?' Sam takes the empty water bottle from me and holds it up in the air with a smile and unbidden, a flashback to the night of the accident bludgeons its way into my brain. Rick said the same thing, held the bottle up in the same way, only that night it was red wine and not water. He'd already drunk far too much and I knew that more would make him worse but I didn't have the nerve to tell him so. Even then, I was afraid of upsetting him; afraid that one wrong word from me and the evening would end in disaster.

Which it did.

I try to push it away; the rage on Rick's face, the fear I felt at his words.

The dawning realisation of what he was truly capable of.

'Hey, are you okay? You look like you've seen a ghost.'

I come back to the present then, to Sam's concerned face. 'No, I'm fine.'

He frowns.

'Honestly.' I manage a weak smile.

'Hey, I'll always be here for you,' he says.

Said with sincerity, the words are familiar.

That's what Rick said, too.

* * *

'Doing anything nice at the weekend?' Rhona asks from her desk opposite me.

An innocent enough question, were it asked by anyone

else. The week has flown by and here we are again; it's the Friday afternoon lull and we're at that hour before we finish work where no one wants to actually do anything but has to look as if they're working. Even the phones are quiet; most of our clients do their utmost to clear the decks by Friday afternoon.

'Nothing special.'

'No plans with your sister-in-law? Although I suppose she's practically ready to drop, isn't she?'

'She's got about four weeks to go, I think.'

'Wow. That's going to be strange, isn't it? Having a new baby in the house.'

Before I can answer, the door to Jeremy's office opens and he comes out, switches the light off inside and closes the door.

'Hard at it, ladies?'

I smile stiffly and Rhona looks down at her keyboard. Jeremy has no people skills at all, given that he's a manager, and seems to think that he simply has to bark at people to get them to do what he wants. He's forty but dresses and behaves as if he's a schoolteacher from the 1950s.

'I have a phone meeting in ten minutes so will take it upstairs in the coffee lounge. Have a good weekend, everyone.'

He says it so quietly no one even hears him, except for me and Rhona and he slips out of the office door.

'Phone meeting, my backside,' Rhona says with a snort. 'I can guarantee that if I went upstairs now, he wouldn't be there. I don't know who he thinks he's kidding.'

I laugh. He does it every Friday without fail and I don't know why he bothers because no one believes him or even cares, they're just relieved to see the back of him. I look around the office to see everyone has already downed tools and is now making no attempt at a pretence of working.

'Your sister-in-law,' Rhona prompts. 'I take it she's staying with you until the baby's born?'

'I think so.'

'Rather you than me. I couldn't put up with a screaming baby and piles of dirty nappies everywhere. You must be super chilled.'

I shrug.

'Are you coming to the pub after work?' she asks. 'It was okay last week, wasn't it?'

'It was,' I admit. 'I'll definitely come, but maybe just for one drink this time because I feel a bit guilty leaving my sister-in-law again. Are you going?'

'Too bloody right. There's a massive glass of Prosecco with my name on it. That's great that you're coming again and I wouldn't worry about your sister-in-law, I'm sure she can look after herself.'

'I just feel a bit bad leaving her, that's all.'

'Why? She's an adult, isn't she?'

'I know, but she's heavily pregnant...'

'She's got your mobile and she can ring you if there's a problem, can't she? Put yourself first and stop worrying about other people,' she says sternly.

'Yes, boss,' I say with a smile.

I sense Sam looking in my direction from his desk further down the office and I can't resist a sneaky look.

'You and Sam seem friendly,' Rhona says.

Obviously I wasn't sneaky enough.

'What makes you say that?'

'Oh, I don't know, the conflabs in the kitchen, the way he hangs around your desk a lot, the way you were glued to each other last Friday night.' She grins.

'It's true, we have been talking a lot,' I say quietly. 'I find it helps to talk and Sam's really not the person I thought he was. He's much more understanding than I imagined.'

'Oh, God, yeah, of course you do. I was only joking, you know, I didn't mean anything by it.'

Her cheeks flush. She's embarrassed now, remembering that I've been recently widowed.

'I know you didn't,' I say, letting her off the hook. 'And Sam and I are friends. Good friends. He's been great, we've been spending a bit of time together and he's also got me back into going to the gym regularly, because I needed someone to push me to do that.'

'That's so sweet,' she says, her eyes lighting up at the potential gossip I've just handed her.

'So although I'm not looking for a relationship, because it's far too soon, when I am ready, I do think I could do a lot worse than look in Sam's direction.'

17

EMILY

How can Keith know?

How?

The only way he could have found out I'm not Emily is for him to have been asking around about me; talking to someone I know.

Just my rotten luck.

I pretended not to know what he was talking about, asked him who Shelley was, put on my very best dumb act. At first, he laughed, but after a while he got nasty, said, 'Stop getting on my fucking nerves and do as you're told.'

Which is to get him money, five hundred pounds, to be precise.

He's given me until next Friday to get it, which, he says, is very generous, considering I've been splashing money around like a millionairess. I told him then that Megan was paying for it all because I didn't want him thinking I had loads and that he could ask for even more. I didn't tell him about the credit card I've been using because I'm not that stupid.

I don't have five hundred pounds. The payment I got from

the social has gone on the back rent I owed and I'm not due the next payment for another few days and even then, it won't be enough. So I have to either find the money from somewhere and pay him or it's all going to come out. I toyed with the idea of telling Megan who I am; get it over and done with and out in the open before he had a chance to tell her. Tell her that I'm not Ricky's sister, but I was his lover and that I want my share of his estate for the baby. Come clean. Tempting though it is to tell her, so she knows Ricky didn't give a shit about her and loved me, I'm not going to. Because the trouble is, if I tell her who I am, things are obviously going to turn nasty. I'll have a fight on my hands because I can't see her just rolling over and handing me a load of money simply because I demand it and right now, I don't feel up to a fight. I'm exhausted most of the time, no matter how many hours I sleep. Carrying this baby is like having a huge bag of coal strapped around me that jumps about all the time and stops me from sleeping. I might lie in bed for a lot of the time, but mostly I'm not asleep or if I am, it's not good sleep. The minute she knows the truth, I'll have to move out of here and back to my flat and although I love my flat, I can't afford to keep it toasty warm like it is here. I'll have to start buying food again and cooking for myself all of the time and I really don't feel like it. As for all the baby stuff I've bought, well, I can't see her letting me keep any of that, so I'm going to end up with nothing for the baby whilst I fight her for what's rightfully mine. Which means I'll have to get myself a solicitor and I don't have any money for that, either.

So in reality, I have to pay him. But the question is, how?

So aside from the baby kicking and punching me and keeping me awake, I've spent the last twenty-four hours trying to work out how I'm going to get my hands on five hundred pounds. I was lying in bed this morning, wide-awake, pondering the problem when I heard Nosebag Elaine turn up at the crack of dawn. I couldn't believe it, it's Saturday, for God's sake. Doesn't she have a life of her own to be getting on with? What a sad-arse. Does she have any idea what her creep of a husband gets up to? I'm guessing she doesn't, because if she did, she wouldn't be so stuck-up and high and mighty.

Unable to sleep, I got out of bed, quietly opened my bedroom door and tiptoed out onto the landing. Megan and Elaine were in the hallway so I stood at the top of the stairs so I could see what they were doing. They were carting my deliveries into the garage, tidying them away out of sight because Megan is absolutely obsessed with cleaning and tidiness. She can't bear a thing out of place and if I leave so much as a cup on a worktop she's whisking it away into the dishwasher. No wonder Ricky didn't want her, she must have driven him mad.

It was annoying that Nosebag had turned up, because being awake so early, I was starving. That's the trouble with me now; if I'm not sleeping, I'm eating. I can't seem to stop. So I was itching to get downstairs and get some breakfast but I didn't want to see either of them because then I'd have to talk to them and I really can't be bothered. I don't like talking to either of them on a normal day and at the moment I haven't got the headspace to hold a conversation without fear of telling one or both of them to fuck right off. If it's not Nosebag giving me the Spanish Inquisition, it's Megan looking down at me because I've dropped a crumb on her bloody carpet.

Luckily, once they came inside, they pretty much then went straight out again. I heard Megan telling Elaine that she was going to the gym and then out for lunch. It sounded like an excuse to me, like she wanted to get rid of her. I gave it ten minutes, when they'd left the house, just to make sure they didn't come back and then I went down and cooked myself a lovely sausage sandwich. I even remembered to shove the frying pan in the dishwasher because she doesn't need to know what I've been eating.

I came back upstairs straight afterwards because I didn't want to chance getting caught by her if she came back. I feel more comfortable when she's out at work because I can please myself, watch as much TV as I like but at weekends, unless I want to put up with having to make conversation with her and looking at her superior, snotty face, I stay in my room. I've got my phone on the Wi-Fi now so I don't have to worry about how much data I use but there's only so much crap on there I can look at. I went back to bed after a while and actually managed to get to sleep because the baby was quiet, for once. Probably all those sausages.

And then she wakes me up.

I'm in a deep and lovely sleep and she knocks on my bloody door. For what? To tell me that she's going out. She was out last night, too; didn't come home from work until gone nine o'clock. She'd prewarned me with me some cock-and-bull story about going for a drink after work for someone's birthday, but I'm not stupid, I know what she's up to. And I had to cook my own dinner again whilst she was out gallivanting and that's not on; I'm pregnant and I need my rest.

Not that I give a shit what she does, and she'd already told me she wouldn't be here tonight so does she think I can't remember anything just because I'm pregnant?

Silly cow. It didn't help that looking at her made me feel even more of a blimp because she was all tarted up in a nice dress and heels with a bit of make-up on and her hair was all curled and fancy. She looked stunning, and I felt so eaten up with jealousy because it's all wasted on her and I feel like absolute shit.

She was clearly meeting a man, because why else would she get tarted up like that?

I stared at her and thought, Ricky's only been dead a couple of months and you're moving on already. You've got all his money and now you've found yourself another bloke who you're probably going to rip off.

What a bitch.

What I was thinking must have been written all over my face because she asked if I was okay, if she'd done something to upset me. I had to think on my feet then because I really wanted to slap her and tell her what I thought of her. But I'm pretty quick-thinking so I managed to put a surprised expression on my face and make up a load of old bull about Wes pestering me and how I wasn't sleeping, although the not sleeping bit is true.

She suggested getting the police involved and I quickly put the kibosh on that, because Wes doesn't even exist and whilst I don't think much of the police, even they'd be able to figure that one out. I couldn't resist telling her she 'looked all done up', then, and she gives me the line that she's going out for a meal with a 'friend'. Yeah, right, I wasn't born yesterday.

I told her to have fun and closed the door on her and went and got back into bed.

I was a bit rude, actually.

But, you know, whatever.

* * *

It's Friday again.

A whole week since that creep told me I had to pay him. I've been dreading this day so of course, the week has flown by in a flash at twice the speed it normally does.

I get up off the sofa, and for the twentieth time this morning

I go over to the window and check the street to see if his battered estate car is outside; it's not. I return to the sofa and huddle back underneath the furry throw, pulling it up to my neck. It's not cold in here because I've turned the heating up to a tropical twenty-five degrees, but even so, I just can't seem to get warm. It's nerves, I think, plus this cold that seems to be hanging around forever, and I have a face full of spots so I look like shit. I think it's the result of the shittiest week ever catching up on me.

But I've got the money to give him and I used Megan's credit card to get it.

Dead easy, it was, after all my fretting about it. I googled getting cash from a credit card because I knew it was possible, but I'd never actually tried it. It's a big no-no, finance-wise, because the amount of interest is astronomical, as it's charged on a daily basis, so it's the worst possible way of getting cash. But short of going to a money lender, it was my only option. If there were any other way I could have got my hands on that cash, I would have done it. My bank account is barely in the black and five hundred pounds might not seem like a lot, but it is when you don't have it. Every penny I get has to go on paying my rent because I need that flat to go back to once I tell Megan who I really am. I've thought ahead and doubled up on some of the baby stuff for when it turns nasty and I've been taking it all round to the flat in a cab. Not big stuff, because I think she'd notice if I had two prams delivered here but the stuff I can manage, I've bought two of. I make sure to use a different cab firm every time because I'm not thick. I'm fairly well set up at my flat now and have loads of stuff there and quite a few new outfits there for myself post-birth, because I have to make hay whilst the sun shines.

Because I think a storm's a-coming, as they say.

Drawing cash on that credit card is risky. So far, she hasn't mentioned how much I've spent using the card, so I'm guessing she hasn't checked it but she's obviously going to find out when the statement comes in. I've spent *a lot* – not that I've added it all up – but it's well into the thousands, not hundreds. Quite a few thousand; more than a few. Although it's still just a drop in the ocean compared to how much money she's got for Ricky dying. Ricky's money. She's got nearly a million by my reckoning and that's without this house, so she's not exactly hard up. When she eventually finds out about me, she can take everything I've spent on her card out of my share of Ricky's estate if she's that bothered.

I got a cab into town on Monday, went straight along to the cashpoint outside my bank and fed the card into the machine. I punched in her number and the amount I wanted, crossed my fingers and hoped for the best. The banknotes swooshed out, no trouble at all. It was such a relief because I was sweating on it a bit; I didn't know if there was a limit on how much I could get out or if the card was even set up for drawing cash, but I needn't have worried, it worked like a dream. I only got two hundred and fifty pounds out that day because I didn't know if there was a daily limit on it and I didn't want to muck it up by asking for too much. I went back on Tuesday and got the other two hundred and fifty pounds.

So I have the money but I wish that sodding Keith hadn't found out I'm not Ricky's sister. Everything was going so well and now he's gone and ruined it. I'm comfortable here and even with all the stuff I've bought on her credit card, I think I'll get away with it because most of it is for the baby and she's unlikely to go through the statement checking every penny I've spent. She's not going to know how much stuff I've bought two lots of. But drawing cash out, that's different. She might not let that go because she could think I'm taking advantage of her, especially if she tells Nosebag Elaine, because the old bag will stick the knife in and try to convince her I'm ripping her off. I think I've got a fighting chance of convincing her that I needed it to pay Wes off or something, to get him out of my life, because it's only five hundred quid at the end of the day. But I won't be able to get away with doing it again; she's not that dumb. No, I can't take any more money out on that credit card, much as I'd like to.

Which could be a real problem, because I have a horrible feeling that Keith is going to come back for more. Because what he's doing is blackmail, and blackmailers always want more, don't they? They never go away; once they have you, they have you forever, or in my case, until Megan finds out the truth about me.

So I've had to come up with a plan B.

I've thought of a way to stop him blackmailing me but it's drastic. I really don't want to have to go through with it because it's an absolute last resort action that could go badly wrong for me. But I have limited choices, as they say, so I'll do it if I have to. I can't allow myself to be blackmailed by him forever.

So this is going to be a one-time only payment and I'm not giving him five hundred; I'm seeing if I can get away with two-fifty. Because five hundred's a bit much, isn't it? I mean, he must know I don't have a lot of money because I'm living here. So it'll be his own fault; if he's greedy, and I think he will be, it'll be plan B.

The sound of the front door opening makes me jump. All that checking the window and he sneaked in without me realising. I push back the throw and haul myself off the sofa. I don't want him coming in here standing over me, putting me at a disadvantage. The thought of him catching me in my nightie was the reason I got up so early and got dressed. I knew he wouldn't wait all day to come and get his money. I've barely stood up before he strides into the lounge, stinking of cigarette smoke.

'Fuck's sake, it's like a sauna in here.'

'God, you stink,' I say, sniffing loudly. 'You make me feel sick.'

He frowns, his mouth twisting. 'You got it?' he snarls.

'Got what?'

'Don't play games with me, fatso, just hand it over if you want me to keep your secrets.'

'I have to go upstairs and get it.'

'You knew I was coming to get it.'

'Yeah, but you didn't tell me what time, did you? I could hardly sit here with an envelope of cash waiting for you. What if Megan decided to come back for some reason?'

I push past him and I feel his eyes on me as I waddle out of the lounge. I go upstairs and into my bedroom and take the cash out of the dressing table drawer.

'Hurry up.' He's standing in the doorway watching, and I never even heard him following behind me. That's what comes of being so skinny, I suppose. Sly and sneaky.

'Get out of my room!' I shout at him. 'You didn't need to come up here, I told you I was getting it.'

'Gimme.' He holds out his hand, waggling his fingers.

I walk over and shove the cash at him. He snatches it from me, licks his fingers and makes a big thing about counting the notes.

What a prick.

'Where's the rest of it?' He looks at me, his mouth twisted. 'I said five hundred, there's only two-fifty here.'

'It's all I could get out in one go.'

He steps towards me and I step backwards.

'You've had all week so don't give me that bullshit. Give me the rest of it.'

'My benefits don't go in until Monday.'

'Give me it or I tell Meg who you are.'

'I'll be overdrawn.'

'Do I look like I give a shit? Get it or she finds out all about you.'

'Okay.' I bite my lip. 'But I'll have to go to the cashpoint and get it out.'

'Whatever. I'll be back this afternoon for it so don't piss me about.'

'I'll get it, I will. Now get out of my room.'

He grins. 'I'm going.' He walks out onto the landing and I grab hold of the handle, ready to slam the door behind him.

'I'll be back later.' He turns. 'So don't even think about messing me around. And after that, it'll be the same time, next week.'

'What?'

'Same time, next week,' he repeats slowly, grinning. 'Five hundred. Every week from now on.'

'But I don't have it.'

He laughs. 'Well then, get it. Sell something, steal it, I don't care. I want the same again next Friday, and every Friday after that.'

'Please, honestly, I don't have it.'

'Not my problem.'

'I can't get any more. I'll give you the other two-fifty today but that's it.'

'You're not listening, fatso. I want five hundred every week or I'll tell Megan everything.'

'You don't know everything about me,' I say.

'What does that mean?' He studies me. 'What don't I know about you?'

I'm tempted then to tell him about me and Ricky but I can't figure out whether that would make things worse or better. He might ask for even more money if he knows I'm carrying Ricky's baby.

'I've got a right to be here,' I say.

He laughs. 'No, you haven't. I'll be back later for the rest. Pay up every week, or I'll tell her everything, *Shelley*.'

He goes out onto the landing and I stand in the doorway and watch him as he saunters down the stairs.

Next week and every week.

It's not my fault, I tell myself, he's forced me into this. I don't want to do it but he's left me with no choice.

When he comes back this afternoon, I'll be putting plan B into operation.

18

MEGAN

I open my eyes to an unfamiliar room; cream painted walls, bare and plain, navy curtains pulled haphazardly across the window. There's a gap in the middle where they're not properly pulled together and sunlight is streaming through. I pull my arm out from underneath the quilt and the air is warm, almost hot. There's no early morning chill in this room which tells me this is a new building, not an old one like mine with its numerous gaps and drafts. I push the duvet down. It has a satin feel to it, slippery almost, I make out dark blue and light-coloured geometric stripes on the material in the light coming through the curtains. Two blond wood chests of drawers sit side by side on the wall next to me, the tops bare of clutter except for a wallet and a watch.

This is a man's bedroom; functional, plain, no frills, no ornaments.

I turn over to face the man lying next to me and study his handsome face. Does he sense me looking at him? Maybe he does, because he opens his eyes.

'Sleep well?' I ask.

He blinks several times as he comes to and then smiles. 'Yes.'

'Thank you,' I say.

'What for?'

'For last night. For making me feel alive again.'

His arm snakes around my waist as he pulls me towards him and I melt into the warmth of his body as he holds me tightly. I slip my arm around his shoulder and stroke his skin. He closes his eyes; thinking he's gone back to sleep, I gently pull away and slide out of bed.

'Hey, where are you going?'

'Bathroom.' I grab my clothes from the chair and saunter into the en suite, conscious of Sam's eyes on my naked body as I go. Maybe I walk a little taller, hold myself differently, tense my stomach muscles.

He's the first man to see me naked since Rick.

Once in the bathroom I turn on the shower and whilst the water runs, I squirt toothpaste onto my finger and rub it around my teeth and tongue. Once underneath the running water, I wash my hair using Sam's herbal shampoo; it smells minty and manly but I like it. Somehow it makes me feels stronger.

Like a new person.

I lather my hair and stand underneath the hot water to rinse, only forcing myself to get out when I realise that I'll use all of the hot water up if I stay any longer. When I've towelled myself dry, I look at yesterday's clothes that I brought into the bathroom with me and feel distaste at the thought of wearing them again. I never wear clothes more than once but there's no way I can borrow any of Sam's gym wear, he's nearly a foot taller than me and twice the size. I pull on yesterday's underwear and tell myself not to be ridiculous.

I stand in front of the mirror and comb my hair with Sam's comb and fluff it up with my fingers. I'm sure he has a hairdryer somewhere but I'll let it dry into natural waves. There's a definite glow to my skin and my eyes look alert. Alive.

I feel good, despite my day-old clothes.

When I return to the bedroom, Sam is sitting up in bed, scrolling through his phone. He looks up at me with a frown.

'You're not going, are you?'

'Of course not.' I go and sit on the edge of the bed next to him. 'Unless you want me to? Have you already made plans for today?'

'No, I mean, don't go. I know we usually meet at the gym but we could give that a miss, today, what do you think? Shall we just spend the day together instead? Go out for lunch, mooch about, have a lazy day?'

'Sounds perfect, but I need to go home and get changed first. I feel like a tramp in yesterday's work clothes.'

'Don't go yet. I'll get up and make breakfast for us. I don't know about you, but I need food and lots of it.' He pulls a face.

'Did I wear you out?'

'No.' He laughs. 'I think I must have drunk too much at the pub last night. After-work drinks for me are usually a tonic water or the occasional beer. God knows what possessed me to indulge in that round of shots. I usually stay well clear because it interferes with my training. I must have lost my tolerance for alcohol because I didn't have that many. I feel quite hungover. How about you?'

'I feel pretty good,' I say. 'After last night.' I give him a meaningful look.

'God, I hope I didn't disappoint you.'

'Sam, you didn't disappoint me in any way, it was a wonderful night. The best. Didn't you think so?' I bite my lip.

'Of course I did. It was perfect. I just wanted to be sure you were happy, because you know how much I think of you.'

'Were you really that drunk? You didn't seem like you'd drunk much.'

He looks uncomfortable.

'You do remember last night, don't you?' I ask, eyes wide.

'Of course I remember, I wasn't that drunk!' He grins. 'As if I could forget! I may have overindulged a bit but I remember every second of it.' He leans forward and kisses me gently on the lips.

'Eew,' I say, as we come up for air. 'Morning breath, or what?'

'Sorry.' He laughs. 'You, of course, are never less than perfect and it's time for me to hit the shower.' He clambers out of bed and struts to the bathroom, fully confident in his nudity. As he reaches the door he turns and winks at me before going inside and closing the door.

I get up and wander out into the lounge and cross to the window. We're on the fourth and top floor of a block of apartments on the edge of town. I look down at the roads below, already busy with cars full of Saturday shoppers heading into the town centre. This apartment is ideally positioned for the centre and, although Sam has a car, I know that he usually walks to work. I go into the kitchen, which is open-plan to the lounge with a worktop bar across and two stools beneath, to add some separation. The walls are painted the same cream as the bedroom and the furnishings are blond wood and pale grey cloth. The kitchen splashbacks and worktops are grey, too.

It's all very new and modern; very Sam.

I didn't see much of it last night when we arrived here.

A sleek, stainless-steel coffee machine sits in the corner of the worktop and I walk over and study it. It's a different model to mine and of a much higher spec, but works on the same principle. The water tank is full but the coffee hopper is nearly empty. I open the wall cupboard in front of me in my search for coffee and am confronted by box upon box of protein bars. The next cupboard contains protein shakes, the one after that, a huge bag of coffee beans and a tiny packet of teabags. I fill the hopper with coffee and begin the search for milk.

I open three cupboards before I find the built-in fridge and I'm impressed with what's in there: lots of fresh vegetables, eggs, fruit, a pack of organic chicken and the only processed meat, a lone packet of bacon. I take out a carton of coconut milk – my favourite – and wonder what Sam will have. I've only ever seen him drink smoothies at the gym and have no idea how he takes his coffee, although he drinks it at work.

'You're making coffee? I knew you were perfect.'

Sam comes up behind me and slides his arms around me. He smells of shower gel and minty toothpaste.

'Yes, I am,' I swivel around to face him. 'But I don't even know how you take yours.'

'Half coffee, half semi-skimmed, no sugar. You have that in yours?' He points at the coconut milk.

'I do. I love coconut.'

'There are so many things I don't know about you.'

'Ditto.'

He leans into the fridge. 'Are we being healthy or do you want a good old-fashioned bacon sandwich? I have proper bread and brown sauce.'

'Sounds perfect.'

I take two cups from the shelf and set about making the coffee whilst Sam busies himself with the frying pan.

'Nice place you have here,' I say, putting our mugs of coffee on the counter and sliding onto a stool. 'How long have you lived here?'

'Just over a year. I bought it off plan and then spent eight months waiting for it to be built.'

'It's lovely.' I look around. 'Like a show home.'

Sam lays bacon in the pan and watches it sizzle before replying.

'It needs a few pictures or something to make it more homely, but I don't have much idea about that sort of stuff. Plus, I'm over-the-top tidy, so it never gets a chance to look lived in.'

'I think it's homely. It doesn't have to be untidy to feel like home. I can't stand mess, so I'm the same.'

'We're perfectly suited, then.' He grins, then opens a cupboard and takes a glass out, fills it with water, pops two paracetamol in his mouth and drinks the water straight down.

'Headache?' I ask.

'Sort of. I'm a bit fuzzy-headed, a bit vague. That'll teach me to over indulge. The brief enjoyment of alcohol is never worth the hangover and because I do it so rarely, I have a low tolerance for it.'

'Same here,' I say. 'A bacon sandwich will sort you out.'

'It will.'

I watch him as he cuts four uniform slices of bread from a loaf and spreads butter onto them.

'Don't let your coffee get cold.'

He comes and sits next me.

'Very good,' he says, taking a sip. 'Just how I like it.'

'Bacon smells good,' I say.

'It does. I don't know about you but I'm starving. What's that noise?' He frowns, his head on one side, listening. 'I can hear something.'

'I think it's my phone,' I say, listening. 'It's in my handbag somewhere.'

'Leave it,' Sam says. 'If it's important they'll ring again.'

'It might be Emily, I should get it.'

'Why? She's not your keeper.'

'What if she's gone into labour early? I should answer it.' I look around the room to see where the ringing is coming from.

'It's coming from there.' Sam stands up, walks into the alcove to the front door, picks my handbag up from the floor and brings it over to me.

'God,' I say, as I unzip it and root around with my fingers. 'That's really bad of me leaving it in there where I can't hear it – she could have been trying to get hold of me and I wouldn't have heard it in your bedroom.' I feel the familiar contours of the phone and as I pull it out, it stops ringing.

'That was Elaine,' I say, staring at the screen. My eyes widen. 'But there are loads of missed calls from Emily last night. Oh my God, I never even thought about her needing me, how selfish am I? If something's happened to her or the baby, I'll never forgive myself.'

I call Emily's number and wait whilst it rings but there's no answer. I cancel the call and try again with no success. I look at Sam with a worried expression. 'I need to go.'

'She'll be sound asleep,' Sam says. 'You said she sleeps a lot and it's still early. Maybe she just wanted to know where you were.'

'That's possible. But why would she ring all those times? It must have been important.' The phone rings again but it's not Emily, it's Elaine.

'Hi, Elaine?'

'He's missing,' Elaine says without preamble, her voice panic-stricken. 'Keith didn't come home last night.'

* * *

'This will sort your hangover out,' I say, as we march along the street in the direction of our office. I left my car parked there last night when we went to the pub with everyone from work.

Sam pulls a face. 'A leisurely lunch somewhere nice would have sorted it out much better. A hair of the dog, even. A small one.'

'Sorry,' I say, for what feels like the millionth time. 'But at least you can go home and have a nap to sleep it off now.'

'You're too nice,' he repeats, also for the millionth time. 'I'm sure Emily is fast asleep and Elaine's husband is sleeping off a massive hangover at one of his mates'.'

I slow down as I spot my car, in the same spot that I parked it in yesterday morning. I click my key fob and it tweets.

I turn to face him. 'I'm sorry to wreck our day, but I need to check Emily is okay, and Elaine's in a right state and I can't just ignore her. She needs me.'

He shrugs. 'Her husband's a grown man, for God's sake. Like I say, he's probably had a skinful and is sleeping it off somewhere. You said he practically lives at the pub, didn't you?'

'He does, but Elaine says he's never stayed out all night before and it's so unlike him. He always comes home, no matter how late it is, according to her. He's not answering his phone and it's not even ringing, which is really frightening her. She's already rung around all of his friends and none of them saw him after he left the pub last night. She's got it into her head that he's lying dead in a ditch somewhere. I promised to go round as soon as I've checked on Emily, so we can go to the police station together to report him missing.'

'I don't think they'll be interested because he's not a kid. I think you have to be missing for twenty-four hours or something before they'll even consider doing anything.'

'Regardless of that, I have to be there for her. It's the least I can do after all she's done for me. But at the moment, I'm more concerned about Emily. Her baby is due in a matter of weeks and she was ringing me again and again and I never heard or even thought about her. Now I can't get hold of her, I'm really worried something bad has happened.'

'Sorry, of course you're worried.' He pulls me to him and wraps his arms around me. 'I'm being a selfish pig, and you're absolutely right, you should be there for her. I'm massively disappointed, that's all. I was looking forward to us spending the day together.'

'Me too.' I look up and kiss him. 'Today might have been ruined but we'll have plenty more days together.'

'Is that a promise?'

'It is. And thank you for last night, and that lovely bacon sandwich this morning.'

'Anytime. Even if we did have to stuff it down, walking along the street.'

We kiss deeply and then I pull away. 'I have to go. I'll keep you posted, okay?'

'Yep.'

'You can go and sleep off that hangover.'

Sam pulls a face at my remark and I climb into the car and start the engine. I see him in the mirror, still standing watching as I pull away.

I drive home, calling Emily on hands-free on my way but I get no response. When I pull up onto the driveway, I grab my handbag and go inside the house. I'm met with silence. No sound of the TV or Emily being up and about upstairs, despite it being nearly twelve o'clock. I slip my shoes off and go straight upstairs. As I get to the top of the landing, I see her bedroom door is open. I go into the room but she's not there, although her bed's all rumpled and looks as if it's been slept in. I come out and carry on down the landing to see that my bedroom door is open, too. I always close it. When I enter the room, there's an Emily-sized mound underneath the duvet, her blonde hair poking out of the top.

'Emily,' I say, walking to the bed and putting my hand on her shoulder. I give her a gentle shake and the mound moves slightly. 'Emily,' I repeat, more loudly this time. 'Are you okay? Emily!'

She moves and after a moment, the quilt is pushed down from her face and she heaves herself upright.

'What?' she says, blinking at me as if she has no idea who I am.

'Oh my God, Emily.' I stare at her in shock.

She has a black eye, a cut lip and a gash on her cheek. A livid purple bruise is blossoming on her forehead.

She puts her hand to her head and winces.

'Thank God you're back,' she whispers. 'I rang you but you never answered. I've been waiting and waiting for you to come home.'

'What happened? Who did this to you?'

She opens her mouth to answer and then bursts into tears.

19

EMILY

A loud banging noise forces its way into my dreams and I open my eyes in panic wondering what the hell it is. It takes a minute to remember where I am, as it does most mornings, and I lie still and listen, telling myself to calm down.

The banging suddenly stops and is then immediately followed by a ringing sound.

It's the doorbell.

I relax and let go of the breath I've been holding. It'll be a delivery of something that I've ordered, although I can't remember what I have ordered right now, because there have been so many deliveries that I've lost track of what's arrived and what hasn't. The keen, new delivery driver who's too frightened to leave it on the doorstep for fear of it being stolen will be the one ringing the bell. All the other drivers give a cursory tap of the letterbox flap and drop the boxes next to the front door. Usually I don't even hear them and only see the deliveries because I check each day. There's no way I can get up and answer the door. He'll give up trying in a minute and leave, no doubt taking the parcel away with him. He'll come back tomorrow. Not that I care whether he leaves the parcel or not, I have far more important things to worry about.

There are several more rings and then silence; he's gone.

I haul myself upright in bed, wincing at the pain in my arm as I do so. My head hurts when I move and I gingerly feel around my eye with my fingertips.

It's sore, very sore. Swollen and puffy too, by the feel of it.

I slowly turn my head to look at the clock; 8.06 a.m.

I lie back down and pull up the duvet. I need to pace myself and take things very slowly. The baby – I'm having second thoughts about calling him Brad, to be honest – kicks me viciously underneath the ribs and despite the pain, I'm flooded with relief. He's fine, there's no need to worry about him; nothing that I've done has in any way affected him.

I know that I should get up soon, even though it's far too early and I don't normally get out of bed until at least midday.

Today is different because it's not going to be like any other day, and I need to prepare myself.

I should have done this last night but Megan fucked up my plan because she wasn't *here*; the one night that I wanted her to be here, she decides not to come home.

Unbelievable.

I sat on the bed with the bedroom door open and waited and waited for her to come back but it got later and later and she never appeared. I rang her loads of times and the bitch never even answered. She's probably with her new man that she pretends doesn't exist. Her 'friend', as she persists in calling him, as if I'm so thick I'll believe her. Here I am, ready to drop at any minute and she doesn't even answer the phone to me. What sort of person does that? The last time I recall looking at the clock, it was nearly midnight. I must have fallen asleep soon after that, despite my agitation. That's the thing with being pregnant; I can toss and turn and not get any meaningful sleep but equally, I can fall asleep at the drop of a hat without intending to. I actually fell asleep sitting on the toilet the other night when I got up for a wee. Disaster was only averted because I hit the side of the bath as I started to keel over.

I feel grubby and a right state because I'm still in the clothes I was wearing yesterday. I can't put clean stuff on because I need to look a mess – it'll be more effective that way. I wonder what time she came back. I assumed she must have gone straight out after work again but I don't remember her telling me about it. She usually makes a right fuss about going out, as if I can't cope with being here on my own. How typical of her that the very time I needed her to be here, she wasn't around.

I lie still and listen but can't hear anything, no sound of her moving around downstairs, or the radio playing in the kitchen. Maybe she's had a late night and isn't up yet. I suppose she could still be asleep, although I've never known her to lie in, even on weekends. Like I say; she's not normal; up at the crack of dawn, every day. I force myself to sit up again, swivel around, swing my legs off the bed and onto the floor. They feel heavy and cumbersome and when I look down, I see that my ankles are swollen and puffy. Quite common, according to my midwife, and nothing to worry unduly about. My legs used to be lovely and slim and one of my best assets; they're still slim but are now cigar-shaped with no discernible ankles at all. Cankles, I think they call them. My toenails need cutting too and a spot of nail polish wouldn't go amiss. The trouble is, my bump gets in the way and I'm finding it really difficult to reach them. I wish I'd treated myself to a manicure and a pedicure whilst I had the chance because I could have used the credit card. It all felt like too much effort, though.

I haul myself onto my feet with all the grace of an elephant, stand still and take a steadying deep breath. I have a headache and my shoulder and arm are throbbing. I feel about a hundred years old. I walk slowly to the door, catching sight of myself in the dressing table mirror as I pass. I come to a halt in shock. The wild-haired woman in crumpled clothes looking back at me in horror is barely recognisable as me. I smile at my reflection but then quickly stop.

It hurts too much and I look awful; an absolute horror show. I remind myself that this is a good thing, because it's exactly how I need to look.

I pick up the carving knife from the bedside table and trudge slowly out onto the landing and along the corridor to Megan's room. I've never been in her room when she's in it but have been in there plenty of times when she's not. I've been through every nook and cranny of this house, several times, and there's nothing I've not seen. Megan's bedroom is an old-fashioned mess of clashing, garish colours that look as if they've been thrown together, or someone's vomited summer berries all over the walls. What's the saying, all the gear and no idea? Well, that's Megan, pots of money to spend but absolutely no clue about decor. God knows how she sleeps with all that going on with the wallpaper, it's enough to give you nightmares or make you think you're tripping on something you regret taking. I'm surprised at how well she dresses, when she clearly has no idea about anything else. Her bedroom does have an en suite, though, so there is that. In keeping with her obsession with housework and cleaning, her room looks as if no one has been in there for years, let alone slept in it. I've had several looks through her wardrobe and it's like something out of the pages of a magazine. No stuff wedged in the bottom or hangers vying for room with several dresses or tops crammed on them, no, everything is as neat as a pin and all of her shoes are in clear plastic boxes. Even her underwear drawer is unbelievably tidy with everything rolled up or standing up like they're files in a cabinet. I mean, seriously, how can anyone live like that? I know Insta is full of people showing you how to roll things up and be tidy but no one actually does that, do they?

Megan does.

I haven't found one thing of interest in that room, not a thing, and it's not for want of trying. No steamy novel on the bedside table, no raunchy underwear, no sex toys, not even so much as a vibrator. Is it any wonder she bored the arse off Ricky and he came to me for some fun? No, it's not.

Her bedroom door is closed when I reach her room, as it always is, so I tap on it.

Silence.

I put my ear to the door and listen, but I can't hear anything. No snoring, obviously, because she's far too uptight to snore. I bet she even sleeps with her mouth closed. I tap again, a little louder and when this gets no response, I turn the handle and quietly open the door.

She's not here.

The bed is pristine, the ghastly duvet pulled neatly over the bed, the cover looking as smooth as if it's been run over with an iron. The pillows are soldiered neatly on the headboard, perfectly plumped with a precision dent in the middle. The curtains are open, the windows closed. There are no clothes strewn across the bed, no hairdryer flung on the floor, no dirty underwear lying on the bed. There's nothing to show that she slept here last night, but there never is, because it looks like this every day, even when she does sleep here. I lay the knife on the bedside table and cross to the en suite, go inside and gaze around at the hideous peach bathroom fittings that might have been fashionable in the 1950s. Who, in their right mind, would choose a peach toilet? Thick white towels hang on the towel rail, neatly folded and exactly lined up with each other, as if she uses a ruler to get them just so. I wouldn't be surprised, actually, if she did use a ruler, she's so obsessive. I reach out and touch one of the towels and it feels dry. There are no drops of water in the shower to show it's been used. It doesn't appear as if she slept in this room last night.

Which means she definitely never came home.

I feel a sudden rage at her; why did she choose last night to stay out? She's never done that in all the time I've been staying here and I *needed* her here last night and the stupid cow has gone and let me down.

She's messed up everything.

Where is she? With the man she's been secretly seeing, it has to be. I can't think of any other reason why she would stay out all night. Most likely she's with the *friend* who she's been getting all tarted up for this week. Three times she went out with her *friend*, as she called him. As if I'm stupid and will believe any old shit. She obviously feels embarrassed in case her sister-in-law finds out that she's got with someone so quickly with Ricky only being dead for five minutes. I don't care that she goes out because it means I can watch telly without her wanting to put shit documentaries on all of the time. But she's always come back at night, and not even late; in the house and in bed by eleven. As soon as I hear her car on the driveway I'd rush upstairs to my bedroom and pretend to be asleep so I didn't have to talk to her. Typical of her to stay out all night when I needed her to be here. I'll make her squirm when she does comes back, make her feel uncomfortable, play the part of the sister-in-law who's disgusted that she's been out all night shagging someone else when she's a new widow.

Putting aside my anger at her for being such a trollop and

treating Ricky in that way, I try to think what I'm going to do. She'll have to come back to the house, if only to change her clothes, so realistically, she'll be back sometime today.

Some time is no good though; I need her to come back right now, so I can put everything into motion. Last night would have been better, much better, but it's not too late if she comes back now. I can come up with a valid reason for waiting for her before doing anything but it had better be soon because otherwise it'll start to look suspicious. I definitely don't need that.

What if she stays out until tonight?

I sit down on her bed and try to think. Plan C, that's what it'll be if I have to carry it out on my own. It would be better with her here for backup, but I might not have any choice. I rub my arms and try to warm up but I'm freezing. I can't concentrate when I'm cold. The heating can't have come on yet because it's normally toasty warm in here. I think she must turn it on when she gets up in the morning. Anyone else would have it on a timer, wouldn't they? Have it set up automatically, but not her.

What a control freak.

What a freak.

I throw back the duvet and burrow my feet underneath it, then pull it up to my neck. It feels heavy and comforting, and smells faintly of lavender, or something flowery. My arms start to defrost and I feel much better, quite cosy, actually. I thump the pillow and lay my head on it and it's so soft and comforting. Plan C, that's what I need, plan C to supersede plan B because she's fucked it up. All I need to do is think it through and everything will work out.

And somehow, without meaning to, I fall asleep.

* * *

Someone's calling my name.

I ignore it but they won't go away. I roll over, cradling my bump, and open my eyes.

'Emily?'

Megan's face swims into focus and she doesn't look happy. She has a snotty look on her face and I can't think why until I remember I'm in her bed. I pull the duvet down and heave myself up a bit and the snotty look turns to horror.

'What?' I say, blinking at her.

'Oh my God, Emily.' She stares at me, a shocked look on her face.

I move and my head starts to pound so I put my hand on my head to rub it. I flinch. God, it hurts.

She's back; plan B it is, then.

'Thank God you're back,' I whisper in my best pathetic way. 'I've been waiting and waiting for you to come home.'

'What happened? Who did this to you?' she asks.

I open my mouth and burst into tears.

20

MEGAN

She buries her head in her hands and sobs. I don't speak but sit down on the bed and wait. I see the knife then, on the bedside table. I recognise it as one of my own from the knife block in the kitchen. It's the biggest knife in there and the steel blade is extremely sharp. I never use it for fear of cutting myself.

'Sorry,' she says through her tears. 'I've been bottling it all up since yesterday. I haven't allowed myself to cry since it happened because I knew once I started, I wouldn't be able to stop.'

She sees me looking at the knife.

'It's for protection,' she states. 'But who knows if I could even bring myself to use it? I was so afraid he'd come back and when you didn't come home it was the only thing I could think of to do.'

'Are you up to telling me what happened?'

She sniffs, bites her lip, takes a deep breath. 'It was Keith.'

'What?' I stare at her in shock. '*Keith* did this to you? He attacked you?'

She nods.

'Ever since I came to stay, he's been coming around here in

the daytime when I'm on my own. The first time, I thought he was okay because he seemed nice, chatty. He offered me a cup of tea so I sat in the kitchen and talked to him because it seemed rude not to. But then he started bringing me things, like chocolates or a cake from the bakery, stuff like that. I thought he was being nice even though I didn't want any of it but I felt it would have looked really ungrateful to refuse it. He'd started to make me feel uncomfortable and I couldn't understand why he kept turning up when you weren't here but, because he's an old friend of yours, I felt I couldn't say anything to you. Soon he was turning up every day and I couldn't even not let him in because he'd just let himself straight in with his key.'

'In what way was he making you uncomfortable?'

'The way he looked at me. It was so creepy. He'd sort of leer and if I was at the table he'd grab a kitchen chair and pull it close to mine and sit right next to me, really close. I thought it would be best to keep out of his way so I started staying upstairs whenever I heard his car pull up outside. I wanted to avoid him. Then one day I came out of the bathroom after I'd had a bath and he was standing right in front of the bathroom door on the landing waiting for me. I only had a towel wrapped around me because I thought I was alone, and he frightened the life out of me. I jumped in surprise and he just stared and stood there, arms folded, watching me as I walked into the bedroom and shut the door. I was totally creeped out. He didn't even apologise. I tried to convince myself it was just coincidence that he was there but I soon found out that it was no good staying upstairs to avoid him because he'd just come up here to find me.'

She looks down at the bed.

'Go on,' I urge.

'One morning when I woke up, he was standing next to the

bed, staring down at me. I screamed when I saw him and he laughed this really weird laugh and said there was no need to be frightened of him because we were friends.'

'Oh God, Emily, why didn't you tell me this?'

She turns her head away and won't look at me.

'Emily?'

'I said I'd tell you and he laughed and told me to "go ahead". He said he'd known you since you were a kid and was like a father to you, that there was no way you'd believe me because you thought the world of him. He threatened to tell you that he'd caught me going through your things and that Elaine would back him up. Said you'd throw me out because you did everything Elaine told you to.'

'What a bastard.' I take hold of her hand to reassure her. 'No way is he like a father to me. He never has been.'

'So, then, yesterday, he turns up here in the afternoon like he usually did. I'd stopped staying upstairs when he came because I felt more trapped up here than downstairs. I was in the kitchen making myself a sandwich and he strolled in, just like normal, but this time he comes straight over to me, grabs my face and says that "it's time to stop messing around". He kissed me, right on the lips. Oh God, it was disgusting. I thought I was going to vomit. I managed to push him away, told him to get out, but he just laughed and said he'd waited long enough.'

She starts to cry again and I wait until she's finished and has composed herself.

'He was going to rape me, I knew it. He put his arms around me and was pulling at my clothes and I knew what was going to happen. I fought back; I scratched him and hit him but he's bigger than me and I was so afraid he'd hurt the baby. He slapped me and when I twisted out of his grip, he grabbed hold of my hair and dragged me closer and punched me on the side of the head. I thought I was going to pass out because I saw all these spots in front of my eyes. The more I begged and cried for him to leave me alone, the more he seemed to enjoy it. I reminded him I was nearly ready to give birth and he laughed and said he'd "never done a pregnant woman before". I was so afraid, Megan, terrified of what would happen to the baby rather than to me. And I was thinking that maybe it would be better if I just gave in and got it over with when the doorbell rang. He stopped for a second, frozen, and I knew that it was my one and only chance so I screamed as loud as I could and ran out of the kitchen. But I didn't get far, he caught me in the lounge, clamped his hand over my mouth and was dragging me into the kitchen when the bell rang again and then stopped.'

'Oh my God.'

'I thought then, this is it; just give in now because it'll be worse if I fight him. But he started talking, quietly, in my ear, said that if I promised not to scream, he'd take his hand away, so I nodded and he uncovered my mouth but kept a tight grip of my arm. Then he said he had to go – I think the doorbell ringing had spooked him – but if I told anyone what had happened, he'd come back and kill me because he could get in here any time he liked and that no one was going to believe a word I said anyway. That's why I've got the knife. In case he comes back. But I feel safer now you're here.'

'You must have been terrified.'

She nods. 'I was. Still am. Even now I can't believe what happened and I know it's going to make things awkward for you. I can't help feeling that somehow it's my fault.'

'Don't ever think it's your fault,' I say. 'You've done nothing wrong. Keith is not my friend, he's married to Elaine, that's all, and he's been taking liberties for as long as I can remember but I never dreamed he was capable of this.'

'You do believe me, don't you?' She looks at me with her huge eyes.

'Of course I believe you. We have to call the police and report him. Get him arrested.'

She shakes her head. 'I don't know if I can face it. I just want him to leave me alone. Police, court, statements, all of that. What if they don't believe me? He'll lie and say he didn't do it and it'll just be awful and go on for ever.'

'They only have to take one look at you to believe you, the evidence will be in front of their eyes, there's no way he'll get away with it. We must go to the police because Keith needs to be stopped. He's dangerous. What if he does it to someone else?'

'But I feel so bad for Elaine. And it'll look bad for me, won't it, that I never called the police straight away? I know I'm weak but I just didn't have the strength to cope with it on my own.'

'You're not weak, you were in shock, and the police will totally understand that. As for Elaine, it can't be helped. Keith can't be allowed to get away with what he's done.'

'Oh God, this is a nightmare. I bet you wish you'd never asked me to stay. You must wish you'd never met me.'

'Of course I don't. It'll be okay,' I say. 'The police will believe you, especially as Keith has gone missing. Why would he do that if he was innocent?'

'Missing?' She looks surprised.

'Yes, Elaine hasn't seen him since she went to work yesterday morning and she has no idea where he is. That, in itself, makes him look as guilty as anything and the police will think the same. He knows he's in big trouble, so he's lying low, isn't he? If you can just wait whilst I quickly get changed then we can talk about contacting the police. Is that okay?'

'Um, all right. Why didn't you come home last night? Why didn't you answer my calls?'

'I stayed over at a friend's. I'm so, so sorry I didn't let you know but we all went out after work and it turned into a late one. I never rang you because I thought you'd be asleep and I'd be back long before you woke up. It was easier to stay over than get a cab as I'd had a couple of drinks so couldn't drive. Stupidly, I left my phone in my handbag in the hallway so never heard it ringing. You'll never know how bad I feel that I wasn't here for you. Truthfully, I'll never be able to forgive myself for that. I should have been here.'

'That's okay,' she mumbles.

'No, Emily, it's not okay, you needed me and I let you down. I hope you can forgive me.'

She doesn't respond but lies back down, pulls the duvet up to her neck and closes her eyes.

'Just stay there,' I say. 'I'll go and get changed and be back in a few minutes.'

* * *

'When did you last eat?' I ask as I take a sip of my tea.

Emily shrugs and pulls the throw more tightly around her shoulders.

'I can make you something and if you don't want to eat it, that's fine, but at least try.'

'Okay. Thank you.' She looks up at me with huge eyes like a child. 'Can I put the TV on?'

'Of course.' I smile. 'You don't need to ask. Here.' I pick up the remote control and give it to her. The sound of a game show soon fills the room and I settle back and drink my tea. Emily is staring at the screen, her hands wrapped around her mug of tea.

I take the last mouthful of my own tea and get up.

'I'll go and make a start.' I turn to go out to the kitchen when she calls me.

'Megan?'

'Yes?'

'Do you mind if we eat in here?'

'No, of course not.'

'It's just, you know, it happened in there. The attack.'

'We'll eat in here,' I say, firmly. 'It'll be more comfortable.'

I head out to the kitchen and open the fridge. I was sure there was a pack of bacon in there but I can't find it so I rummage around in the freezer and take out a bag of vegetarian sausages. Much healthier, but I won't be having any as it's not long since I ate the bacon sandwich Sam made me. I open up the air fryer to find it full of grease, maybe from cooking the bacon I couldn't find. I quickly wash and dry it, put the sausages in and set them cooking before going back into the lounge.

The TV channel has been changed from the game show to a rerun of a reality TV dating show.

'Sure you're okay?' I ask Emily.

She nods, but doesn't reply.

'So have you thought any more about reporting Keith's attack to the police?'

She looks up at me in alarm.

'I can't. No police. I can't face it.'

'It's your choice entirely but have you thought this through properly?'

'I have and I don't want to tell them. I want to forget about it, put it behind me.'

'I understand that and you know you have my full support no matter what you decide to do, but they'd be sympathetic and Keith needs to be stopped.'

'I've decided,' she says, quietly. 'No police.'

'Okay. If you're sure. I'll have to ring Elaine because she's expecting me to go to hers. I'll finish making you something to eat and then I'll ring her.'

'What are you going to say to her?'

'Quite honestly, I have no idea. She's like family to me and was my mother's dearest friend so it's not a phone call I'm relishing, which is probably why I'm putting it off. How do you tell someone that their husband is a rapist?'

Emily flinches.

'Oh, God.' I rush over and kneel down in front of the sofa. 'How stupid of me. Me and my big mouth. I'm so, so, sorry.'

'It's okay.' She pulls the throw down from her face. 'It's not like he actually raped me, but it's the thought of what could have happened, you know? If the doorbell hadn't rung.'

'Try to rest and once you've had something to eat, I'll run you a nice warm bath, yeah?'

'That would be so nice. I feel so much safer with you here in the house. He won't come back now, will he?'

'Honestly, Emily, I don't know. The only way to prevent that for sure is to report him because then he'll be arrested. I've already arranged for a locksmith to come out later today to change all of the locks, so that'll ensure he won't be able to get in here any more, but I can't make promises about what he might do.'

She doesn't answer but fixes her gaze on the TV. I pick up her cup and go back out to the kitchen. I check the air fryer and take out the sausages and put them on a plate to cool, then fill the kettle for more tea. Whilst the kettle boils, I cut two slices of bread and butter them and put them on the plate, add the sausages and make a sandwich and carry the plate through to the lounge.

'They might be hot,' I say, as I hand her the plate.

She gives me a wan smile and balances the plate on her knee, picks up one sandwich and takes a bite.

'Aren't you having anything?' she asks, as I marvel at her ability to bite into a piping hot sausage.

'No, I'm fine. I had breakfast at my friend's.'

My phone shrills from the coffee table, making us both start. I glance over to see *Elaine* flashing on the screen.

'It's okay,' I say, seeing Emily's expression. 'I'll take it out in the hallway.' I pick up my phone, press to accept the call and leave the room.

This isn't going to be a good conversation.

'Hello, Elaine,' I say quietly.

'Oh, God, Meg, I don't know what to do.'

'It'll be okay, Elaine,' I lie, in a soothing tone.

'No it won't, it'll never be okay. Keith's dead, Meg, he's dead.'

21

EMILY

She's in the bathroom, getting changed out of yesterday's clothes.

Dirty stop out.

I'm feeling rather pleased with myself because it went much better than I thought it would. She fell for it like a charm once I turned on the tears and started blubbering. Once I got going, it all flowed out of me as if it had really happened and at times, I almost believed it myself. Had things been different in my life and I'd had a better upbringing, I could definitely have been an actress; a very good one, too. I couldn't see even the tiniest hint of a doubt on her face at all so I must have been convincing, although the state of me was the clincher, so it was well worth doing it even though it hurts like hell. I look as if I've taken a proper beating and there's no denying what's in front of your eyes, is there? The horror on her face when she saw me was priceless, I wish I could have got a photograph of her expression. I badly wanted to laugh even though I was half asleep and I think I could even have got away with that, because I could have pleaded hysteria.

The added bonus is that she feels really guilty too, for not answering the phone to me last night. I didn't let her off the hook about that either because whilst she was shagging some bloke, I needed her here and she ignored me. Obviously she was having far too good a time to worry about her heavily pregnant sister-in-law left all on her own. She said that she never heard her phone because she'd left it in another room and I actually believe that, because there was no disguising how bad she felt. And as it's turned out, she's played right into my hands by not answering because I'll use that guilt to get her to do what I want. So it's turned out to be a good thing that she never came back last night, although it didn't feel like it at the time.

It's all working out perfectly.

She blathered on about reporting Keith's attack on me to the police but no way will I be going anywhere near them. The police won't be as easy to convince because, unlike Megan, they know full well what people are capable of doing. I'll be under suspicion and having to lie through my teeth as soon as they find out I'm not Emily and Keith turns up and tells them I'm lying. The whole thing will blow up then and it'll all come out and I don't want that, not yet. Also, I'm not entirely sure that pretending to be someone else is legal, especially when you've been using your pretend sister-in-law's credit card.

I pull myself up onto the pillows, make myself comfortable and ready myself to do a bit more acting. I do feel better now I've told her and as long as I can convince her we're not going to the police, everything will be hunky-dory. She'll be out of the bathroom at any minute so I have to persuade her to put the whole 'reporting Keith to the police' thing to bed. Incredibly, he's even thicker than I gave him credit for, because he's played right into my hands and done a disappearing act.

What a stupid idiot; innocent people don't do a runner, do they?

His face was a picture yesterday, when I put my plan into action. He couldn't believe what I was doing and stood there gawping at me, his mouth hanging open. He'd turned up all cocky, strolled in as if he owned the place and said, 'I've come for the rest of my money.' I was sitting in the kitchen waiting for him. Without the two hundred and fifty pounds, of course, because no way was I giving it to him. I was nervous, though, all those old photographs of Megan's creepy relatives that are poked into every nook and cranny were making me feel as if I was being watched and I had to remind myself that there's no such thing as ghosts. Why have pictures of dead people watching over you? The place is like a junk shop. God knows how Ricky stood living here for so long.

Anyway, I'd rehearsed over and over in my head what I was going to do but knowing and doing are two very different things and quite honestly, I just wanted it over with. And what with having got up so up early, I was knackered.

So once he was in the kitchen, he sat himself down at the table and I got up straight away and said I'd go upstairs and get his money. He smirked as I walked past him and, when I stopped by the massive built-in fridge and asked him if he was quite sure he wanted to do this, he frowned and looked a bit puzzled and asked me what I was on about, so I told him: 'I don't have the rest of your money but we can call an end to this now. You go back to your life and I'll go back to mine and we'll leave it at that. No harm done.' He laughed, then, and he was still laughing as I slammed the side of my head into the fridge. Christ, it hurt, but after the third time I was getting into the swing of it and I think the adrenaline was stopping it from hurting so much. He shot out of that chair like a rat out of a trap and came racing towards me. When he got close to me I put out my hand and raked my nails down his face, shouting, 'Please, please, don't hurt me any more.' I'd filed them into sharp points in readiness so they'd leave big scratches. He's going to have to explain them to Nosebag Elaine and anyone else who asks, so if he decides to be really stupid and try to tell anyone what really happened, how's he going to explain that? He stepped back, trying to get away from me and I was relieved then, because I wasn't completely sure how it would go. I'd sussed him out as a verbal bully who didn't have it in him for physical violence, what with him being so weedy, but you never know until you come to the crunch and I *had* just attacked him. He was still standing there, stunned, blood already filling one of the scratches from my nails, when I punched myself in the eye. The first one didn't do a lot so I really had to put some effort in on the next one and I couldn't have aimed very well because I managed to catch my lip as well. It's quite hard to punch yourself in the face, difficult to aim it right. I hope I never have to do it again.

He did touch me then, caught hold of my arm to try to stop me. Told me I was 'fucking mental'. I twisted around to try and get out of his grip and for a skinny weed, he was surprisingly strong. I reckon that's when I wrenched my arm. I smiled at him and said, 'Nasty scratch you've got there, Keith.' He let go of me as if I'd scalded him and ran from the kitchen as if his backside was on fire. Seconds later, I heard the front door slam. Megan says he never went home, so I assume he headed straight for the pub and started drinking. Probably waiting for the scratch to calm down.

He played right into my hands.

What a stupid prick; but, equally, what else could he do? No one would believe him if he told the truth, because why would a pregnant woman deliberately hurt herself? It would sound far-fetched and ridiculous. He'd have to come clean about black-mailing me and no one is going to believe a word he says after that or if he didn't tell them that bit, why was he even here?

So it was a big relief when he'd gone, because I knew it had worked and he wouldn't be round here asking for any more money. Reporting him to the police was never in my plan, and once I've convinced Megan of that, I'll never have to see Keith again, because he can't ever come here again, can he? And I don't think Elaine will be popping round now, despite being Megan's friend, because it'll all be far too awkward with me here, so it's a win-win. After I've had the baby and I tell Megan who I really am, they might put two and two together, but by then it'll be too late. And, if they did want to make anything of it, it'd be my word against his. There's no proof, so I think I'm safe.

I was done in afterwards, though, felt absolutely drained. I think I might have overdone the head banging on the fridge because I had one hell of a headache and I was concerned I might have concussion. I looked up the symptoms on the internet and I didn't lose consciousness so hopefully I'm all right. My headache has gone now, although it was a shock when the bruises started coming out so quickly even though that was the whole point of doing it. My face is a right state.

I had a good look at the door on the fridge and amazingly, there's barely a mark on it unless you look really closely. The kitchen may be an ancient oak monstrosity but it was certainly built to last. God knows how she stands all that wood and clut-ter, though. And those photographs. Ugh.

There are none of Ricky, though, which I think is weird. There's only one of him and that's in the lounge. It's a big one of their wedding day, slap bang in the middle of the mantelpiece and he looks so handsome. And happy. That was before he found out what she was really like. I want to cover it up when she's not here and I'm watching telly. I don't want to have to look at it but I daren't do it because I know I'd forget to uncover it one day and she'd come back and see what I've done. Even with my acting skills, that would be a hard one to explain, what with Ricky supposedly being my brother and everything.

I close my eyes for a moment and breathe deeply.

It's been one hell of a twenty-four hours.

* * *

She's out in the kitchen cooking me something to eat. I might have given her the impression that I haven't eaten since Keith attacked me but I've just remembered that there was a pack of bacon in the fridge and I had a bit of a pig-out and ate it all.

I don't think she'll notice.

She's got too much else to worry about, like telling her best friend that her husband is a rapist and that basically, they're not going to be friends any more.

No more Nosebag Elaine coming around here sticking her beak in and questioning me.

I did a good job of persuading her to not contact the police because it's my decision, isn't it? She said I might be making a mistake but she understands that 'it's my choice'. That's big of her, considering she's not the one who was nearly raped. Well, I wasn't either, obviously, but that's not the point.

Anyway, she's promised to get the locks changed so Keith will no longer be able to get in. The locksmith is coming this afternoon and he's doing the back door, too, just in case Keith has a key to that. I wonder if she'll give Elaine a key to the new lock? I badly wanted to ask her but I thought it might seem a bit off if I did. That's a question for another day.

When we got downstairs, she helped me onto the sofa like I was an invalid and then went and made a cup of tea and brought it to me. We sat in silence, drinking it. Excruciating, it was, the silence. She asked, yet again, if I was sure about not going to the police and I thought, for Christ's sake, give it a rest. But I kept my cool and said I was sure so maybe she'll shut up about it now. I asked what she was going to say to Elaine and she said, 'Quite honestly, I have no idea. She's like family to me and was my mother's dearest friend so it's not a phone call I'm relishing, which is probably why I'm putting it off. How do you tell someone that their husband is a rapist?' I pretended to be all emotional then and she apologised, but all I could think was, well, would I want to be friends with a rapist's wife? No, I wouldn't, because the wife always know, doesn't she?

So then she said she'd make me something to eat and after that she'd run me a nice warm bath and I really wanted to tell her to fuck off because I can run my own bath and I'd had enough of her hanging around me.

I pretended to be all frightened of going into the kitchen again after what happened, which I thought was very clever of me but really it was a way of getting rid of her and having a bit of peace. At least she's out there and I'm in here on my own whilst she's cooking. I got her to turn the telly on before she went and I stared at it like I was in a trance but as soon as she was out of the way, I turned it over to a rerun of *Married at First Sight*. It's one of my all-time favourite programmes. I even toyed with applying to go on it, until someone told me that you have to apply for everything, including the one where you have to strip off and shave all your bits and go on a date if you win.

No, thanks.

Although I don't suppose I'd stand a chance now anyway; no one wants a beached whale on their show. Or maybe they would; going by the episodes I've seen, the bar's not set very high. I was quite enjoying it until she came back in and gave me the sausage sandwich, or should I say, not-sausage sandwich. I tried to look grateful, but really? Do I look like I eat crappy vegan food? I started to eat it and it wasn't as bad as I thought it would be but it wasn't great, but as I'm pregnant and constantly starving, I can't be too fussy.

And then her phone rang.

I could see it was Elaine flashing up on the screen and Megan swooped on it and said she'd take it in the hallway, which is annoying, because I want to hear what she was saying. She's out there now, talking quietly so I can't hear a bloody word, even when I stop chewing. I'm swallowing the last piece of rubbish non-sausage when she comes back in.

I put my best sad voice on and ask her how it went and she sits down on the sofa and stares into space.

'That bad?' I ask, twisting the sides of my mouth down to stop myself from laughing at the thought of Nosebag Elaine's face on hearing the news about her ratbag husband. 'Maybe you should have done it in person.'

'Um, I didn't tell her.'

'What?' This time my shock is real.

'It didn't seem appropriate.'

'What's wrong?' Shit, has he told his nosebag wife the truth and she believes him? Is Megan starting to believe him?

'Sorry.' She rubs her hand across her face. 'It's just a bit of a shock, that's all.'

I stare at her.

'Keith's dead,' she says quietly. 'They pulled him out of the canal this morning.'

22

MEGAN

I end the call and walk slowly back into the lounge.

'That was quick. I'm guessing she didn't take it well?' Emily asks, looking up at me.

I sit down on the sofa and stare into space before I shakily fill her in. When I've finished Emily's mouth drops open and her eyes widen.

'I know. It's a hell of a shock, isn't it?' I say. 'You know where the allotments run along the canal? Well, Keith has a plot there. *Had*. Elaine says he spent a lot of his time there and it was a bit of a bolthole for him. If he's not in the pub and she doesn't know where he is, he'd be at the allotment. She'd already been down there looking for him first thing this morning when she rang me, but there was no sign of him. One of the other allotment owners, an elderly man, found him later. He was opening up his shed when he thought he saw something in the canal. At first, he thought it was old clothes or some junk, because they get a lot of fly-tipping there so he went and had a look to make sure before he reported it to the council. He prodded it with a stick and then realised it was a body. He rang the police but by the time they arrived, he was in such a state of shock that he was suffering from chest pains, so they had to take him to hospital.'

'God, that's awful. I can't believe it. I know he tried to rape me but...'

'I know. Poor Elaine is in pieces. I don't want to leave you but I'm going to have to go round to hers, she doesn't have anyone else close by, you see. No family apart from her sister who lives hours away. I need to be there for her because she's always been there for me.'

'I totally understand,' Emily says. 'You should go. Don't worry about me, I'll be okay here on my own. There's nothing for me to fear now, is there?'

'No,' I say, quietly. 'There's not. He can't hurt you now. But we can't keep what Keith did to you between us now.'

'Why not?'

'Because everything has changed now. You'll have to speak to the police and tell them what happened.'

'Why?' She looks alarmed. 'What's the point in telling them now? We'd agreed that I wasn't going to and I don't see any reason to change that.'

'But things are different now. Keith is dead. They'll want to know his last movements, where he was, who he saw, that sort of thing. His dying has changed everything.'

'No, I don't agree. What has it changed? If anything, there's even more reason not to tell them because what will the truth do to Elaine? As if it's not bad enough that her husband's dead, she then finds out that he's a rapist. It'll absolutely destroy her. Wouldn't it be better for her to think the best of him rather than find out the horrible truth?'

'I know what you're saying,' I say, after a while. 'And I do worry how she's going to cope with it all as it is. She's devastated and this will make it so much worse for her but we can't lie to the police, can we? You've told me what happened so now I'm implicated. I didn't feel comfortable about not reporting it but I believed it was your choice and not mine. But now it's different. A man has died. I'm sorry, but I can't lie.'

'But it wouldn't be lying,' Emily says. 'It would be not telling them. Two very different things. After everything he did to me, *I'm* the one who has to relive it and tell them everything and I can't face that. I don't want to relive it. I'm prepared to keep it a secret because the truth isn't going to achieve anything or help anyone, least of all me. Only me and you know about it, no one else, and it has to stay that way.' Emily's trying to contain it but I can see the anger in her eyes, hear it in her voice.

'It might not be actually lying and more withholding information but I don't think the police will see it the way you do. We have to tell them.'

My phone rings in my hand and I look at the screen to see Elaine's name flash up again. I answer it, turning my body away from Emily's angry eyes.

'Are you coming over?' Elaine asks between sobs. 'I'm so sorry to ask you but I can't stand it here on my own. Please come now? I can't bear it, Meg, I just can't bear it.'

'Yes, yes, of course I'm coming. I'm leaving right now, there's no need to worry. Just try to stay calm and I'll be with you very soon.'

Elaine ends the call without saying goodbye and I turn to Emily.

'I'm really sorry, Emily, but I have to go, Elaine is in such a state, she shouldn't be on her own because I fear for her, for what she might do. I feel really bad leaving you after everything you've been through but I'm seriously concerned for her. I've never heard her like this before.'

'And you're going to make it worse.' Emily stares at me, her expression grim.

'What?'

'By telling her what he did to me. It's the worst day of her entire life and you're going to pile on even more misery. I should think she'll want to end it all when she finds out what he's done.'

'Emily!' I stare at her in shock.

'Sorry.' She looks sheepish. 'That was uncalled for, especially, you know...'

'Look, I know this is hard for you but we have to do the right thing, whether we like it or not. The right actions are not always the easy ones.'

Emily stares at me, unsmilingly.

'If you need anything at all, just ring me.' I go out into the hallway, take my coat off the peg and put it on before going back into the lounge. 'I'll ring the locksmith and cancel him as there's no point in changing the locks now.'

'Okay.' She pulls the throw up to her chin, her huge eyes glaring at me. If it weren't for her massive bump, she'd look like a truculent child.

'I'm sorry,' I say, going over and sitting down on the edge of the sofa. I put my hand on her shoulder. 'I know it's going to be really hard for you to go through it all again but we don't have any choice.'

'There's always a choice,' she says, and with that she turns her head away from me and closes her eyes.

'Do you want anything before I go? A hot drink? A glass of water?' I offer.

I think she's going to ignore me before I hear a muffled 'No, thanks'.

'I'll be back later.' I get up, slip my phone in my pocket and head out of the house.

I'm not relishing seeing Elaine. This morning's breakfast with Sam seems like a lifetime ago.

* * *

'Are you sure you're going to be okay? I can stay longer, it's not a problem.'

Elaine shakes her head. 'My sister, Susan, is on her way. She should be here by seven.'

'Well, then, let me wait with you until she gets here, you shouldn't be alone.'

'No, you go home. To be honest, lovey, I'd like a bit of time on my own before she gets here. She's full-on at the best of times.' Sitting at the kitchen table, a full cup of cold, undrunk tea in front of her, she drags a hand through her hair and stares into the distance. In a matter of hours she seems to have aged; her once carefully coiffed, always immaculately highlighted hair looks greasy, the grey showing through at the roots, her face drawn and sagging under the weight of her grief. Hardly surprising with recent events.

'You'll let me know when she gets here?'

'Of course, now get off home.' She flaps her hand at me and I lean down and hug her, despite my aversion to social affection. She doesn't resist but she doesn't hug me back; this isn't the Elaine I know.

I take one last look at her and decide I can't leave her in this state but as I open my mouth to tell her, she pre-empts me.

'Please, Meg, just leave me be for a while. I promise I'm not going to do anything stupid.' She looks up at me with a wan smile.

'Okay, but if I don't hear that Susan has arrived in the next hour, I'll be back, okay?'

'Okay.'

I leave her and go through the lounge to the hallway, passing Keith's now-empty armchair. There's no disputing he always sat there; the rest of the three-piece-suite is pristine and nearly new, the leather on the arms of his chair is worn and lighter in colour than the rest, the seat cushion baggy from constant use. A small side table holds his ashtray and lighter, and the smell of stale cigarette smoke still lingers in the air. He refused to go outside to smoke in the garden, not caring that Elaine had never smoked herself. Well, not her own cigarettes anyway, she'll have passively smoked plenty of Keith's.

I'm in the car and plugging in my seatbelt when my phone rings. I look at it, expecting it to be Emily, but it's Sam. I realise that I haven't messaged or spoken to him since I left him this morning.

'Hi, Sam.'

'Hey, how are you? I've just woken up and when I saw there were no messages from you, I got worried.'

'You've just woken up?' I ask in surprise.

'Yeah. Embarrassing, isn't it? After I left you I went back home and thought I'll go back to bed because I felt knackered. I slept like the dead, Meg, the absolute dead. I think I'd still be asleep now if my next-door neighbour's car alarm hadn't started honking.'

'That's *hours*.'

'I know. I'm a bit concerned.'

'Concerned?'

'Yeah, I mean I've never slept like that before and it's not as if we were that late last night, was it? I did wonder if someone might have spiked my drink when we were in the pub.'

'Really? I suppose it's possible. Although you were fine when we got back to yours.'

'I was, and that's the really weird thing. I don't know. Maybe I'm just a lazy arse or I'm coming down with the flu, or something.'

'Do you feel ill?'

'No, not ill. Just knackered. Anyway, I didn't ring you to whinge. How is Elaine, have they found her husband yet?'

'He has been found; they dragged his body out of the canal this morning.'

Sam gasps. I set my phone on the stand and put it on hands-free and start the car.

'Jesus, what happened?'

'Hang on a minute whilst I get out of this parking space and I'll fill you in as I drive.'

* * *

By the time I pull up onto the driveway it's nearly six o'clock. It feels like days ago when I left here to go to Elaine's, not hours. I let myself into the house and am immediately sweating from the heat. It's cold outside but inside it's like a hot summer's day. I put my fingers on the radiator underneath the mirror and immediately take them off. Blistering hot, I could probably get a third-degree burn off it and it's no wonder; when I check the thermostat on the wall, it's set at twenty-five degrees. I turn it down to twenty.

I go into the lounge to find Emily lying on the sofa underneath the throw. Has she been there all this time and not moved at all? She must be suffocating in this heat, especially bundled up in that fur throw. She sits up when she sees me and I see she's wearing different clothes from this morning.

'Hi. How are you feeling?'

'Not great,' she says. 'I have a bit of a headache, although that might be because I haven't eaten. I just haven't felt well enough to go out into the kitchen and make anything.'

'I can make you something if you like? Elaine's sister is on her way down from Wales and should be arriving soon, so I don't need to go back there tonight.' A plate is lying on the floor next to a mug so I guess she's eaten *something*. I need something to eat, anyway. I must have made twenty cups of tea for Elaine but she wouldn't eat a thing, no matter how much I tried to persuade her. I didn't feel I could eat if she wasn't.

'I think I could manage to eat something,' she says, quietly.

'Okay, I'll make us something in a minute. I have to tell you that I've spoken to the police. I rang them from Elaine's.'

I leave the news to sink in whilst I go out into the hallway and hang up my coat. When I go back in, she doesn't look very happy but I carry on and get it over with.

'They wanted to talk to you today but I told them how heavily pregnant you are and they're prepared to wait until tomorrow morning, if you go in first thing. They took some persuading and were all set to come around here to speak to you but I managed to put them off.'

'Why the urgency? It's not exactly important, is it?' She's annoyed with me and not attempting to hide it.

I sit down on the sofa, suddenly tired. It's been quite a day; comforting Elaine would have been exhausting enough without the late night with Sam. I try to keep my voice level when I reply.

'They were going to come here to interview you but I persuaded them to wait. The police officer I spoke to was sympathetic to your advanced pregnancy but she said that you have to go in and speak to them tomorrow.'

'What an absolute waste of time.'

'You have to do as they ask.'

'Why?' She pulls herself upright. 'Keith decided to kill himself, so what does it matter now? He obviously couldn't live with the guilt and nothing I say is going to change that.'

She's jumped to completely the wrong conclusion and now I have to put her right.

'What makes you think he committed suicide?' I ask.

'You said so.'

'No,' I say, carefully. 'I said that he was pulled from the canal. I never said he'd committed suicide and I'm sorry if you thought that.'

'What?' She looks at me in confusion.

'No,' I say. 'It definitely wasn't suicide. Keith was murdered.'

23

EMILY

I'm absolutely fuming.

What did the stupid prick have to go and kill himself for?

Not that I care one bit about him being dead, because I don't. It's not as if the world is losing anything by him topping himself. He was, as my mother was fond of saying, a waste of skin. His nosebag wife will miss him but aside from her, who's going to care?

No one.

The most annoying thing is that had I known he was dead before Megan came back this morning, I wouldn't have needed to tell her all that crap about him attempting to rape me. I could have pretended I'd fallen and hurt myself; falling down the stairs would have been a good one, and then I'd have avoided the absolute shitstorm that I now find myself in. Keith deciding to kill himself would have been a good thing because there'd be no more threat of him blackmailing me.

Life is all about timing, isn't it?

Yet again, bad timing has massively cocked up my life and it seems to be a running theme throughout it. If Ricky hadn't been driving by the river on the night of the worst storm that we've had in living memory, he'd still be here now. He'd have left Megan and we'd be together and looking forward to the birth of our boy together. I'd have a bright and secure future ahead of me because he'd get his half of this house and we'd be well set up. I wouldn't be in this absolute mess. When am I ever going to catch a break? What, exactly, have I done to deserve this?

I didn't need to pretend to be horrified when Megan told me because as soon as she said the words it was all whirling around in my head; how I'm going to lose everything and how fucking selfish killing yourself is. What a cowardly thing to do; too weak and afraid to face the music.

Not that there would have been anything to face.

When she said they'd fished him out of the canal, I knew that there'd be no way to avoid the police knowing what happened yesterday; my story, that is, not the truth. There'll be an investigation into why he did it, questions will be asked about where he went on his last day on earth, who he saw, what his state of mind was, what could have driven him to it. All pointless as far as I'm concerned, because does that help anyone? Will it bring him back?

No.

But I'm going to have to fess up to the police because Megan will make sure of it. All that effort of persuading her to let it go and then this happens. I could see she was itching to ring them even as she was telling me about it because she always has to do the right fucking thing.

So very *Megan*; boring, dull and intent on obeying the letter of the law.

Apparently, Keith was found when one of the other allotment owners was opening up his shed; he saw something bobbing along the canal and went to investigate. Nosey, just like

Elaine. He was prodding it with a stick when he realised it was a body. Why couldn't he just mind his own business? But he didn't; he rang the police and by the time they arrived, the old codger was having a heart attack from the shock of it all. It's a good job they sent an ambulance for the body in the canal – I've never understood why they do this when someone is clearly dead – so they carted him off to hospital in it. Doesn't that just show you that you shouldn't go poking your nose in where it's not wanted?

Yes, it does.

I asked her if telling the police what Keith had done to me was the right thing to do because it'll paint him in a very bad light. Does she really want to do that to Elaine, who is already grieving her husband? Wouldn't it be better for her to remember him as he was? I said I was willing to let her believe the best of him as he's dead and no longer a threat to me. I told her that there's nothing to be gained from telling the truth. Very generous and noble of me, I thought.

She looked shocked when I said it; said that we couldn't not tell the police, that they needed to know. Why? What good will it do now? All it will achieve is that it'll all come out about who I am, or rather, who I'm not, and that'll be the end of my comfortable life here whilst I wait for the baby to arrive. I'll be turfed out quicker than you can say *liar*. I'll be back at my flat with no money to have the heating on and a long legal fight ahead of me, which I'm somehow going to have to fund. The only proof I have that I'm carrying Ricky's baby will be the DNA that I hope they're going to find on the toothbrush I stole out of the bathroom. If they can't get his DNA off that, I'm stuffed, because *she* had him cremated.

I'm trying not to think about that.

I know I'll have to do the DNA thing anyway but at least I

can have a bit of comfort and save a bit of money whilst I'm staying here. And what about all the baby stuff I've bought, what will happen to that? I can't see her letting me take it all with me.

It's not fair.

Whilst she was sitting there all pious, talking about ringing the police and being 'kind to Elaine and being there for her', and them 'wanting to know his last movements', all I could think was, what about me? I wanted to scream it at her but I huddled underneath the throw whilst she droned on and on, loving the sound of her own voice. After she'd talked about *poor Elaine* for what seemed like forever, she said she didn't want to leave me but felt that she had to go and see her because Elaine has no one else. 'GO,' I wanted to shout at her. 'Just fuck right off and leave me alone before I lump you one.' At least whilst she's fussing around her creepy friend, she's not going to be forcing me to go to the police station. I looked at her and her mouth was moving but I wasn't listening and I thought, whilst she's at Elaine's, I'm safe for a while. She could be there for a long time because she'll tell Elaine what Keith did and Elaine will be hysterical and need calming down. Maybe she'd even stay overnight with her. At least with her out of the house it meant I could have a bath, wash my hair and get dressed because I was still wearing yesterday's clothes and I felt pretty gross. I wondered if I'd have enough time to call a cab and take everything that's left here that I've bought and ferry it round to my flat whilst she was away. Maybe if I called a black cab they'd even be able to fit in the pram, high chair and cot. I was already mentally moving out and going back to my chilly flat with sod all to show for the weeks I've spent putting up with her. Yes, I thought, if I could manage to take everything with me, it wouldn't be a complete loss. I was trying to figure out the logistics of actually doing it, when it came to me.

I don't have to give up anything.

I can stay.

Because if she wants me out of this house, she's going to have to drag me down those stairs and physically throw me out, because I'm not leaving. I've got as much right to be here as her – more, actually – because I'm carrying Ricky's baby and but for that accident, he'd be with *me* now, not her.

I don't think there's much chance of her manhandling a pregnant woman who could give birth at any time out of this house, is there? I'm certain of it; she's far too stuck-up and prim to do anything like that. So what if I've lied to her about who I really am? It's not an offence, is it? At least I don't think it is, because I haven't tricked her into giving me anything, she offered it. She *offered* me a place to stay, she asked me to move in. I've not asked her for a single thing, she's freely given it all. She *gave* me her credit card and pin number; it was totally her idea and not mine. She's been lugging all of the stuff I've bought out to her garage so she can't pretend that she didn't know how much I was spending, because she's seen it all. Well, aside from all the stuff stashed in my room. Not that I can see her lying to the police; she's far too upright and old-fashioned for that.

The police have terrible trouble getting squatters out of houses and that's what I'll be – a squatter. I'm here and I'm not leaving voluntarily so she can get stuffed. I've got all the baby stuff sorted now so there's no need for me to go out to get anything else so even if she changed the locks, it wouldn't do any good because I won't give her the chance to lock me out. She can't starve me out, either, because I can live on takeaways because I do have a bit of money in my own account.

I'll give birth to this baby in that bedroom if necessary.

So, that's it, if she wants a fight, she's got one.

I'm going nowhere.

* * *

I turn off the taps, clamber carefully over the side of the bath and slowly lower myself into the water. By the time I'm settled, the water is lapping an inch from the top and I've drained every last drop of hot water from the tank.

Deliberately.

I feel the pent-up tension begin to ease from my body and I relax into the warmth of the water, lay my head back and close my eyes. Peace at last from her incessant yapping about doing the *right thing*. When she took the call from Elaine, I could hear Elaine sobbing, even though Megan had the phone clamped tightly to her ear. She sounded nearly hysterical and I felt a fleeting sympathy for her until I remembered how unpleasant and snotty she's been to me. Megan wants to tell her the truth about her husband and make it worse for her, so what sort of friend does that make her?

Completely selfish and unfeeling. Cold; that's what Ricky said about her, and he was right.

Plus, Elaine already hates my guts so she's bound to blame me, isn't she? No way will she believe anything bad about *him*. It won't matter that he's a rapist, none of that will matter because all she'll see is that he killed himself because of me, so it'll be my fault. She won't want to admit she was married to a sleazebag rapist. I can cope with that, though, because she's hardly going to want to come around here any more when I'm still living here. Which will be a bonus because once it all comes out, the gloves will be off and her pretence of being polite to me will be gone. Not that I care; I'm more than a match for her.

I wash my hair and wallow in the bath until the water cools so much that I'm shivering. I haul myself out, wrap a towel around my ever-growing bump and pad along to my bedroom. I pull on a pair of leggings and a nice dress with a big cosy jumper over the top. The jumper is new, I bought it from Next last week on a trip into town. It's not maternity wear, it's just big, although I doubt I'll be able to wear it afterwards because it'll be all stretched. I'll miss going shopping with the credit card and buying whatever I want. She's going to want the card back and whilst I'm not refusing to leave, I can't keep her card because I'd be on dodgy ground. She'd block it anyway. I wish I'd got some more cash out now whilst I had the chance; built up a little nest egg to help when I eventually leave. I'm too nice, that's my trouble; I should have taken advantage when I could, like most people would, but at least I still the have the two hundred and fifty pounds I drew out.

Once dressed, I make myself a nice big cheese sandwich as all of my exertions have made me hungry again. This is a good sign, because it means that I'm not letting the situation get to me. Once finished, I make myself a cup of hot chocolate and, armed with a packet of chocolate digestives, I head back to the lounge to resume my position on the sofa. I put Catch Up on so I can watch all of the programmes I've missed and before I know it, I've polished off the whole packet of biscuits. I screw the wrapper up and tie it into a knot and stuff it down the side of the seat cushion. I'll put it in the bin later. If I remember.

I snuggle back down under the throw. I may not like Megan but she doesn't stint on the groceries; every Sunday morning without fail, a big shop arrives from Tesco. The cupboards and fridge are always packed full of food and I never have to go without anything like I did when I was at the flat. Likewise with toiletries, I haven't bought so much as a bottle of shower gel since I've been here, it always appears like magic in my bathroom along with a plentiful supply of toilet rolls.

Will she try and starve me out?

I hope not. I don't think she will because she's too uptight and fixated on doing the right thing to behave like that. But we'll see; like I say, I can order takeaways even if I have to use my own money.

She's no match for me.

I spend the afternoon drifting in and out of sleep, watching telly and mulling over what I'm going to say to the police. I've decided to go down the traumatised route; less is more, as they say. In other words, they're going to have to drag every single word out of me. I'll say as little as possible. Less likely that I'll fuck it up that way. The only thing I can't decide it whether to fess up right away that I'm not Ricky's sister; would that make things worse or better? I can't decide. I think I'll wait and see and do what feels right at the time.

I'm just starting to get hungry again when I hear the front door opening. A quick glance at my watch confirms it's six o'clock, so she's been gone for around five hours. There are no voices so she hasn't brought Elaine with her, which is a relief. I didn't think she would but you never know; Megan is so gormless that she wouldn't understand why bringing her here wouldn't be a good idea.

'Hi.' She walks into the lounge, bringing the cold of the night air with her. 'How are you feeling?'

'Not great,' I lie, pretending that I have a headache due to not eating.

She takes the hint and offers to cook me dinner. And then drops the bombshell that she's spoken to the police. Called them from Elaine's.

Of course you called them, you interfering cow.

She drags it out, of course, going out into the hallway to hang her bloody coat up just to make me wait. I sit and seethe and when she returns, she tells me that the police wanted to talk to me today but she's persuaded them to wait until tomorrow morning, saying it as if she's done me some massive favour.

So now I'll have to get up early tomorrow. Why doesn't she just keep her nose out?

'Why the urgency? It's not exactly important, is it?' I ask, trying to keep the fact that I'm royally pissed off with her out of my voice.

She sits down on the sofa; a sure sign that a lecture is about to be delivered. I bite down on my impatience whilst she tells me yet again that she's managed to convince the police to wait until tomorrow to talk to me. What does she want, a medal? I don't even attempt to hide how annoyed I am and I give it to her straight and tell her that I can't see the point of talking to them when Keith has killed himself.

This strange look comes over her face that I can't fathom and I feel the faintest stirring of unease.

'What makes you think he committed suicide?' she asks and I want to shout at her, because that's what you told me, you silly cow. I don't, obviously, I restrain myself and try to stay calm. So then she witters on and tells me that she never said that when she clearly did, and I start to feel really uneasy then, because I know something is majorly wrong. I want to cover my ears and block it all out even before she says it but I can't. I have to listen to it and I want to scream.

Keith didn't commit suicide, he was murdered.

24

EMILY

No way did I want to do it but here I am at the police station, giving a statement. Because of her.

Big mouth Megan.

I had to get up super early this morning so I could come and tell them how Keith tried to rape me. We got here at ten o'clock which is quite early enough for anyone but according to Megan, 'first thing' meant nine o'clock on the dot. I just ignored her when she kept calling through the bedroom door asking if I was getting up; short of her coming into my room and dragging me out of bed, what could she do? It worked for a while but eventually I couldn't stand any more of her constant nagging and tapping on the door so I dragged myself out of bed just to shut the stupid cow up. She was shocked when I yanked the door open and stalked past her to the bathroom. As I slammed the bathroom door I caught sight of her face. It was a picture of shock and almost made the getting up so early worthwhile.

I had to compose myself when I went downstairs after I was washed and dressed, because I want to keep things civil, at least until she finds out who I really am.

Then the gloves will be off.

She'd made me scrambled eggs on toast and brewed some tea so I forgave her as she fussed around me. In the car on the way here, she still couldn't shut up; kept banging on about 'telling the truth' and how I didn't need to worry. I wasn't worried, and then I wondered if I should be. I watched her mouth as she drove and it never stopped; for the love of God, woman, I thought, put a sock in it. No wonder Ricky came to me, because she's enough to drive any man away. In the end, I zoned out because I couldn't stand any more of her. Then I fell asleep and she had to wake me up when we arrived in the police station car park. I opened my eyes and didn't know where the hell I was and it took a few moments for me to come round.

So. Here I am – and let me tell you, the wheels of justice move excruciatingly slowly and although I've already told them what happened when Keith attacked me, we're going over and over it a million times whilst they think of ever more mind-numbingly boring questions to ask me. I thought that Megan could have come into the room with me, because she could have chivvied them up a bit with her schoolteacher manner. Helped things along a bit, you know, but no, that's not allowed, apparently. The last I saw of her she was at the desk in reception, probably boring them to death.

Once we were settled in here – a policewoman and a man – it did cross my mind to kick up a fuss and use the baby card, but then I thought that might drag it out even longer so I decided not to. Just get on and get it over with, I decided. But I've been in here for a couple of hours already and I can't see an end in sight. You'd think there would be a limit to how many ways they can ask the same question, but incredibly, I don't think there is.

Both of the officers have been at great pains to tell me that I'm not under arrest and I looked at the policeman blankly when he said it the first time because I didn't think for one minute that I was. I'll admit, when Megan told me Keith was dead, I experienced a distinct pang of unease because I would have had a motive for killing him, if the story about the rape were true. I soon calmed myself down when I realised what a ridiculous notion that was. Who is going to suspect a massively pregnant woman weeks away from giving birth, of murder?

No one, that's who.

I'd hazard a guess that as Keith was blackmailing me, he was also involved in other unsavoury things and one of them came back to bite him on the backside. Obviously, he tried to black-mail the wrong person and they were a lot tougher than me and he's now paid the ultimate price. Hit around the head with a blunt instrument and thrown into the canal. One blow, apparently, and he wasn't dead when he went in, just unconscious, so he drowned.

Serves him right.

The woman officer kept asking me every five minutes if I wanted a break but aside from going to the loo once, I refused because that would just prolong things even more. I want it over and done with so I can go back to the house, put my feet up and watch telly. I guess that Megan will be going out to fuss around Elaine at some point so with a bit of luck, she'll be gone for ages and I'll have the place to myself. The tedious questioning continued until lunchtime and then the policewoman, Jess, said that we should stop for a break. I was disappointed because that meant it wasn't finished, but at least it meant I could get out of this bloody room and we could go round the corner to the McDonald's or maybe one of the pubs in the high street and Megan could buy me some lunch. But no; I'm still stuck here in this room because a really young PC who looked like he should still be at school appeared at the door with a sandwich and a bottle of fruit juice for me. I was a bit surprised but also starving and the sandwich looked good, not what I was expecting; nice chunky, posh bread with thickly cut ham inside, presented on a proper plate with a bit of salad and some fancy crisps on the side. The two officers got up and left me to it so I thought, why not just eat it and when they come back we can get the statement done and I can leave and never come back.

Although they haven't actually mentioned making a statement yet; the man did drone on when I got in here but I wasn't really paying attention because I was rehearsing in my head what I was going to say to them. But they're recording everything, so they can get all they need off that and maybe I can sign it another day. Although I have to admit that the longer this is taking, the more nervous I become. I have a niggling feeling that something isn't right but I can't quite put my finger on it. I haven't figured out exactly what it is yet, but the police don't seem quite as sympathetic as I expected them to be. Not even when I squeezed a few tears out and that's a worry, because crying generally does the trick. Although perhaps they become immune to tears in this job because they must see a lot of it. They're very polite, but considering I've told them how Keith tried to rape me and then beat me up, they're not making a super big fuss of me in the way I expected. Maybe they have to be like that, you know, to be professional, but they can see the bruises and the cut on my head so the evidence is right in front of their eyes. All they seem really bothered about is Keith; as if he's the important one just because someone decided to murder him. They've told me I could be the last person to have seen him alive. The third time Jess said it, I corrected her, I can't be, can I? Because the person who murdered him was the last person to see him alive.

I haven't told them my real name and hopefully, I've got

away with that. I didn't make that decision until I actually got in here and they asked for my name, age and address. I told them I was staying with Megan and they asked for my previous address, so I just made up an address in Newcastle. They never batted an eyelid and when I thought about it, why would they even check? I'm here as a witness or whatever it is they call it, nothing else. Although I did think that I should have been a bit more prepared and googled a real address and postcode; I made it up on the spur of the moment, so the chances of the postcode I made up being a proper one are pretty remote. Although if I don't know, they won't either, will they? I don't think it'll matter. Aside from that, the other thing is that with my baby brain, I've already forgotten the address so I'll be stumped if they ask for it again.

But it's too late now anyway so there's no point in dwelling on it. And they won't ask. Why would they? I hope they don't.

I drink the last of the juice and screw the top back on the bottle. I feel quite full up now; that was a very good sandwich, I'll give them that. I wonder if the prisoners they hold in the cells get such good food?

I stretch out my arms on the table and rest my head on them. That's the trouble with eating, it makes me sleepy.

I'll just rest my eyes for a minute until they come back.

* * *

'Emily?'

I open my eyes, lift up my head and wince at the crick in my neck. God, that hurts. I pull myself upright and blink as I come to. I've fallen asleep sitting in a chair at a table, hardly comfortable, but I've managed it. Since I've been pregnant, I actually think I could sleep on a washing line.

'Emily.'

It's the man, Matthew, his name is. He's staring at me.

It takes a second for me to remember that to him, I'm Emily.

'Sorry.' I run a hand over my face, hoping that I haven't been drooling. I think I'm okay, I can't feel anything wet on my face. 'I dozed off,' I explain. 'It's the baby.' I pull an apologetic face, pat my bump and wait for him to smile.

He doesn't.

I sneak a glance at the clock on the wall and am shocked to see that I've been asleep for over two hours.

'If you're ready?' he asks, shuffling papers from a file that he's brought in with him.

'Yes.' I pull myself upright and take a deep breath.

'So, Emily, just for our records, do you have a driving licence or similar that we can see? We always ask for ID but somehow you slipped through the net when you arrived this morning.'

'Oh. No. Sorry. I didn't bring any ID with me.'

'Not a problem. You'd be able to bring it into the station though? First thing tomorrow?'

I pull a worried face. 'Well, that might be a bit of a problem.'

He looks at me, a questioning look on his face.

'I left all my ID behind in Newcastle. When I came for my brother's funeral I wasn't planning on staying for more than a few days. My circumstances changed and I decided to stay and I haven't been back to collect anything so it's all up there.'

'Can I ask how your circumstances changed?'

'I left my partner. He's still in Newcastle. He was abusive and wouldn't leave me alone and kept on pestering me even though we were finished. I moved out of our house into a place on my own but he'd tracked me down and was making life extremely difficult for me. I told Megan about it and she offered to help me so I decided not to go back to him and to use this opportunity to escape him for good. I knew he wouldn't find me here.'

'I see. Okay. The trouble is, we couldn't find any record of you at the address you gave us. In fact, we couldn't find that address at all. Are you sure you gave us the correct details? Could we check them with you again?'

'Yes, of course.'

'So what was the address?'

I stare at him. I have no idea what I told him and I think he knows that.

'Why don't you read it back and I'll check it's correct?' I can hear a quiver in my voice. If I can hear it, so can they.

The woman officer, Jess, stares at me and there's no hint of a smile from her. The man puts down his pen, laces his fingers underneath his chin and studies me. All pretence at niceness has gone now; they know that I've lied and they're not happy about it. I feel my face heat up, and no doubt it's flashing beetroot red right now.

Could I look any more guilty?

'I understand you wanting to escape an abusive relationship, but lying to the police really isn't a good idea. You have to be honest with us. If you're concerned that your ex might be able to trace you, I can assure you that our records are completely confidential and there's no way he'd be able to find you through us. If you want to stop him harassing you, the best thing to do would be to report him and get an injunction against him.' He sounds stern now and I feel like a naughty schoolchild.

'Shall we start again, Emily?' Jess asks. 'You give us your correct address and also your correct date of birth and we'll check with the DVLA and then we can forget about the misinformation you've given us.'

I could lie, prolong it, but they're going to keep me here until they can verify who I am. I take a deep breath and go for it.

'So the thing is,' I say, in a mouse-like voice. 'Is that my name isn't Emily Fordham.'

Silence.

'It's Shelley Beech.'

'Right,' he says, after an uncomfortable silence 'So, Ms Beech, why have you lied to us about who you are?'

'It's complicated.'

He raises an eyebrow.

'As you can see, I'm expecting a baby. The father of my baby is Ricky Fordham, the late husband of Megan Fordham. We were having an affair and he died in a car crash before he got a chance to leave her. He was definitely going to leave her and set up home with me but his death stopped that. I wanted to go to the funeral and pay my respects, you know? But I couldn't tell his wife who I really was, could I? So I pretended to be his sister. Ricky had told me about his sister. He hadn't seen her for years so it seemed a safe thing to do because Megan had never met her. I was pretty sure his sister wasn't going to turn up so I pretended to be her.'

A look passes between them.

'And now you're living in Mrs Fordham's house?'

'Yes. But she doesn't know who I am. She thinks I'm Emily, Ricky's sister.'

There's a stunned silence and I try to read their faces but I can't; they're too well practised to give their feelings away.

'And you've continued with the deception for, how long?'

'Two months.'

'And Mrs Fordham genuinely believes you are her late husband's sister?'

'Yes, she does. When I met her at the funeral and told her I was Ricky's sister, she couldn't do enough for me. Fell over herself to help. She thinks this baby is her nephew and practically begged me to move in with her. I know it sounds weird but I was absolutely desperate. With Ricky dying, I'm in big trouble financially and I have no one to turn to. I only planned on staying for a few weeks until I'd sorted myself out but the weeks have just gone by so quickly.'

'So the abusive ex in Newcastle was a lie?'

'Yes. I live here, on the other side of town from Megan.' I put my head down and try to look ashamed. 'I was struggling to get by and like I say, I was desperate. She offered help so I took it, it's as simple as that. I only went to that funeral to say goodbye to the man I love and when she offered to help, it felt as if Ricky was looking down on me, looking after me, you know?' I manage to squeeze a couple of tears out and look at them both, biting my bottom lip. They stare back at me stone-faced, my display of sorrow lost on them. I suppose that's what happens when you do a job like this, you lose all feeling for people. I wait for them to speak but they don't, so I plough on.

'Once the baby's born I'm going to tell her the truth and then contest the will or whatever it is I need to do. I have Ricky's DNA so I can apply for maintenance for our baby.'

He studies me for a moment.

'So let me get this right. You moved into your dead lover's house with his widow and pretended to be his sister-in-law. But once the baby is born, you're planning to tell her who you really are?'

'Yes.'

'So what's your real address?'

I give him the address of my flat and there's silence as he writes it down.

'We'll check those details with the DVLA in a moment but

for now, returning to the matter of Keith Foster. You claim that on the day before yesterday, he attempted to rape you and beat you badly before fleeing when a delivery driver called at the house and disturbed him. Has that claim changed in any way in light of your recent admission?'

'No.' I don't like the way he said 'claim'; as if I'm making it up.

'Okay. And did you tell anyone else about this attack? Are there any witnesses?'

'No witnesses, no, because it was only me and him there. But I told Megan about it, when she came home yesterday morning. I would have told her that night but she stayed out all night. She knows all about it and that's why I'm here, because she said that you need to know what happened because of Keith dying.'

Both of them look at me and I have the distinct feeling that I'm missing something.

'Why are you looking at me like that?' I ask.

'Well, Shelley,' he says. 'The thing is, there's been a development.'

25

MEGAN

Revenge. That's a good word, isn't it?

There is a saying that revenge is a dish best served cold and I think that's right. Spot on, as Mum used to say.

The water in the river was very cold that night; mind-numbingly, brain-freezingly cold. The shock, apparently, is what kills most people when accidents involve water. Not just the physical shock but the unexpectedness of it all. The terror freezes you into inaction, makes clear thinking impossible. All your brain can do is panic in those first few vital seconds when the car plunges into the water. Seconds that are vital to any possibility of surviving. Most people are too dazed and horrified to think their way out of drowning.

And then it's too late.

Unless you're expecting it, of course.

I was expecting it and I was prepared. Rick, sadly, was not. As we fought over the steering wheel, he was already in shock; shock that I was trying to steer the car into the river, shock at how strong I was.

How much stronger than him I was.

Me, a little slip of a thing.

I'd already unclicked my seatbelt before we left the road, my window was fully open before we sank beneath the water. I'm quick, as well as strong, and being small, getting through that window wasn't a problem. I'm also a very good swimmer, not that I told the police that. I told them I was amazed that I managed to make it to the riverbank, that it was more luck than anything else. And they didn't check, of course, especially when they discovered that Rick was well over the drink-driving alcohol limit.

How remiss of them.

Rick, on the other hand, hated the water and couldn't swim properly because he'd never bothered to learn. Not that it mattered; he was still fumbling around to release his seatbelt when I eased myself through the window and struck out towards land. He used to sneer at my daily thirty laps at the gym, especially in the winter, said he couldn't think of anything worse.

Except drowning, maybe.

Of course, I'd known about Shelley, the tramp, long before that night. Rick thought he was so clever and I was so unworldly, so old-fashioned, so gullible.

So stupid.

He took me for a fool and I couldn't forgive him for that. He lied to me that night, told me that he'd married me because he loved me, that he was blinded by my beauty but had realised how incompatible we were. We had nothing in common he said; we viewed the world in a different way. Much better that we part now, amicably, with no hard feelings before we destroyed each other completely.

I didn't want him to leave; I loved him when I married him

and I still did, despite his cheating. I could have forgiven his cheating, eventually, but he never gave me a chance.

He didn't want me.

No; he wanted 'his share', as he called it.

He thought he was entitled to half of this house. My house. Not his. Married barely a year and he expected me to sell my house so he could walk away with half of the proceeds to set up home with *her*, the tramp. So I made a decision; he would never get half of my house. Over my dead body, as Mum used to say, or in this case, his.

He never told me about her, or the baby she was expecting. Laughably, he thought he'd managed to keep it all a secret. That's my only regret, that he didn't know that I knew exactly what he'd done and that he was paying with his life for his betrayal. He probably guessed as his lungs filled with water but it would have been nice to have told him, to have seen the expression on his face, but some things just aren't possible, are they?

I'd read all of their sickening messages to each other because he made it so easy for me. He always left his phone lying around, thinking I was too trusting, too stupid, to snoop. Such an obvious thing, to use your own birthdate as the lock code. I knew everything; all the money he'd spent on her, the number of times he saw her, the places he took her, the pregnancy, his promises to her, everything. I even followed him to her flat one night. I felt like a spy, trailing behind him in the car, and he was so sure of himself that he never even noticed me behind him. Once I knew where she lived it was so easy to find out about her, to go back in the daytime and get a good look at her as I sat in my car parked outside her flat, a woolly hat hiding my hair. To see what it was about her that had attracted him to her.

She was the cheap version of me; bleached hair and a face full of make-up.

I feel no guilt about what I've done; Rick brought about his own death through his greed for something that was never his to begin with. If he hadn't tried to take what was mine, maybe I'd have let him live.

Maybe. Or maybe not.

And as for the tramp, I'd always intended my revenge on her one day but I hadn't decided how I would exact that revenge, it was something I was still thinking about. And then she turned up at Rick's funeral and made it so easy for me.

So ridiculously easy.

Almost as if it was meant to be.

I didn't show it but I was shocked when she walked into the wake; shocked at the sheer front of her. I was sure she was going to announce to everyone present that she was Rick's secret lover, that she'd come there to cause a scene to embarrass me. I was still considering how I was going to react when she came over and she told me she was Rick's sister.

I knew then that she was up to something, that she had some sort of plan, so I went along with it, pretended to believe her, pretended not to know that the real Emily lived in Australia. Because of course I knew where his sister was, even though Rick never talked to me about her. I'd read all of his emails to the tracing agency; it was the only way I could find out what was going on in his life. His email account was always left logged in on his laptop and when he was out, playing sport or seeing the tramp, it was easy to check up and see what he'd been up to. The truly hilarious thing was that the tramp thought she was the clever one; she thought, like Rick, that I was an unsuspecting, gullible fool and that she'd fooled me at the funeral. She thought that I'd played right into her hands and not the other way around. She took that credit card from me and abused it, as I knew she would. Even drew cash on it when that idiot Keith tried to blackmail her. When I was at work she searched my house, went through all of my private belongings, rifled through every single file in Rick's office, read every piece of paper.

Left her fingerprints everywhere.

In other words, did exactly what I expected her to do.

The photographs of me and Mum, my grandparents and other members of my family, the ornaments full of sentimental value collected over years that the tramp hated so much because I could see it on her face; maybe she should have looked a little closer. She'd have seen them then, the tiny cameras that recorded her every move in the kitchen, lounge and study. And my own moves too, but as I'm the only one who knows about them, I'll be the only person who will ever view that footage. I saw her sneers and the faces she pulled behind my back when she thought I couldn't see her. Her ingratitude when I was making food for her or clearing up her mess. I watched her as she slumped on the sofa stuffing her face with all the food I'd bought, wallowing like a fat pig in a stye.

How I wish I could have been in the interview room when they charged her with theft, could have heard her protesting that she was innocent and that I gave her that credit card. The police had already been to the house to remove files from the study for evidence, files with her fingerprints all over them, files with my pin numbers and passwords on sticky notes inside. They believed me totally when I told them that I believed she was paying for all of the things she was buying, that I was oblivious to her using my credit card until I received a phone call from the card provider asking me if I'd like to increase the credit limit. Suspecting fraud, I looked through the account and discovered that she'd been using it to pay for all of her purchases. They didn't doubt me when, in desperation, I asked them to look into it because I was a little afraid of her and she scared me with her explosive temper. I told them how she intimidated me and had outstayed her welcome but was refusing to leave, even though I'd asked her to go, how I'd even offered money to help with a deposit for somewhere for her to live. How she bullied me and threatened violence if I suggested she move out. When the police gently explained to me that she wasn't Rick's sister at all, but his lover, I broke down in front of them, unable to believe her deception. They had to suspend the interview to allow me to compose myself. They brought me a cup of tea and a box of tissues.

They believed every single word that I said, because why wouldn't they? She was the liar, the thief, not me.

I'm the grieving widow. The poor woman who's shown a lying, scheming woman nothing but kindness and been rewarded with nastiness and stealing.

So she's in trouble; not only for her theft and intimidation of me, but also as a suspect in Keith's murder.

Ah, yes, Keith.

I've always hated Keith; since I was a child he's been there, hanging around like a bad smell, literally a bad smell, stinking of cigarettes and beer, watching and waiting.

Waiting to rip me off.

When I was at work, I'd watch him in my house nosing around, going through my stuff, poking about, seeing what he could help himself to, thinking that I wouldn't miss the odd banknote from my purse or the bottles of wine he regularly took from the wine rack. Small, petty thefts, but stealing, nonetheless. They were alike, the tramp and Keith, and he knew it, he knew what she was, right from the start. It takes one to know one. As I watched him blackmail her, I wondered how she'd wriggle out of that and when I saw her hitting her own head against the fridge to make it look as if he'd attacked her, I knew then what she was truly capable of. I'll admit to being slightly impressed because I didn't think she had it in her, and I hadn't known how far she would go to get what she wanted. But I felt sad for the baby; no child deserves a mother like that. As I sat in the car park at work and watched the video, it came to me that I could kill two birds with one stone. I could make life extremely difficult for the tramp and be rid of Keith forever. Going for after-work drinks that night gave me the opportunity to be rid of both her and Keith without incriminating myself and if my plan didn't work, she'd still be charged with stealing.

So what of Sam? Had I always planned to use him as an alibi? No; he was simply a distraction, a way to get away from her, because it was wearing being in the same house as the tramp, even when she was in her bedroom. She was a malevolent presence, I could feel her evilness. If I didn't get away from her, I was afraid I'd be the one doing something stupid, that I'd forget myself one day and lace my fingers around her throat and squeeze...

Sam was sweet and hopelessly infatuated with me. He was also very hot and I'm only human. Although we haven't actually had sex yet, even if he thinks we did. His pride won't allow him to believe that I shared his bed and we didn't do the deed, because I told him that we did and even though he can't remember, he's convinced himself that we enjoyed a night of passion. He'll tell himself that he can't remember because he was drunk, which he was, but he was also drugged. I wasn't sure how many sleeping tablets to give him so I overcompensated, I think. Mixed with the alcohol, he was practically comatose. The tablets were prescribed for me after Mum died and I did wonder if they might have gone off but they obviously hadn't. I knew there was a reason I'd been carrying them around in my handbag all of this time, so I knew it was meant to be. Those tablets gave me confidence; all the pieces of my plan fit perfectly together, like a puzzle. I didn't tell Sam I was going back to his flat until the end of the night because I knew if he had prior warning, he would have stuck rigidly to soft drinks. He prides himself on his performance, you see, and not just in the gym. And he drank far more than he thought he did because I had to remain sober, and deal with Keith. It was the work of a few seconds to make sure that all of my shots found their way into Sam's glass.

Getting Keith to meet me at the allotments was the only niggle; how could I get him there without incriminating myself? I couldn't see a way around it and in the end, I did the only thing possible, I rang him. I slipped away from Sam and the work crowd, telling him I was going to the toilet, but I really went outside to the car park at the back. Keith was in the pub, as I knew he'd be, drowning his sorrows. He always spent Friday afternoons and evenings at the pub, come rain or shine, that's where he would be. When he answered his phone, I told him not to speak, not to give any indication that he was talking to me. Shocked into silence by my tone, he listened as I told him that he had to meet me at his allotment after the pub closed that night, that he was to wait there until I arrived.

That I needed to talk to him about Shelley.

Just uttering her name was enough. He knew he'd been caught and was desperate to appease me. The rest was easy; once back at Sam's flat, Sam opened a bottle of wine at my insistence and when his back was turned, I laced his with the sleeping tablets. We drank the glass of wine quickly because I'd made the promise of sex afterwards. Not in an obvious way, of course, because I'm not like the tramp, but I seduced him, none-

theless. We moved into the bedroom because Sam needed to be
undressed and in bed to believe that we'd slept together. Once
down to our underwear, I excused myself to go to the bathroom
and by the time I came back he was asleep and snoring. I
quickly dressed in the gym gear that was still in my bag from the
morning, and even though it was rather sweaty, it did the job. I
needed to wear something suitable for what I was going to do,
heels and a skirt just wouldn't do it. Sam had expressed surprise
that I needed to return to my car after we left the pub that night.
I told him I needed to collect my gym bag, that I was uncomfortable leaving it in the car overnight. He told me it would be fine
and I confided in him that the bag had sentimental value, that
Rick had bought it for me and I couldn't risk ever losing it. He'd
smiled sadly and wordlessly taken it from me to carry it himself.

I'd thought of everything.

Satisfied Sam was fast asleep, I pulled the quilt over him and
quietly let myself out of the flat and ran to the allotments, down
back alleys and dark streets, avoiding the main roads. It didn't
take much more than fifteen minutes because I'm fast as well as
strong.

When I arrived there, Keith was waiting inside his shed,
exactly as I'd told him to be. I told him to come outside and talk
to me, that I didn't want to sit in his disgusting cigarette-smoke-
filled shed. He reluctantly walked down to the canal with me.
He was still staggering drunk as I knew he would be, alternating
between taking sips from a whisky bottle that he'd pull from his
coat pocket and inhaling drags from a cigarette. I told him I
knew what had happened that morning, that I knew who Emily
really was and that I would deal with her. I said that I would
forgive him this time but if I ever caught him doing anything
again, I would tell Elaine. He was pathetically grateful and
proceeded to light up yet another cigarette, shielding the flame

with his hand. Whilst he was struggling to get it to light, I picked up a hefty branch from the debris littered around the ground and hit him around the head with it, swinging it, rounders-style.

Keith wasn't a big man; he was a scrawny weed who smoked and drank too much so was not in good shape at all. I put a lot of force behind that blow but somehow, after I'd hit him, he remained upright for a moment and managed to put his hand out towards me and grab hold of my arm. I pushed him away with as much force as I could muster and he spun around and fell straight into the water, face down. He didn't move, not once, and I watched him for a while to satisfy myself he was dead before throwing the branch into the undergrowth and running back to Sam's flat.

It bothered me, though, that I'd rung him from my phone, because that could be traced. It was a loose end. But after thinking for a while, I came up with the simplest of solutions; it was a pocket dial. Happens all the time, doesn't it? My phone had rung his number from the pub whilst it was in my pocket. All those people jostling around me, forcing their way past me to the bar on a busy Friday night. I hadn't realised at the time and never even noticed that I'd called him. There would be no evidence that I had anything to do with Keith's death because, once I've washed the gym gear that I wore that night, which I'm planning to do the very minute I get home, there will be nothing to tie me to his death. I would have washed it before now but with so much going on, I haven't had the chance. Once that's done, I'm home free.

Not that I'm in the least bit worried, because the police wouldn't be looking at me.

Because I have an alibi.

Sam.

* * *

As I drive home from the gym I feel exhilarated and pumped; Sam and I took several classes together before I persuaded him to come for a swim, all topped off with a very nice lunch. He wanted me to go back to his but I put him off, pleading exhaustion from the events of the last few days. He couldn't really argue, but that excuse will eventually wear thin and I'll have to decide whether to continue seeing him. He's eager for a repeat performance of our fantastic night of forgotten sex together. So it's a case of put out or dump him.

I suppose I'll also have to decide what to do with all the baby equipment that the tramp bought. I could return it to the shops, I suppose, get a refund. Or maybe I'll just give it all to charity; ring one of them up and get them to come around and collect it all. There's no rush, although I don't want it hanging around here for too long. Yes, charity, I think.

I debate whether to call into Elaine's to see her but decide not; she has her sister, Susan, staying with her now so there's no need for me to be there too. Frankly, there's only so much misery I can take. Eventually, she'll realise that she's better off without Keith, but it's early days. She has to grieve for him even though he was a poor excuse for a man. I never told Elaine about Shelley's rape accusation, because there's no need for her to suffer any more because of Shelley's lies. I apprised Susan of Shelley's arrest by telephone and have left it to her as to how much or how little she tells Elaine. I think Elaine has enough going on at the moment without adding my problems to the mix.

As I turn down into my street and approach my house, I'm surprised to see a police car parked outside. As I draw closer I see there's another police car parked on my driveway as well as a van parked on the road behind the first police car. A man in a white boilersuit is carrying a box into the back of the van and I pull up behind the van, get out of the car and hurry up the driveway. The front door is wide open and several officers are milling around inside the hallway and lounge. I storm inside, furious. How dare they enter my house without my permission? How did they even get in here?

'What the hell do you think you're doing?' I demand, stalking into the lounge. A grey-haired man turns around from the man he's talking to. I've not seen him before, he's wearing plain clothes and not in uniform, so I guess he's senior.

'How dare you come into my house without asking! You've already taken all the files from the office so why are you here? Who gave you permission to come in here whilst I was out? And how did you even get in here? You'd better not have broken the door down or damaged it in any way.' My voice is shrill but the man doesn't seem worried by my words at all.

'Ah, Mrs Fordham,' he says smoothly. 'We do have a warrant. And also, a key.' He waves at one of the other officers and she scurries over and hands him a piece of paper which he holds towards me.

'I don't care if you've got a warrant.' I ignore the paper in front of me. 'You should have waited for me to come back. And where did you get the key from?' I glare at him and wait for the grovelling apology. It isn't forthcoming. I notice then that the wedding picture of me and Rick that's usually on the mantelpiece isn't there; everything else is, but not the picture.

The one in the frame with the camera; they've taken it. Have they found the other cameras, too? I want to know. I need to know.

'We'd like you to come down to the station, Mrs Fordham,'

he says, not answering my questions. 'We have questions we need to ask you.'

Fear trickles down my spine. What do they know, suspect? A vision of my gym bag in the boot of my car sears itself into my brain. No, it's fine, I tell myself, they have more questions about Shelley, that's all.

'I've spent quite long enough there, thank you,' I say, in my best haughty manner. 'I've told you everything I know about Emily or whatever she's calling herself today.'

'If we go to the station now, I'm sure we can get this all cleared up in no time,' he persists.

'No. Absolutely not. Ask me your questions here, and hurry up. And then you all need to leave.'

'I'm afraid I have to insist. And the questions aren't about Shelley Beech, they're about Keith Foster. We've received new information regarding his death.'

'New information?' My mouth is suddenly dry and I can barely breathe.

He sighs then, rather theatrically, I think, before he speaks.

'Megan Fordham, I'm arresting you on suspicion of the murder of Keith Foster...'

26

ELAINE

Caroline, Megan's mother, and I were best friends since we met on our first day at school – a very long time ago now. We were more than friends, we were like sisters, 'joined at the hip', as my mother used to say. I can honestly say that I was closer to Caroline than I was to my own sister, Susan. Even now, I still miss Caroline dreadfully, we spoke every day when she was here, not a day passed without us having some sort of contact and I still can't get used to not seeing her.

I don't know if I ever will.

Caroline was a single parent from the off, Meg's father having long gone by the time she was born. I loved Meg from the moment she came screaming into the world after a long and protracted labour. I was there in the delivery room, holding Caroline's hand. I shared in all Meg's firsts; first word, first steps, first day at school, everything. Caroline was a sharing person, never jealous of how I felt about Meg, she was happy and grateful to have my friendship, my help. I've always thought of Meg as the daughter Keith and I were never blessed with.

And I still love her, despite everything she's done.

We knew from an early age that there was something not quite right with Meg. It's why I saw so much of her after Caroline died, why I still went to the house so often. Even after she married Rick, I stayed close, although I could tell it annoyed him. He thought I was an interfering old woman, but I'd promised Caroline I'd look after Meg, make sure that she didn't get into trouble, look out for her. It was a deathbed promise; the last thing that Caroline asked of me.

Watch over her. Please.

Because Caroline knew, as I did, that for all her beauty, there's a darkness inside Meg; there's something not quite right, something missing. I don't know exactly what it is but there's a reason she doesn't have any proper friends, apart from me. Even as a young child, she was a loner. She'd make friends easily enough because people are drawn to beauty, even children, but they never stuck around for very long. And she never seemed to care when they drifted away. I'd catch her watching other children with detachment when they fell over or scraped a knee, when they cried. She'd look at them as if they were some sort of experiment, a thing to be studied. We gradually realised that Meg lacked any empathy for others; she's learned to fake it as she's grown older, but Caroline and I could see that it wasn't real, because we knew her so well. The swimming – that was something Caroline and I encouraged at the start because it gave her something to focus on. We thought she needed something, that it would do her good to have an activity to concentrate her energy on but she soon became obsessed with it, with winning.

She had to win, no matter what.

In no time at all, she became the star of the swimming club. She was dedicated, never complaining as the other girls did about the early morning practice, the constant travelling to competitions, the chilly pool, the constant warm-up lengths. Caroline and I used to take it in turns to run her to practice early in the morning and she was always ready and waiting when I arrived to pick her up, never oversleeping. At first, we took her eagerness for dedication but soon we realised it was obsession. She travelled all round the country taking part in swimming competitions and Caroline and I would go and watch her, so proud of her as she collected trophy after trophy and for a while, we breathed easier. But there's always someone better waiting in the wings, isn't there? It's a fact of life, but Meg couldn't take it. When a new girl joined and started winning more than her, she couldn't cope with it. She hid her feelings well to others but we could see the cold rage in her eyes as she watched the other girl win the races that she thought belonged to her. Then one morning there was an incident with the girl when the two of them were practising. The girl swore that Meg had tried to drown her, forcing her under water whilst the instructor had popped away from the pool to get herself a coffee. Meg laughed it off; said that the girl was lying because she didn't like her, was jealous of her, but there was no denying the girl's hysteria or her real fear of Meg. The instructor couldn't do anything about the girl's accusation because she wasn't there and there were no witnesses. It was one girl's word against another. But I saw the rest of the girls in the swimming club's expressions, the way they looked at Meg, how they distanced themselves from her and stopped speaking to her. Caroline and I watched on as the other parents at the poolside eyed Meg with ill-concealed suspicion when they thought no one was looking, the whispers, the aloofness when we tried to engage any of them in conversation.

They knew, or at least suspected, the truth.

After a few weeks, Megan announced that she no longer

wanted to swim, she was bored, she'd won everything possible so what was the point in continuing? She refused to go back to the club and it was left to Caroline to tell them she wouldn't be returning. Caroline lied and said that Meg had to concentrate on her schoolwork but she needn't have bothered; the club were as relieved as we were. We could relax now it was over and life returned to normal once more. There were other incidents over the years but never anything that stuck. We lied to ourselves that Meg was fine but we both knew deep down what she really was. But she was, and is, very clever. She made sure she never got caught or suspected again.

When Rick died, I had my doubts about the accident but I pushed them to the back of my mind, not wanting to believe she could do such a terrible thing. When the coroner found it was death by misadventure, well, who was I to argue? They had all of the facts and I didn't; I had to believe that they knew better than me because it was just an uneasy feeling I had, that's all.

And I wanted so badly to believe that Meg had nothing to do with Rick's death.

I overheard her the day she told the police she didn't know how she'd made it to the riverbank. I tried to put it to the back of my mind but deep down I knew she was lying. She's still an excellent swimmer and swims daily at the gym but I didn't want to believe the worst of her, didn't want to believe that she wouldn't have saved Rick if she could.

To my shame, I stayed silent.

But I couldn't let her get away with murdering Keith. I could no longer pretend to myself.

Keith wasn't perfect; far from it. He could be very selfish and was overly fond of a pint and a cigarette but I loved him despite his faults, just as I loved Meg. Other people saw only the selfish side of him but when we were alone together, he was completely different, he was the real Keith. He never liked to show his feelings for me in public; he was a man's man and didn't believe in 'soppiness', as he called it, but when we were alone together he could be himself. Other men might have been threatened by my friendship with Caroline but Keith never was because he knew how much she meant to me. He never asked me to choose between them like a lot of men would.

We were happy together; I looked after him and he looked after me, in his own way. No one, not even Caroline, realised how very close Keith and I were. He rang me that night, the night he went missing; the night Meg murdered him. He was in a hell of a state; convinced that Emily was going to report him to the police for rape and he was going to prison for something he hadn't done. He told me it all; his attempt to blackmail her, who Emily really was. Keith was always looking for a get-rich-quick scheme, a way to make money with hardly any effort but this time, it had all gone horribly wrong. I was so angry with him. I shouted at him and that's hard to bear, knowing that the last time I spoke to him was in anger. He was so, so sorry and kept telling me so over and over again. He was in the pub drinking, not drunk when I spoke to him but I knew he'd carry on knocking back the pints, even though I begged him not to. I told him that he needed to keep a clear head but I knew my Keith; he found his courage in the bottom of a bottle.

And then he never came home.

He sent me a message though, late that night. Told me that Meg had asked him to meet her at the allotment and he messaged me as he was waiting for her. I messaged him back immediately but he never replied. I tried to tell myself he hadn't looked at his phone, hadn't heard my message arrive but I think part of me knew, then, that Meg had done something to him. I never told her that Keith had rung me that night, I wanted to give her a chance to tell me herself, to reassure me that she didn't have anything to do with him being missing. To tell me herself why she rang him, to tell me that the last time she saw him he was alive and well, convince me that she hadn't killed him even though I feared deep down that she had.

But she never said a word about the phone call, not a thing. All the time I was panicking over him being missing and fearing the worst, she stayed silent. I knew that something terrible had happened to him because he always came home.

The really funny thing was – well, not funny but strange – was that Keith found out Emily wasn't who she said she was quite by accident. He thought she was dodgy, as did I, but he didn't go looking to find out about her. It was one of the drivers who was delivering all the stuff that Emily had bought, who told him about her. He was a regular at the pub Keith went to and they bumped into each other when Keith popped round Meg's one day to check on the boiler. He'd noticed it had been making a funny noise when he was there previously and was going to have a look at it. He was good like that, always looking out for her; looking after her. Trying to do her a kindness, be the father she never had. Just as he was getting out of his car, the delivery driver was leaving, having just left a load of parcels on the doorstep. He said hello to Keith and something about him being all right for a haircut. They stopped and chatted and Keith asked him what he meant about the haircut and it all came out. Turns out that Emily, or rather Shelley, used to regularly cut his wife's hair so he knew her well. She wasn't who she said she was. She'd wheedled her way into Meg's house and was taking advantage of her by pretending to be Rick's sister.

What sort of person does that?

So Keith took it into his head to blackmail her.

And it worked at first. Even Keith didn't really get why she would pretend to be Rick's sister, because he couldn't see any connection between Emily and Meg. And then he thought about it and remembered Emily saying that there were things he didn't know about her, and that she had a right to be in the house, stuff like that, and he twigged what she meant, because Keith was good at working things out.

Emily was Rick's bit on the side and the baby was his.

Because Keith never liked Rick and always had him pegged as a charmer who was after Meg's money. I can't say I took to Rick either, but maybe that was because he called me the 'old biddy' behind my back, but loud enough so I could hear. He didn't try very hard to disguise his dislike of me and was only civil if Meg was around. Still, for all that, he didn't deserve to die.

So Keith's attempt at blackmail all turned to disaster, and he thought he was going to prison, for sure, after she'd thrown herself around the kitchen to make it look as if he'd had attacked her. He fled the house and went straight to the pub to drown his sorrows and that's when Meg rang him and told him to meet her at the allotment. So I think Meg knew who Emily was then, and I wonder if she always knew. Was Meg trying to set Emily up for Keith's murder? Because I'm pretty certain Meg killed Keith, just like she killed Rick.

Because it's clear Rick was going to leave Meg. When I look back, I remember he was always going out somewhere or going away on business, as he put it; he was hardly ever home and they'd only been married five minutes. And now we know he was seeing Shelley. Meg wouldn't have been able to cope with the rejection of him leaving her, not after he'd pursued her the way he did. I could sometimes see he'd lost interest in her by the expression on his face when he looked at her.

She wouldn't have been able to take him leaving her.

She'd had boyfriends before Rick but none of them lasted very long and she never seemed bothered about any of them, until Rick. I think in her warped way, she loved him.

So I knew that I couldn't lie for her or stay silent, not like I had when Rick died. I had to tell the police that she'd arranged to meet Keith that night. There'll be a record of that call on both of their phones, won't there, and his message to me? I told them the truth of what happened with Shelley, too, because why should Keith's memory be blackened by her lies?

I told them about Meg being an excellent swimmer, too, but who knows whether they'll bother to look into Rick's accident.

I hope that once they start investigating, there will be evidence that she killed Keith though. The allotment is covered by CCTV on the gate because incredibly, people steal plants and vegetables from there. The allotment owners clubbed together and got the CCTV put in because it was becoming a joke; as soon as someone had put new plants in, a couple of nights later it would all be gone, so there must be footage of Meg being there that night. The police will have already started looking into it so maybe they didn't even need me to tell them what I know. I have faith that the police will find out what happened to my Keith.

Meg will have to face the consequences for what she's done.

But I'll be here to support her, whatever happens; I'll always be here for her.

Because, despite what she's done, she's like a daughter to me.

ACKNOWLEDGEMENTS

Thank you to the wonderful team at Boldwood for all of their help and support in producing this book, with special thanks to my editor, Isobel Akenhead. Thank you to Peter, my husband, for his unending support and enthusiasm and, last but not least, a big thank you to all of my readers.

ABOUT THE AUTHOR

Joanne Ryan is the author of several well-reviewed psychological thrillers. After realising she loved writing thrillers, Joanne left her office job and has been writing full time ever since.

Sign up to Joanne Ryan's mailing list for news, competitions and update on future books.

Follow Joanne on social media here:

instagram.com/authorjoanneryan

bookbub.com/authors/joanne-ryan

ALSO BY JOANNE RYAN

Keep Your Friends Close

Don't Let Her In

Alone in the Dark

The Sister-in-Law

THE

Murder

LIST

**THE MURDER LIST IS A NEWSLETTER
DEDICATED TO SPINE-CHILLING FICTION
AND GRIPPING PAGE-TURNERS!**

**SIGN UP TO MAKE SURE YOU'RE ON OUR
HIT LIST FOR EXCLUSIVE DEALS, AUTHOR
CONTENT, AND COMPETITIONS.**

SIGN UP TO OUR NEWSLETTER

BIT.LY/THEMURDERLISTNEWS

Boldwood

Boldwood Books is an award-winning fiction publishing company seeking out the best stories from around the world.

Find out more at www.boldwoodbooks.com

Join our reader community for brilliant books, competitions and offers!

Follow us
@BoldwoodBooks
@TheBoldBookClub

Sign up to our weekly
deals newsletter

https://bit.ly/BoldwoodBNewsletter